Nobody loves you Better

Cover Design: Uplifting Designs/Alyssa Garcia

Editing: Jillian Rivera Editing

PRAISE FOR SAMANTHA CHASE

"If you can't get enough of stories that get inside your heart and soul and stay there long after you've read the last page, then Samantha Chase is for you!"

-NY *Times & USA Today* Bestselling Author **Melanie Shawn**

"A fun, flirty, sweet romance filled with romance and character growth and a perfect happily ever after."

-NY *Times & USA Today* Bestselling Author **Carly Phillips**

"Samantha Chase writes my kind of happily ever after!"

-NY *Times & USA Today* Bestselling Author **Erin Nicholas**

"The openness between the lovers is refreshing, and their interactions are a balanced blend of sweet and spice. The planets may not have aligned, but the elements of this winning romance are definitely in sync."

- ***Publishers Weekly, STARRED review***

"A true romantic delight, *A Sky Full of Stars* is one of the top gems of romance this year."

- ***Night Owl Reviews, TOP PICK***

"Great writing, a winsome ensemble, and the perfect blend of heart and sass."

1

It's James Bond...

Peyton Bishop knew she sometimes romanticized things going on around her, but when the perfect man walks into a room wearing a tuxedo and oozing confidence, it's hard not to think of one of her favorite action heroes.

She pressed herself back against the wall of her café so she'd be in the shadows while she watched this magnificent man. He was tall with broad shoulders, dark hair and even darker eyes, and Peyton felt her heart flutter when his lips lifted with a small smile as he looked around.

Like what you see? I know I do.

He might have been smiling as he looked around Café Magnolia, but Peyton only had eyes for him.

They'd been at a handful of events at the same time, the two of them, but they'd never been introduced. Well, people had always wanted to introduce her to him, but Peyton always ran away like a scared schoolgirl, nervous giggle and all, because Ryder Ashford was like something off a movie screen. He was the epitome of tall, dark, and handsome, and the thought of going anywhere near him intimidated the crap out of her.

But then again, the same thing happened the first time she met author Mia Kingsley, who was now engaged to Peyton's cousin Austin. She had declined an introduction multiple times and when she finally caved, Mia was an absolute delight and now the two of them were good friends.

Somehow she doubted she'd get the same results from being introduced to Ryder.

Sneaking another glance, she wondered what he was doing here at her little café.

And dressed in a tuxedo.

He was no stranger to Magnolia Sound–he'd already purchased several homes, property, and the veterinary clinic that her cousin Garrett now ran. Ryder never came in here before, though. And again, why the tuxedo?

From where she was standing, Peyton admired his strong jaw and the smile on his face as he took in his surroundings. When she inherited the café several years ago, it was somewhat outdated. Truth be told, it still was. But she was doing the updates a little at a time so she wouldn't have to shut down for any extended period of time. Basically, she'd updated the menu, bought new tables and chairs, painted the walls, purchased new artwork–all cosmetic fixes. The kitchen was next on her list and fortunately, she would be able to do it all without disrupting business. The new appliances were being delivered this coming weekend and the work to take out the old ones and install the new ones would be done overnight. She was proud of what she'd done here and her customers loved it.

It was her next endeavor, however, that she was most looking forward to.

In a matter of days, she would finally be able to put in an offer on a small piece of property she'd been eyeing for a while. Her dream was to build a place of her own–literally from the ground up. For years, Peyton had dreamed of what it would look like, what she wanted on the menu, and already had her sign and logo designed.

She was nothing if not thorough.

Out of the corner of her eye, she saw Ryder chatting with her hostess, Dana. Then she saw Dana turn and point in her direction, and damn if Ryder wasn't looking directly at her.

Busted.

Straightening, Peyton willed her heart rate to calm down. This was so not the way she wanted to meet him. She wasn't dressed to impress, but...there wasn't anything she had in her wardrobe that would wow a guy in what could only be described as a custom-made tuxedo. Still, she seriously wished she was dressed in something a little more stylish rather than a pair of navy capris and a white t-shirt. Her hand smoothed up over her sleek ponytail as she sighed. This morning she swore she looked cute. Now? Not so much.

Straightening, she threw her shoulders back and stepped out from behind the large potted dragon tree with all the confidence she could muster.

"Oh, here she is now," Dana said with a smile. "Peyton, this is Mr. Ashford. He was looking to speak to the owner." She stepped away to seat a party of two, leaving Peyton alone with Ryder.

Holding out her hand, she smiled up at him. "It's nice to meet you, Mr. Ashford. I'm Peyton Bishop. How can I help you?"

His large hand enveloped hers in a gentle clasp, but he wasn't smiling.

Not even a little.

Releasing her hand, Ryder cleared his throat. "Are you the manager?"

"Um... no," she replied, confused.

"I was looking for the owner," he said slowly, as if she wouldn't understand.

"Then you've found her," she stated, her smile feeling a little stiff, and her tone carried just a hint of annoyance.

"Do your folks own the place and you're just running it?"

"Excuse me?" Okay, now she was more than a little annoyed.

"It's just..." He looked her up and down—and not in a flattering way. "You don't quite look old enough to own this place."

It didn't matter how many people said that to her in the past; this time it really bothered her. He said it with just enough condescension to truly rub her the wrong way.

"Trust me, Mr. Ashford, I'm the owner and I'm old enough. Is there something I can do for you?" And yeah, her polite tone and smile were gone.

Not that it mattered. He didn't look the least bit sheepish or apologetic. "I need a dinner catered tonight and I was told this was the place to go. Austin Coleman recommended you."

Normally she loved a recommendation from her family, but right now she didn't feel like basking in it. "Of course. How many people will be attending?"

"Four."

"Okay. Do you know what you want to order? Have you looked at the menu?" Reaching for one, she held it out for him and was dying to know if they were all going to be in tuxes and evening gowns. It was on the tip of her tongue to suggest he go to the Magnolia Country Club, but figured Austin had to know what he was doing by suggesting the café.

"This is a very important dinner and I was told you do custom menus," he replied, ignoring the menu in her hand.

With a serene smile that she totally wasn't feeling, she put the menu down. "With advanced notice we do, but considering it's after three..."

"It's still advanced notice," he interrupted smoothly. "It will need to be delivered promptly at seven and delivered hot. We won't be reheating."

This guy...

Peyton forced herself to mentally count to ten before speaking. "Mr. Ashford, I appreciate your inquiry, but unfortunately we cannot accommodate your request. If you'd like to order something off the menu, then I'd be more than happy to take your order. As for delivering it, I'm afraid we can't accommodate that either."

And just like that, Ryder's expression hardened and Peyton was sure that look caused many a person to fall in line. But so far, he'd been condescending and insulting and she wasn't having any more of it. So she met his gaze and waited for whatever insult was coming next.

"Miss Bishop," he began after a moment. "In this day and age, I would think delivery would be an obvious service to offer. Even a small-town café..." He paused to look around with disdain... "should keep up with the current trends. Especially when so many new eateries are coming into the area. Surely you don't want the competition to put you out of business."

Wait... new eateries? What new eateries? And was he threatening her? Seriously?

Her brother Mason worked for the town and always kept her up to date on any new businesses moving in. So if Mason hadn't mentioned it, that meant Ryder was either bluffing to get his way or planning to open someplace himself.

Which made him a major jerk right now.

"I don't see that happening," she told him levelly. And because she was feeling a little extra bold right now, she added, "And I would think if this dinner were so important, you would have made arrangements more than four hours before it begins."

One corner of his mouth lifted slightly. "Touché."

"I wish you luck with your dinner, Mr. Ashford. Have a wonderful day!" Feeling rather proud of herself, she turned and made it all of three steps before he called out to her again.

So close...

Glancing over her shoulder, she replied, "Yes?"

He slowly walked over to her and it was hard not to hum with appreciation. Ryder Ashford in a tux was stunning enough, but Ryder Ashford in motion was almost like watching porn.

Or... so she thought.

"Surely you could help out a friend of your cousin's," he said, his voice low and gruff and damn if she didn't want to promise him whatever he wanted. "You'll be paid handsomely for it." Then he glanced around again. "And from the looks of things, you can use a good infusion of cash."

And that was it. Now she was officially done.

"Thanks, but I'm good," she said and turned and walked away, her heart hammering hard in her chest the entire time. It wasn't until she was in her office with the door closed that Peyton finally let herself breathe. Collapsing in her desk chair, she let out a long breath. "What a jerk!"

Eyeing her phone, she considered calling Austin and telling him just how awful his friend was, but she also considered calling her brother to see if what Ryder just said was true. Unfortunately, she wasn't sure her heart was up for hearing if it was. She already overcame so many obstacles with the café and it finally felt like things were going her way. Why did Mr. Looks-Too-Sexy-in-a-Tuxedo have to come in and ruin that for her?

Ownership should have been a no-brainer. Café Magnolia was already wildly successful when she inherited it. All she had to do was keep doing what the staff was already doing and she'd be fine. But when you're young and things are handed to you, the critics seemed to take great joy in waiting for you to fail. It didn't matter that her great-grandfather was from the founding family of Magnolia Sound and it didn't matter that her parents were very prominent in the community.

If anything, that one seemed to work against her.

But she persevered and practically killed herself trying to prove to everyone that she was smart enough and more than competent enough not only to continue the café's success, but to succeed with other places as well. Two years ago, she stepped in and helped her brother make a success of the pub he'd inherited from their great-grandfather. After a traumatic fire, she helped redesign the space and then reworked the menu and trained the staff of The Mystic Magnolia. Now it was one of the most successful eateries in town. Peyton took great pride in knowing she helped make that happen.

Damn Ryder Ashford for getting in her head like this.

It had been a long time since she'd second-guessed herself and it was an awful feeling.

"Call Austin or call Mason? Call Austin or call Mason?" she murmured as she slowly spun herself around in her chair. A soft knock on the door had her pausing and straightening. "Come in!"

Dana popped her head inside with a nervous smile. "Um... Mr. Ashford placed a rather large order and asked if anyone would be able to deliver it." She hesitated a moment before stepping fully into the office. "Landon offered to do it, but I thought I should check with you and see if it was okay for him to do that."

Peyton took a moment to think on it. "What did he order?"

"Um..."

"Did he order from the menu?"

She nodded. "He ordered a couple of pints of the She-crab soup, four of the Southern loaded sweet potatoes, two orders of the Peach-Chipotle Baby Back Ribs, two orders of the shrimp and cheddar grits, two of the baked catfish specials, two orders of crab cakes, um... an order of the seaside egg rolls, a whole sweet tea cake, a whole pecan pie... and... some cornbread and biscuits."

Nodding, Peyton was mildly impressed. He caved and ordered. If he simply did that while they were talking, she wouldn't be sitting here thinking negative things about him.

And herself.

Still, she had to wonder what kind of dinner party consisted of grits and tuxes...

"So?" Dana asked, interrupting her thoughts. "Is that all okay with you? Mr. Ashford was insistent that Landon get your approval."

She fought hard to hide her smile. "As long as Landon knows he's off the clock..."

"Oh, yeah. He does. His shift ends at seven and that's what he told Mr. Ashford." She paused and stepped in a little closer to Peyton as she whispered, "And he's paying him fifty bucks to deliver it!"

It seemed Ryder was the kind of person who believed throwing cash at people was the way to get what he wanted rather than simply following the rules. Still, Peyton knew that Landon and his wife had a new baby, so the extra money would probably come in handy. "Tell them both I'm more than fine with it and be sure to thank Mr. Ashford for his business."

"Thanks, Peyton," Dana said with a smile as she walked out of the office.

Once the door was closed, Peyton leaned back in her chair and sighed. It boggled her mind how some people simply *had* to be difficult. Would it have killed the man to simply accept the way she did business graciously? Did he have to use veiled threats and intimidation? Is that how he ran his businesses?

"Probably," she murmured before straightening and dealing with some paperwork she'd been putting off.

She was tired–exhausted, really. And now she was cranky, too. It seemed like her life was consumed with the café, consulting with The Mystic Magnolia, and her plans for the new place. There was very little time left over for... well... a life. It had been a long time since she'd gone out with friends or seen anyone socially except for her family. She missed going to lunch with her sister and her cousin Mallory and going for pedicures and catching up on all the town gossip. It had been a couple of months since she'd done any of that, and even longer since she'd gone out on a date.

Groaning, she forced herself to acknowledge what she really missed.

Sex.

Yeah, and thanks to Ryder looking like sex on a stick in his tux, that's what she had on the brain right now.

Hot, sweaty, sex.

Damn him.

"Bills," she blurted out as she booted up her computer. "Pay some bills. There is nothing even remotely sexy about that." And sure enough, an hour later all thoughts of Ryder were pushed aside as she paid the last invoice and pulled up her plans for her new venture. Pretty soon, she'd have a little piece of Magnolia Sound for herself and no one could say she hadn't earned it.

"This is... quite a variety of dishes, Ry. Nice of you to put in the effort."

Stepping out of his bedroom and into the living room, Ryder glared at the snarky remark from his brother. "Well, maybe if they had given me more than a few hours' notice, I could have gone a little more gourmet."

Patrick Ashford laughed as he shook his head. "You think you had short notice; I was getting ready to leave for work when they called. So instead of driving to work, I had to drive almost four hours to get here."

"You could have flown."

"It seemed like a lot of effort when it was just easier to drive. Besides, it gave me to time to clear my head a bit. You know how exhausting they can be."

The *they* in question were their parents and the reason for this thrown-together family dinner.

And he was already exhausted.

Looking around, he noticed it was relatively quiet. "Where are they?"

"Freshening up. I told them dinner was here so..." Pausing, he studied the table again. "Why are we eating here instead of going out?"

"Mom requested a quiet dinner–just the four of us," Ryder explained. "Besides, you drove through the town. Did you see anyplace worthy of Helen and Jonathan Ashford?"

"I wasn't paying much attention but...I'm not sure how the foil and Styrofoam containers are going to go over."

Ryder hadn't thought of that, but it was too late now.

Glancing at his watch again, he wondered how much freshening they could possibly need to do. Raking a hand through his hair, he fought the urge to growl. He hated when people weren't considerate of other people's time. He'd spent the earlier part of the day being photographed for an article in GQ where he'd finally had to call a stop to it because the shoot was taking longer than they agreed upon. Then his mother called and dropped the news that they were on their way to Magnolia to sit down with him and his brother, which meant he had to cancel meetings and rearrange his schedule to accommodate them, so the least they could do was come to the table when the food arrived.

Walking over to the dining room table, Ryder looked at all the food and had to admit he was impressed. Each tray of food was beautifully plated and presented–albeit in disposable containers–and it all smelled delicious. The café might not have looked like much, but clearly he'd judged too quickly.

Reaching out, he carefully straightened plates before walking over to pour himself a glass of wine. "So what do you think this is all about?"

"No idea," his brother said as he moved over to accept a glass for himself. "Mom was pretty tight-lipped."

That was typical, he thought to himself. Neither parent felt the need to share what they were doing or ask their sons how they felt about it. Ryder wasn't sure why it still bothered him, but... it did.

"Oh, something smells wonderful!" his mother said as she came up the stairs. The house had a reverse floor plan which meant the main living area and kitchen were up on the third floor. "And I'm starving!" Helen Ashford had sleek, silver hair, a full face of makeup, and dressed like she was ready to dine at a five-star restaurant.

Again he had to stifle a groan.

His father was right behind her and he walked over and gave Ryder a firm handshake. Heaven forbid the man give his son a hug or a sign of affection. "Thank you for dinner, Ryder," was all he said before walking to the table and sitting down.

Just another cozy dinner with the Ashfords...

They all took their seats and immediately began passing plates around. This certainly wasn't the kind of meal he envisioned serving, but he'd suffer through it for tonight.

His mother served herself one of the Southern loaded sweet potatoes and stared at it for a solid minute as if expecting it to do something. "My goodness, Ryder, I don't know what this is exactly, but it looks...interesting."

"It's pulled pork and coleslaw served in a baked sweet potato. I was told they're a local favorite," he explained, although for the life of him, he couldn't imagine why.

Then he tried one and...

The combination shouldn't have worked, but it did and it was spectacular. Flavors burst on his tongue and he actually moaned with the pure delight of it. Fortunately, so was everyone else at the table and that had him reaching to try something else and seeing if it was just this one particular dish or if the chefs at Café Magnolia were truly that good.

Crab cakes? Fried to perfection.

Seaside egg rolls? Inspired and delicious.

The catfish? Savory and positively superb.

Honestly, he was more interested in the meal than the reason for it. But then again, it seemed his family felt the same way because they were all raving about the food and that was the topic throughout the meal. When they were done, he and Patrick handled the cleanup—which was fairly quick and painless thanks to the disposable containers—and once everything was in its place, Ryder braced himself for whatever this visit was about.

"You know, Ryder, don't you find living in a house like this to be a little...beneath you?" his father asked. "What on earth are you doing in this tiny little town?"

Here we go...

"I happen to like it here, Dad," he said evenly. "When I came to check out the town, I found that I enjoyed living on the water. Most of the houses—as I'm sure you noticed when you drove in—are like this. Besides, this is just temporary. I purchased it and plan on renting it out once I'm done. It's an investment. My other place is much bigger."

"That's right," his mother chimed in as she sat herself down on one of the sofas. "I thought your place was finished. Why aren't you living there?"

"I wasn't prepared to use it full-time and I had some friends who needed a place to live while their house is being built." Honestly, he didn't mind renting the house to Austin and Mia, but he couldn't wait until he could finally move in himself. This house was fine temporarily, but it was definitely not his style. After designing the other house so meticulously, he was getting antsy to actually be able to live in it.

"Then why not just let them live here and you live in your own house?" she asked, interrupting his thoughts.

"It's not really a big deal," he said before sitting on the opposite sofa. "So why don't you tell me what brings you here? Patrick and I are curious." His brother sat beside him as his father took his place beside his mother.

"I'm retiring."

"Seriously?" Patrick asked with a small, nervous laugh. "I thought you were going to give it another five years or so."

Waving him off, their father explained. "We talked about it and I could still do it, but we've decided that we wanted to move it up so we can spend some time traveling to all the places we always said we were going to go to but never did."

Patrick started rattling off a ton of questions, but Ryder simply sat back and observed.

The Ashfords came from old money. There were many stories about where their wealth originated, but Ryder had never quite believed some of the theories. Either way, his father had made a fortune in the financial business whereas Ryder had opted to take a different approach and went with industrial conglomerates and, more recently, real estate.

The topic of retirement had always been pointless because his father vowed he'd work until he died because he loved what he did. So what changed? And besides that, why bother telling him and Patrick about it? They never discussed their decisions before. Most of the time they made big, life-altering decisions and didn't consult with anyone.

When he and Patrick were growing up, they rarely saw their parents. So why share the news now?

Sitting across from him, he watched as his mother stared lovingly at his father, but she seemed a little... restless.

Which was completely out of character for her.

Something was going on and it had nothing to do with traveling for pleasure, but he wasn't going to get to the bottom of it tonight. For now, he'd bide his time and figure it out.

"So where do you plan on going first?" Patrick asked.

"Alaska," his mother replied. "I've always wanted to go. We're going to do one of those cruises." She smiled at Ryder. "We're going to go whale watching."

Thrilling...

For the better part of an hour, he listened to their proposed travel itinerary, and what stuck out to him the most was that they had no plans to spend time with either of their sons. Not that he was surprised, but... it definitely irked him a bit.

But he brushed it off like he always did.

"How about some dessert?" he suggested as he stood and stretched. "Dad, I got a pecan pie. I know that's one of your favorites. And Mom, I got a sweet tea cake. It sounded interesting and I thought you might enjoy it."

"That's very considerate of you, Ryder. Thank you," she said as she walked into the kitchen. "Do you happen to have any decaf coffee?"

"Of course." And following her, he brewed her a cup. "What about you, Dad? Decaf?"

"Sure, why not? You didn't order it from the café, too, did you? Hopefully we won't have to drink out of Styrofoam cups."

Ryder chose to ignore the comment and made them all

coffee before sitting back down at the table for dessert. Fortunately, the topic of travel had been exhausted and Patrick decided to talk about what was going on in his life.

His brother had no interest in finance or business, but he was making a decent living as a civil engineer. He was living up in Virginia and seemed happy enough. Honestly, Ryder had no idea how he did it–working at one job day in and day out. It would make him crazy. Instead, Ryder spent years investing in different businesses and trying his hand in a multitude of things. His newest venture was the resort he was planning on building here in Magnolia, and he couldn't wait to get the ball rolling. There wasn't a doubt in his mind that the additions he was making to the town would benefit everyone, and it wouldn't be long until it was literally the perfect place to live.

And that was his end game–settling in one perfect place that he chose rather than constantly being told where he should live based on his last name. The choice was his and no one was going to dictate that to him ever again.

The remainder of the evening was relatively boring and uneventful. His father went to bed, Patrick said he had work to do, and it was down to just Ryder and his mother to clean up dessert.

"Everything was wonderful tonight," she said as she loaded the dishwasher. "Wherever you got the food from, it was delicious. I was pleasantly surprised. I wouldn't mind seeing if they can pack up some of those dishes for us to take home with us."

With a soft laugh, Ryder wiped down the table. "What time are you flying back tomorrow?"

"I believe we decided on after lunch, so maybe we can order something and pick it up on the way to the airport. What do you think?"

"I don't know if they're open early enough for that to happen..." But then again, he wasn't sure. "Hang on and I'll check." Picking up his phone, he searched online for Café Magnolia and found himself smiling when a picture of the building came up right next to a picture of Peyton Bishop. She really didn't look old enough to own the business, but it was obvious now that she did and that she knew what she was doing.

He wondered if she would be interested in sitting down with him and advising him on the restaurant he planned on putting in the resort.

Stepping up beside him, his mother glanced at the screen. "Who's that? She's very pretty."

Ryder had to agree, but he kept it to himself. "That's Peyton Bishop. She owns the café where I got tonight's dinner."

"Are they open in the morning? Maybe we can all go there for breakfast," she suggested.

"They open at eight," he read when he clicked on the website. "But unfortunately, I have a meeting at that time so I won't be able to join you."

"Oh, Ryder, you work too hard," she said as she gently patted his arm. "The world won't fall apart if you skip a meeting or work a little less. Maybe ask out a pretty girl..."

Good Lord...

"Mom, I already had to skip two meetings today. I can't skip another one in the morning."

"And the pretty girl?" she prompted, taking the phone from his hand and looking over the café's site.

"I ask out plenty of beautiful women," he assured her.

"Hmm..." After a moment, she handed his phone back to him. "All I'm saying is that it's okay to take a little time for yourself. Life is too short and you should take the time to enjoy it instead of working all the time."

He was about to ask her what exactly she meant and if that had anything to do with his father's decision to retire when she wished him a good night and walked away.

Scrubbing a hand over his face, Ryder decided he might as well call it a night, too. It wasn't particularly late, but he knew he'd sit in bed with his laptop and work for a while before actually going to sleep. After walking around and turning off all the lights, he went into his bedroom, quietly closing the door behind him. Within minutes, he was down to his boxer briefs and in bed, looking over several financial statements. But his attention span was short tonight and his mind was wandering to other things.

Specifically, Peyton Bishop.

He thought about how she stood her ground with him and how at first he'd been offended. Annoyed.

Then he'd been mildly impressed.

And after tasting her food, he was downright dazzled.

He thought of the look on her face as she walked away from him and smiled. She might be young, but she was certainly unafraid to speak her mind.

Young. That kept playing over and over in his mind, and now he was curious about just how young she was and how she managed to own her own business already. Ryder knew he could simply ask Austin the next time they spoke, but he wasn't sure he could explain why he was so curious.

So he decided to do his own sleuthing to find out what he could–searching the usual social media sites. There were tons of pictures of her–always smiling, always laughing–and he found himself drawn to her smile. She was beautiful in a wholesome, girl-next-door way and not the kind of woman he ever gave much thought to, but as he continued to scroll through her posts, there was no denying he was attracted to her.

It felt wrong, not only because of the age difference, but because of his friendship with Austin. He knew they were only cousins, but it still felt like he was breaking some kind of unwritten rule.

And yet he still kept reading her posts—some about the café, some about local events—but nothing told him much about her personally.

Until he spotted a recent post titled "My 25th Birthday" and Ryder suddenly felt like a total jerk for searching like this. She was eleven years younger than him and it felt like he was some seriously creepy old guy stalking her and immediately left the site.

And shut his laptop.

It wasn't until the lights were out that he allowed himself to think about the events of the day *after* meeting Peyton Bishop.

Primarily tonight's family dinner.

First, his father was retiring—out of the blue—and he was certain there was more to that story. Second, he had a feeling his mother had something to do with it, but he was more focused on her comment about him dating a pretty girl. It was the closest she'd ever come to nudging him toward meeting someone and settling down—or even any interest in his personal life. It wasn't something he normally thought about—primarily because he was busy running his businesses and traveling and making money. All those things were very fulfilling and satisfying.

But...were they?

For some reason, he was beginning to feel like they weren't. Maybe that's why he was pushing so hard to right all the wrongs he found here in Magnolia Sound. There were only a few parcels of land that were zoned for commercial use, and he planned on buying them and making sure the town had everything it could possibly need. Besides the resort, he planned on building another restaurant–something a little more upscale than The Sand Bar or The Mystic Magnolia–then he'd like to see a bookstore, a coffee shop, and one of those old-fashioned candy shops. At least...that was his vision right now. It was so close to being perfect, and once it was, he knew this was where he'd make his permanent home.

Maybe ask out a pretty girl...

Peyton Bishop's face came to mind again. He'd seen her at several Coleman family events, he realized that now, and he had to wonder how it was that they'd never been introduced. But now that they had? Ryder knew he'd be seeking her out again.

And not only for her catering skills.

It had been a long time since he'd pursued a woman–too long. So many projects were going on right now, but for the foreseeable future, he was going to be in Magnolia Sound. They were in the final planning stages for his new resort and other than some occasional trips out of town to deal with a few of his other investments, this was where he was going to spend the bulk of his time. Why not fill up his free time with a beautiful woman?

There was Peyton's face again and he couldn't imagine any reason why the two of them couldn't go out to dinner sometime–regardless of the age difference.

Although...if he allowed himself to think a little deeper, he realized that Peyton was still a small-town girl–the kind who maybe didn't do casual relationships. Up until now, that was the only kind Ryder did.

But maybe it's time to change that, he thought.

Maybe ask out a pretty girl...

Rolling onto his side, he got more comfortable and thought of the best way to approach Peyton again. He hoped by ordering such a large dinner tonight she'd see he wasn't such a bad guy. Now he'd give her a day or two before he reached out to her again with a gesture that had nothing to do with food and was perhaps just verging on a hint of romantic.

It was a pleasant final thought before he fell asleep.

2

My compliments to your chef. The food was amazing. Thank you for such an enjoyable dinner. Ryder.

Peyton stared at the card in her hands and then the gorgeous bouquet of flowers it came with in stunned silence. She'd never received flowers from a customer because of her food and it was kind of an awesome compliment.

Even more so because of who they came from and how their awkward encounter had gone two days ago. Still...it was nice to be appreciated.

It had been a long time since a man sent her flowers, and for just the shortest of moments she pretended they meant something more.

Something from a satisfied lover rather than a satisfied catering client.

Ugh...I really miss sex...

Pushing her silly and wayward thoughts aside, she carefully placed the bouquet and the gorgeous crystal vase it came in on the corner of her desk. Then read the card one last time with a soft sigh before placing it gently within the arrangement. Today was a big day for her and she hoped these flowers were some kind of sign that good things were going to go her way.

She'd planned everything out meticulously–had been speaking to both the bank and the realtor once a week for the last three months just to make sure no one else was interested. Of course, they always told her that there were inquiries, but they couldn't divulge who they were from. But Peyton was confident the property was going to be hers.

"And once it is, I'll finally be able to prove to everyone that I'm a serious businesswoman," she murmured.

The first thing she was going to do was go to her parents and show them how she had sealed the deal and how she was finally making her silly dream a reality all by herself.

Ha! I'll show them…

Yeah, they still didn't take her career seriously and were constantly encouraging her to settle down and let the café simply be a hobby while her husband took care of her. Ugh…that was so not the life she wanted. Mainly because it was her mother's life and, from everything Peyton had seen growing up, it didn't make anyone happy.

And it certainly didn't make her mother a nicer person.

It always bothered her that no one seemed to have faith in her capabilities–like all she was supposed to aspire to was finding a suitable husband and being a soccer mom. Well… she did want both of those things, but she wanted her career too.

Much to her mother's chagrin.

She always felt like she'd been stifled growing up. As the middle child to Georgia and Beau Bishop, she'd been the quiet one, the agreeable one. With a charming older brother who succeeded at everything and an uber-outgoing younger sister who made friends everywhere she went,

Peyton had a hard time being seen. And when she finally was, it was with disapproval because she'd finally pushed back. If it weren't for her great-grandfather, God only knows what she'd be doing now.

"Certainly not buying my own little piece of Magnolia Sound," she said as she picked up her folder with all her paperwork in it before grabbing her phone, purse, and keys. Walking out of the office, she called out some last-minute instructions to her staff and promised to be back before the dinner crowd. She didn't realize her hands were shaking until she was in her car and she dropped her keys.

Three times.

Taking a moment to calm herself down, Peyton gave herself a mini pep-talk about all the ways she was prepared for this and how good it was going to feel to finally take the plunge and do it. If anything, she had a long line of relatives who were putting their stamp on the town so it was only fitting that it was now her turn. She wanted to be a part of that little club and honor her great-grandfather's legacy.

And with that thought, she pulled out of the parking lot and made the short drive across town to her realtor's office. Jenna Walsh was a friend of her brother's and came highly recommended and Peyton was a little intimidated by her take-charge and firm businesslike attitude. She was a fantastic realtor though, who really knew how to make a deal.

"And she's going to make one for me today," she said happily as she drove through town. Every place she passed seemed to be owned by someone she knew and loved and it was such a wonderful feeling to know how the whole town was steeped in history and how so much of it started with her family.

Five minutes later, she was parked and felt like she

could take on the world. She walked across the parking lot with more confidence than she ever remembered having. Inside the office, Peyton took off her sunglasses and smiled at the receptionist.

"May I help you?"

"Hi, is Jenna in?"

"Who may I say is asking?"

"Peyton Bishop."

"One moment please."

Peyton took a seat, but she spotted Jenna across the room and gave her a small wave.

And was a little perplexed why Jenna didn't smile back.

It took a solid five minutes for her to walk over, and when she did, she asked if Peyton would follow her to her office. It wasn't until they were alone with the door was shut and they were both seated that Jenna faced her, looking incredibly uncomfortable.

"I'm guessing you're here because you heard the news," Jenna began.

"News?"

Nodding, she explained. "I was planning on calling you and letting you know myself, but things got somewhat hectic and...honestly..." Pausing, she let out a long sigh. "I wasn't sure what to even say, Peyton. It all happened so fast and I know how much you wanted this..."

"Wait, wait, wait," she interrupted, holding up her hand to stop her. "What are you talking about?"

"The property," Jenna said sadly, sympathetically. "It sold this morning."

"*What?!*" she cried. "How? How is that possible? Did they just put in an offer? Don't I get the chance to counter or something?" Her heart was racing like mad, and she seriously felt like she was going to be sick. "I...I don't understand how this could happen! You and I just talked late last week!"

"I know and I really am sorry, Peyton. Apparently the buyer went directly to the seller. I've never had something like this happen before and I just feel terrible!" She reached across her desk as if to give Peyton some kind of comforting gesture, but it sort of fell short. "When I got the call this morning, you were the first person I thought of. Then we had to handle some paperwork since we technically weren't the ones to sell the property..."

She didn't want to hear anymore. Tears stung her eyes and all she could think about was going home, letting out a primal scream, and then crying. Her dream was over–gone. It was devastating and completely unfair and she couldn't understand how it happened.

"But considering he's building a resort on the north end of town," Jenna was saying, completely oblivious to Peyton's turmoil, "I'm guessing he wants to invest in as much of the town as he can."

"Wait...Ryder Ashford bought my property?" she asked in disbelief.

"I'm not really at liberty to say..."

"Technically, you already did!" she reminded her. Even without naming him directly, she said enough for Peyton to figure it out. "Why would he need the one little piece of property that I've been eyeing for well over a year? And why go directly to the seller without coming to you? It doesn't make sense! It's dishonest! Unethical! Is there any way to stop the sale?"

"Peyton, I know you're upset, but...I'm surprised no one bought the land sooner. You know we talked about this a year ago when you first came and talked to me."

It was true. Jenna had told her not to get her hopes up

because it was a very real possibility the property would be sold before she was ready to buy.

She just didn't think it would happen on the same day she was ready to hand over a check.

Or that she'd lose it to Ryder.

With a nervous smile, Jenna said, "In some ways, you could say he's a little like your great-grandfather! He's really investing in the town!"

That was it. It was more than she could bear. And as she jumped to her feet, Peyton didn't care how crazy she sounded. "Ryder Ashford is *nothing* like my great-grandfather! *Nothing!* Ezekiel Coleman *never* would have sneaked around to make a deal!"

"Peyton, I..."

"I need to go," she murmured, scooping up her folder and purse. "I just..." She was out of Jenna's office and out the main door without looking back. Jenna called out to her but Peyton was too distraught to respond. Out in her car, she tossed her things onto the floor and was out of the parking lot without even paying attention to her surroundings. It was a miracle she didn't hit anything.

As she drove across town, all she knew was that she was going to go home and scream and cry and potentially break things. It was so unfair and really, what she wanted to do was confront Ryder and demand that he back out of the deal.

After she yelled at him for destroying her dream.

That's when an idea came to her.

Peyton had no idea where the man worked or how to find him on her own, but her cousin would.

Her tires screeched as she made a hasty U-turn, but she didn't care. Now that she had a destination and a possible chance to vent all of her frustrations, it didn't matter how she got there. Hopefully Austin would be in the office and not on a job site, but she'd deal with that when she actually got to the office.

Ten minutes later, she smiled when she spotted his truck.

Storming through the doors, she spotted him sitting at his desk and walked directly toward him. He saw her coming and smiled. As she got closer, he must have noticed how furious she looked and instantly sobered. Austin stood and walked to his door and closed it as soon as Peyton was inside.

"Hey," he said softly, calmly. "This is a surprise. Everything okay?"

"No, Austin, everything is most definitely *not* okay," she snapped.

"Um..."

Throwing her purse on the nearest chair, she rounded on him. "Do you know what today was supposed to be?"

He took a nervous step back. "Uh, no..."

"Today was *supposed* to be the day that I finally bought the property over near Main and Channel! And do you know what happened when I went to Jenna Walsh's office?" she asked, but didn't wait for him to answer. "I was told the property sold this morning. *This* morning, Austin! And do you know who bought it?"

Silently, he shook his head.

"Your friend Ryder Ashford! I lost my damn dream because of your stupid, egotistical, condescending friend, Mr. Moneybags! Do you have any idea how I feel right now?"

"I'm kind of getting an idea..." he murmured as he went to sit behind his desk.

Slamming her fist down on the desk, she leaned in close.

"I have been working on plans for that property for a year, Austin! *A year!* And you knew that! How could you let him swoop in and steal it out from under me?"

Eyes wide, he stared up at her. "How could I?" he repeated. "Peyton, believe it or not, Ryder doesn't discuss his business with me or what he plans to buy and where. I mean, we talk about stuff but he doesn't consult me first." With a sympathetic smile, he motioned for her to sit. "I know you're disappointed and I am so sorry that this happened, but...maybe this just wasn't meant to be."

She was going to strangle him.

"Now...hear me out," he quickly said, obviously sensing her murderous intent. "There are plenty of buildings around town that need to be rehabbed that we can make work. You pick the building and I'll do all the planning for it to your specifications. I promise."

With a weary sigh, she shook her head. "You don't get it. That property was important to me. It had everything I wanted–the location, the mature trees, just...everything. In my mind, when I envisioned my restaurant, that's where it was. None of the vacant buildings around town have that kind of landscape potential, and the renovations we'd have to do to make it exactly what I want are just too much." Tears threatened to fall again. "Are you sure you can't talk to Ryder about this? Maybe convince him to find some other piece of property...?"

"Pey, it's not my place to tell him how to run his business. We haven't spoken recently and it's not like he would look to me for business advice."

There was a knock on the door and before Austin could say anything it swung open and in walked Peyton's worst nightmare.

He didn't spot her–he was focused on Austin. "Hey,

sorry to show up unannounced but I just sealed the deal on a sweet little piece of property and you know you're my go-to guy for advice on the town and what it needs," Ryder said as he reached out and shook Austin's hand.

"Um, Ryder, this really isn't a good time..."

"I know, I know, I should have called first, but things sort of snowballed and I have a ton of ideas but wanted to run them by you first. I trust you to advise me on what I need to be doing here in Magnolia."

She was going to murder them both, she thought.

Austin nervously glanced her way and that's when Ryder noticed her. He smiled as he held out his hand to her. "Peyton Bishop! What a nice surprise. Did you get my flowers this morning?"

Slowly, she got to her feet. Austin said her name softly—warning her—but she'd deal with him later. Right now, there was only one enemy she could deal with, and that was Ryder.

"Do you know what you can do with your flowers?" she said menacingly. "You can take them and shove them right up your ass!"

To his credit, Ryder's initial reaction was a raised eyebrow.

"Do you have any idea what you've done?" she went on, thankful to be able to unload directly on him now. "You just swooped into our town and you're trying to change every-thing! You think you can just go wherever you want and throw your money around to get what you want. Well... newsflash, buddy! We don't want you changing things! Magnolia Sound was doing just fine before you came along!"

Ryder glanced briefly at Austin before giving her his full attention. "I'm afraid you have me at a bit of a disadvantage, sweetheart," he began calmly. "What is it exactly that has you all riled up?"

"Oh, no..." Austin mumbled.

"Did you seriously just call me sweetheart?" she asked through clenched teeth.

"Um..."

"You really shouldn't have done that," Austin said quietly, shaking his head.

Peyton stepped in close and had to look up because he was that much taller than her before poking him in the chest. "Do you even care who you step on to get what you want? Have you ever once considered that someone other than you has dreams?"

"Peyton," he interrupted. "What is this...?"

"That property you bought this morning was supposed to be mine!" she shouted. "I've had plans for it for over a year and today was the day I was finally able to go in and give Jenna a check!" Stepping away from him, she looked at him with disgust. "That was supposed to be the site of my own restaurant! Not one that I inherited, not one that I helped rehab, but one of my very own. And now, thanks to you, that's all gone!"

Crossing his arms over his massive chest, he studied her for a minute and didn't look the least bit put out by her little outburst. "I'd apologize, but I didn't do anything wrong, Peyton. Granted, I had no idea you were interested in the land, but even if I did, it wouldn't have changed anything. It's business, not personal."

Her mouth was moving–she knew it was–but she couldn't seem to make herself say anything.

"There are plenty of buildings for lease around town. Maybe you can take on one of them and use it for whatever it was you were going to do with the property."

"I don't want a building for lease! I wanted the property so I could build exactly what I wanted! Someplace that had my stamp on it from the ground up!"

"Maybe there's someplace down the coast—maybe in Laurel Bay—somewhere that's better suited to your needs?"

She saw red and was about to lay into him again when he held up a hand to her.

"How about we go somewhere and talk? I'd love to hire you as a consultant for the restaurants I'm planning."

Beside them, Austin groaned.

Loudly.

So many responses were on the tip of her tongue, but she was too much of a lady to say any of them out loud. Instead, she picked up her purse, squared her shoulders, and faced him. "You can take your flowers, your property, and your job offer and go straight to hell, Ryder Ashford." Stepping around him, she strode to the door. She glanced over her shoulder one last time and figured, what the hell before adding, "And you can go frack yourself."

"I can go *frack* myself?" Ryder asked once she was gone. He looked over at Austin in confusion. "What the hell was that all about?"

Sighing wearily, Austin scrubbed a hand over his face as he sat back down. "Anyone ever tell you you have lousy timing?"

That made him laugh. "Never. If anything, I've been told my timing is perfect. I know when to buy, sell, invest... you name it." He sat down and shook his head. "You have to know I had no idea your cousin was interested in the property."

Austin met his gaze. "Not that it would have mattered, right?"

He groaned. "Austin, come on. You know what I was saying."

All his friend did was hold up his hands in surrender.

It took a lot to surprise Ryder and somehow Peyton Bishop managed to do that twice in one week. Raking a hand through his hair, he let out a long breath. "Okay, do I need to do something about this situation with your cousin? Should I order a month's worth of food from the café? Send her some kind of gourmet chocolate? Jewelry? There's got to be something she likes since flowers clearly aren't her thing."

Shaking his head, Austin let out a low laugh. "Would you consider backing out of the deal on the property?"

"No."

"Then there's nothing you can do. Trust me." He paused before adding, "It's just a crappy situation."

"Well, she's young, she'll get over it," he murmured.

And hoped he was right.

He'd meant what he said to her—it was only business—but the look of utter devastation on her face was going to haunt him for a while. Ryder wasn't stupid. In order for him to win a deal usually meant someone had to lose. He'd just never been there to see the look on their faces when it happened. Maybe he was getting old—something he was feeling a lot more these last few days—or maybe he was getting soft, but the thought of hurting someone like that didn't sit right with him.

Especially since he'd planned on going to the café today to ask her to dinner.

Blew that one, didn't I?

His mind immediately began to work through ways they

could both get what they wanted. Obviously dating her was off the table for now, but maybe he could work with her and prove to her that he wasn't such a bad guy.

Leaning forward, Ryder braced his elbows on his knees. "I can mentor her. I can totally help her find a way to channel her business skills into finding something else—another location—and how to do it without getting so emotional over it. Do you think she'd go for it?"

"I believe she told you—not five minutes ago—what you can do with your job offer."

"That was different. This isn't me giving her a token job or a pat on the head. I'm talking about legit teaching her about the business world so she can double her business at the café or open another one and make it even more successful. Come on...I feel bad."

Austin laughed out loud. "You? Seriously?"

"I know! You know I never feel bad about anything, but this..." Straightening, he shrugged. "I have to do something."

"I really wish you wouldn't," Austin said carefully. "Peyton is...well...she's struggled to come into her own. This was going to be her big stand—something she did completely on her own. You unknowingly took that from her. She's angry and she's hurt, and you are pretty much always going to be the guy who killed her dream."

"Oh, come on! No one really thinks like that!" he countered. "I get that she's young, but she has to be smart enough to know that we don't always get our way in the real world! Like I said, it's just business, not personal."

"I know my cousin and believe me, she'd disagree."

Standing, Ryder huffed with frustration. "Then she needs to grow up, Austin!"

Pushing back from his desk, Austin leaned back with a mirthless laugh. "What's going on with you?"

"What do you mean?"

"Why all the comments about Peyton's age and needing to grow up? It's not like you to fixate on something like that."

"Yeah, well..." Shit, how did he even explain it? "Let's just say that I met her the other day at her café and she didn't strike me as being old enough to be the owner."

"Oh, God. You didn't say that to her, did you?"

He nodded.

"You know, for such a brilliant businessman, you're kind of clueless. Why would you say that to her?"

"I don't know! It just sort of came out and then she acted a little bratty about delivering my order and it just made her seem even more immature." He shrugged.

"Ryder..." Austin groaned.

"Yeah, yeah, yeah...I was a jerk. Got it." Pausing, he walked over to the large window and looked out. The view was of a small courtyard–nothing special–but it was better than looking at the disappointment on his friend's face. "The thing is...later that night I sort of tried looking her up on social media and it made me feel like...you know...a creepy old dude."

"If you're stalking anyone online, you *are* a creepy old dude."

Ryder's head fell forward. This was getting them nowhere.

Next thing he knew, Austin was standing beside him. "Let me ask you something–why were you looking her up on social media?"

Turning his head, he frowned. "What?"

"You heard me," Austin said, his voice low with just a hint of hostility. "Why go checking her out online when you could have just called me with any questions?"

Shit. Shit. Shit.

"Austin..."

"Look, I know it's not my place to speak for Peyton. She's an attractive woman but...she's a little young for you."

Ryder wanted to be offended, but...it was no more than what he'd been telling himself.

And then told himself it didn't matter.

"I mean, it's not like you're ancient or anything," Austin went on. "But...she's definitely not for you, so...if you have any questions about her, please ask me. Don't be...you know...that guy."

Yeah, he definitely didn't want to be that guy.

Sliding his hands into his trouser pockets, he sighed. "I really would like to help her." Then he shook his head. "And that's a legit offer, not some excuse to be with her."

At least...not that he was willing to admit out loud.

"Like I said, I can't speak for Peyton but I can't see her taking you up on that."

"Maybe she just needs a few days to calm down..."

Austin clapped him on the back. "Don't hold your breath." His phone rang and he walked over to his desk and looked at it. "Listen, Ry, I need to take this call. Why don't we get together next week and talk about your plans?"

"Sure. No problem." With a nod, he walked out, and it wasn't until he was standing in the middle of the parking lot that he realized he had no place to go. In his mind he figured he and Austin would spend some time discussing plans for the property and then maybe go get something to eat–like the café–and that was when he planned on asking Peyton out. Now he had the whole afternoon and evening ahead of him and wasn't sure what to do with himself.

Knowing he couldn't stand there all day, he got in his car and decided to drive around for a while. It was this sort of thing that often gave him his greatest inspirations. This town–this sleepy little coastal town–had drawn him in from the beginning. It started with the house Austin renovated for him and just took off from there. Now he owned three houses in town–the renovated one that Austin and his fiancée Mia were currently living in, and two smaller ones. He'd rented out one of them to Austin's younger brother Garrett and his fiancée Emma and the other one he was currently living in. Once he moved out, he'd turn it over to a management company to be used as a vacation rental. Real estate was always a good investment, he believed.

After the houses came the ten acres of property he purchased thanks to a tip from Austin. And after that, he took on the local veterinary clinic that Garrett was running. That one had totally not been part of his plan, but after a bit of persuasion, he decided it was a smart investment as well. A soft laugh was out before he could stop it because it seemed he owed a lot of his dealings to the Coleman family. Never before had he entered into this many dealings with the same people, but Austin hadn't steered him wrong yet.

Probably should have talked to him before buying that property then...

Yeah, hindsight and all that.

Still, as he drove through town, he spotted several vacant buildings. Spaces he wanted to fill with the kind of places that would round out the town, except...they would need a lot of work to fit what he had in mind.

So maybe he could understand why Peyton felt the way she did about the buildings. It was odd how they had that in common, but...he wasn't going to let that sway him. And there certainly was no way he was going to back out of a deal simply because some...some...*girl* basically called him a bully.

Who could go frack himself.

She had a lot to learn about business and how to be professional about deals that don't go her way, which was why he felt so strongly about mentoring her.

And, on some level, her bold declarations made her that much more attractive to him.

There is definitely something wrong with me...

Austin was probably right, though. She was too angry with him right now and wouldn't take him up on it, but maybe in a week or two she'd feel differently. Maybe if he simply bided his time and came up with the right strategy, she'd want to work with him in a way that would benefit them both. Ryder's plan was to put a restaurant in the resort, and it was clear that Peyton had a knack for that sort of thing. Perhaps he could teach her about business and she could consult with him on the kind of things he'd need for the food portion of his plan.

Feeling invigorated and inspired, Ryder smiled.

It was good to have a plan—a business model.

And that involved wooing Peyton Bishop in a completely professional manner.

For now.

3

"So when are you coming home, Parks? I seriously miss you."

Her younger sister laughed softly. "I'm not sure. It turns out I really like it down here. Luckily I can work remotely so..."

"You don't work remotely, you job-hop. It's completely two different things."

"Tomato-tomahto," Parker replied.

"Parker..."

"What do you want me to do? Lie to you? I really don't know when I'm going to be home because I'm enjoying myself here in Florida. I'm house-sitting and doing some odd jobs and...I don't know, it sort of fits my mood right now."

"Which is...?"

"To have no real responsibilities. I've tried college, I've done some traveling, and I haven't decided what it is I want to be when I grow up."

"You *are* grown up," Peyton reminded her. "You're

twenty-three years old. It's time to start making some decisions about your life and figuring things out."

The loud sigh was Parker's first response followed by, "Okay, I can see you're still in a pissy mood and if being like mom makes you feel better, then have at it."

"Wow, that was insulting and insensitive on so many levels."

"Look, I get it. You're still disappointed about losing the property to Austin's super-hot friend, but it's over and done with and you need to move on! What would you have done if it sold at any other time over the last year? Would you be this pissed off about it?"

"Of course I would!"

"Liar."

"What? Why would you even say that?"

"From everything you've been saying for the last few weeks, your anger is more about Ryder buying the property than anything else," her sister reasoned. "I think if it were anyone else–specifically someone local–you wouldn't be so...squinky about this."

"Squinky? Seriously?" Peyton asked wearily.

"Fine, um...pissy, ragey, murdery...better?"

"Come on, Parks, you have to admit that I've got a good reason to be upset. This guy is swooping in and trying to change Magnolia Sound! It's not right!"

"To you," Parker countered. "Is anyone else complaining?"

"I...I'm not sure." But now that the idea was out there, she knew she'd be asking around town to find out if she was alone in this rage toward Ryder Ashford.

"You need to let this go. I know you're disappointed and I hate it for you, but...it's not going to change anything."

Slouching down in her chair, she sighed. "I know."

"You need to go out and do something just for you. Go get a pedicure or binge on some of your favorite foods. Give yourself a night to have one last pity party and start tomorrow fresh."

"It's much more fun going for a pedicure when you're with me. And it would be even better if we were at the spa you always talked about opening one day. What happened to that?"

Sighing, Parker replied, "You know me, I'm flaky like that. Big dreams and no discipline to make it happen. Besides, I think we both know I'd probably suck at it."

"Parker..."

"And don't go changing the subject! This is about you needing to move on from all this hater-rage you have!"

It had been two weeks and Peyton knew her sister was right. This anger wasn't getting her anywhere and maybe it was time to move on and just forget about Ryder Ashford and the property. Of course, that wouldn't be completely possible since he was such good friends with Austin and Garrett–and probably half the town–but that didn't mean she had to let him live rent-free in her head.

"You're right, Parks. I think I'm going to cut out of here and go do something. Hopefully clear my head." She was about to say more when there was a knock on her office door. "Come in!"

Dana opened the door and walked in carrying a white box with a giant gold bow on it and Peyton immediate groaned.

"What? What's going on?" Parker asked.

"I'm going to throttle Austin; that's what's going on."

"You lost me."

With an apologetic smile, Dana put the box down on Peyton's desk before quickly leaving the room. "Austin's clearly mentioned some things that I like. This is the third box to arrive this week," she murmured.

"Third box of what?"

Cradling the phone against her shoulder, she carefully opened the box and sighed. "More chocolates."

"Ooh...you love chocolate! You're like the ultimate chocoholic! It's like...wait. Who's sending you candy?"

"Ryder."

"Oh my God! We've been on the phone for almost an hour and you're just *now* telling me about the chocolates? What kind are they? Are they yummy? Does he send a card? Has he asked you out? What's going on? Details, Peyton! I need details!"

"There isn't much to tell," she said wearily, as she began picking which piece to sample first. "On Monday a box arrived from a chocolatier in Paris. Yesterday one came from Switzerland, and today's is from...oh, back to Paris. So yeah. There you go."

"That was the worst story ever," Parker deadpanned. "Seriously, how are you so blasé about this? Gourmet chocolate from around the world and you're just like...meh. What is wrong with you?"

"This is Ryder's MO, I'm guessing. He just throws money or expensive gifts at people to get his way. It's not a big deal."

"Well...it kind of *is* a big deal."

"Why?"

"Pey, think about it. He has nothing to get his way about. Technically, he won. He got the property. End of story. Why does he need to send you anything?"

Good question.

"There was the job offer," she murmured. "You know, the one where I was a consultant for him."

"And you didn't take it...why?"

Another good question.

Looking back, Peyton knew it was because, in the moment, she was furious with him. She still was. But the idea of consulting and maybe having a little something to say about what he brought into Magnolia Sound was tempting. Unfortunately, she didn't think she could work with him. Not only because it would be a constant reminder of what he'd cost her, but she had a feeling she'd be majorly distracted by him. Ryder Ashford was just larger than life, and sexier and more masculine than any man she'd ever been around.

The image of him in his tuxedo came to mind, and it was almost enough to make her sigh.

Stop it! He's the devil!

"Um...Peyton?"

"Oh, sorry! My mind wandered." She popped a white chocolate truffle into her mouth and moaned with pleasure. "Damn that's good."

"I'm *so* jealous of you right now!" Parker said, and Peyton could practically see her pouting. They shared a love of candy and if her sister were here right now, half the box would already be gone. "You have a seriously hot guy practically begging for your attention *and* gourmet chocolate. Your life is so much better than mine."

"I'm not so sure..."

"Okay, I need to go. I've got some dogs to walk and you need to go and get a pedicure while eating chocolate and drinking wine. Go and enjoy yourself and I'll talk to you soon."

"You sure you don't want to come home? I'll save you some chocolate."

"You're adorable, but I'm good. Although...if you see

Ryder, maybe tell him it will help him get on your good side if he sends some of those truffles to me!" With a laugh, she added, "And maybe some chocolate-covered strawberries! I love those things."

"You're ridiculous. Go. I love you."

"Love you too! Go pamper yourself!"

She hung up and took another truffle and popped it into her mouth. She hated how good they were. Well, not *hated,* but...it would be easier to keep despising Ryder if he sent her subpar chocolates. But no, leave it to him to find the most decadent candy on the planet and send it to her wrapped up in a big, beautiful bow.

The bastard.

Placing the lid back on the box, she picked it up along with her purse and phone and walked out of the office. It was a little after four and the dinner crowd hadn't come in yet, so she was able to leave without too much fuss.

A pedicure did sound good, but she wanted to run home and change first.

And drop off her chocolates so they didn't melt in the car.

Once she was home, however, the thought of going out suddenly wasn't quite so appealing. Her house was a small rental right on the beach. Her brother had rented it back before he met his wife, Scarlett, and they'd lived there together until their house was built. Peyton loved the little place and was mildly envious of it, so when Mason was ready to move out, Peyton took over the lease. It was her own little haven and maybe what she needed was to soak in a hot bath, sip some wine, eat some chocolate, and maybe walk along the beach to unwind. As soon as the thought was out there, she knew it was what she was going to do.

Besides, going for pedicures was only fun when it turned into a girls' day with either a friend, her sister, her cousin...

With a soft sigh, she decided she was going to take the bath first–with a small tray of chocolate and a glass of wine– and then go for the walk. In the bathroom, she ran the water, added some bath salts, and clipped her long hair up before going back out to the kitchen to prepare her tray.

On her way back to the bathroom, she turned on some soft music and began to feel herself relax. But as soon as she was naked and submerged in the fragrant water and biting into yet another truffle, all the tension left her body.

"So good," she moaned, and wondered why she didn't indulge like this more often. The water was hot, the chocolate was sweet, and the wine was smooth. All in all, it was absolute perfection. All thoughts of work, properties, and consultation offers were pushed aside and in their place were thoughts of making an appointment to go for a massage, ordering herself a pizza for dinner, and looking into flying down to Florida to see her sister. By the time the water cooled, Peyton felt like a wet noodle and it was glorious.

After drying off, she padded into her bedroom and slipped on a pair of wide-legged capri yoga pants and a cami. Opting to keep her hair up, she walked out to the living room and took her phone out of her purse. She was hungry and it would take an hour for a pizza to get delivered, so the sooner she ordered, the better. When she swiped the screen, however, she noticed a text from Austin.

Austin: Hey! Are you at the café?

Peyton: No. Left early today. What's up?

Austin: So you're home?

This was a little weird, she thought.

Peyton: Yes. Why? What's up?

Austin: Just wanted to apologize in advance

Oh, no…

Peyton: What did you do now?

Her phone dinged with an incoming text at the same time someone knocked on her door. With her phone in hand, she walked over to the door and looked through the peephole.

And immediately groaned.

"Seriously, Austin," she muttered before typing out one last response to him.

Peyton: You better pray I don't see you any time soon because if I do, I promise I WILL hurt you!

Austin: Don't worry, Mia will hold me down so you can do it

Peyton: Thank her for me

Peyton: Oh, and you suck!

The doorbell rang, and she knew she couldn't ignore it much longer. With a huff of irritation, she pulled the door open and glared at Ryder Ashford.

Ryder knew he was in trouble the moment Peyton opened the door.

It wasn't the death glare she was giving him or the open hostility radiating off of her.

It was how she looked. She was beautiful–like heart-stopping, breathtakingly beautiful.

Swallowing hard, he forced himself to smile. "I was hoping to find you at home. May I come in?"

The look of utter annoyance almost made him reconsider, but he enjoyed a good challenge and Peyton Bishop was certainly lining up to be one.

"What do you want, Mr. Ashford?" she said coolly.

"That's a bit formal, don't you think?" he teased, and realized she wasn't remotely amused. "Please, Peyton. I'd really like to talk to you."

"And you thought coming to my home uninvited was the smart thing to do?" Shaking her head, she took a step back. "You've got five minutes."

It was pointless to argue that with her, but he knew he wasn't leaving that quickly. With a murmur of thanks, he stepped into her home and jumped at the sound of the slamming door.

He knew she wasn't a fan of his, but he hoped after two weeks and numerous boxes of chocolate–which Austin assured him were her favorites–that she'd be slightly less hostile.

She walked past him and said, "I just spent the last hour relaxing and it's the best I've felt in weeks, so proceed with caution."

It didn't seem possible that this woman was trying to intimidate him, and yet...she was.

And she did.

Ryder knew he was a master of negotiating and putting potential business allies at ease. He just needed to look at Peyton the same way.

And not as a woman who smelled like wildflowers wearing clingy clothes that showed some amazing curves.

Letting out a breath, he walked over to her sofa and sat down. "Your house is lovely, Peyton."

"It's a rental," she told him, sitting in the oversized chair next to the sofa. "My brother rented it a few years ago before he got married and I sort of fell in love with it and the location." With a shrug, she added, "Even though I've lived in Magnolia my whole life, I still haven't grown tired of the view."

"I can understand that. It's one of the reasons I bought the house that Austin renovated."

"You mean the one you haven't lived in yet?"

Her lips twitched and he knew she was making fun, but he didn't take offense. "Yeah, I'm hoping to be in there early next year. The house he and Mia are building is well underway, and I'm more than happy to wait for it to be done. It seemed crazy to make them move twice."

"Most people wouldn't be so gracious," she said, and he had a feeling it hurt her to say something nice about him.

"Austin's a good friend and I'm happy to help." Which was now the perfect opening for him to say what he came here to say. He got a little more comfortable before meeting her gaze. "You may not want to believe this about me, but I genuinely do enjoy helping people, Peyton. And I would think you'd know that considering it's not just Austin I've helped, but Garrett too. Buying the veterinary clinic wasn't something I planned on, but when Emma shared her proposal with me, it was a no-brainer."

The bored expression on her face told him he wasn't winning any points with her by mentioning the ways he'd helped her family.

"I meant what I said to you that day in Austin's office. I genuinely want to hire you as a consultant for the restaurant I'm putting in at the new resort. Everyone has been singing your praises about the way you turned things around for both Café Magnolia and The Mystic Magnolia." Pausing, he chuckled. "Sorry, it's still kind of funny to me how many businesses around here use the word 'magnolia' in them."

"Are you planning on using it on any of the properties you've taken?"

He arched a brow at her choice of words and didn't think he could let it simply slide.

Leaning forward, he told her, "You're going to need to get over that mindset, Duchess. I have never taken anything. Ever," he said with a little more heat than he intended. "I bought that house your cousin worked on for me and paid a lot of damn money for it. It was the same with the veterinary clinic. And that property that the resort is going to be built on? That one cost me a cool two million dollars." Gently clearing his throat, Ryder sat up straight. "And the property you were interested in? I paid the full asking price for it. Not once–on any of those deals–did I try to haggle, negotiate, or *take* anything. Everything I have I came about honestly and I resent the implication to the contrary."

Her eyes went wide and she visibly paled before looking away from him. "You're right," she said quietly. "I'm sorry. That was unfair of me to accuse you." Then she looked him right in the eye and added, "But considering the only thing I personally know of you is how I lost the property I'd been saving for to you, you'll understand why I feel the way I do."

Damn, she was stubborn, he thought.

"It's not the only thing you know of me," he reminded her. "And we've already discussed it and I don't plan on rehashing it considering my five minutes are almost up."

All she did was give him a curt nod.

"You obviously know what you're doing in the food business, Peyton, and everyone here in town adores you. I don't want to bring in some restaurant that no one is going to have any interest in. I want someone who is going to help me make it a place the locals will want to come to and that visitors and tourists will find as appealing as the town itself. Does that make sense?"

She nodded.

"You're very talented and you've certainly picked some fine chefs–particularly at the café, because the menu is extremely original. Is that what you looked for when you hired them? Creativity?"

A slow, smug smile crossed her face before she replied. "Actually, I created the menu. Almost every item on it is an original recipe of mine. I kept some guest favorites from the previous management, but I wanted to put my own stamp on it. If a chef could follow my recipes and make the proper presentation, then I hire them."

Ryder was...stunned. "So...you went to culinary school?"

"No. My parents thought the idea of me wanting to be a chef was laughable and forced me to take business courses. I went to UNC in Wilmington and majored in business, but I worked for several different restaurants during my time there and learned everything I could from the various chefs. Plus, when I inherited the café, I was still in school and needed to keep things going as they were. I eased my way in there and made my changes slowly and I think I'm finally at a point where I'm happy with all of it. That's why I felt it was time to make the leap into buying the property and building something of my own."

Damn. He had to respect that. She was working her way up, she wasn't impulsive, and clearly she had a good head on her shoulders for someone so young.

"All the more reason I believe you'd be the perfect choice to work with on this project," he said pleasantly. "We'd not only work on a menu, but I'd also want your input on the overall restaurant design, décor, and, most importantly, setting up the kitchen. I have no doubt that you know all the best equipment to buy and the kind of layout required for maximum efficiency. I want top-of-the-line all the way. I'll admit I've done some research but I'm certainly no expert on it."

Her laugh was loud and unexpected. "And you think I am? Ryder, come on. I don't think we need to pretend with each other. You offered this position because you felt bad, but I'll bet you can hire someone with a lot more qualifications to do this with you. And with the money it sounds like you're willing to spend, I would highly recommend you hire someone with more experience in the business. You deserve to hire the best in order to achieve what you're looking to do. I know my limitations, but thank you for the offer."

"But..."

Peyton stood and smiled down at him. "Now if you don't mind, your arrival interrupted my dinner plans, so..."

He had no choice but to come to his feet, and he couldn't believe she was turning him down. And not just out of dislike for him, but because she didn't think she was good enough. In all his years in business, he'd never met someone who willingly walked away from an opportunity that would greatly benefit them.

"Fifty thousand dollars," he blurted out and watched as her eyes went wide again.

"Ex...excuse me?"

"That's what I'll pay you for your help on this project. I'm expecting it to take around three months to plan everything out, meet with Austin on the designs, hammer out a menu...and at the end of that, you get the money to do whatever you want with it."

With a mirthless laugh, Peyton walked away from him and went to her kitchen and got herself a bottle of water without offering him one. She took a long drink before looking at him again. "You're crazy. You know that, right?"

"Why? Because I know what I want and I believe you're the person to help me achieve it?"

"Ryder, be serious! That's a ridiculous amount of money for three months' worth of consulting, for starters. Money that would be better put to use by hiring someone with more experience."

"Seventy-five thousand," he countered.

"You're not listening to me," she said with annoyance as she walked back over and stood in front of him. "I'm not qualified for this. What you're looking to do is way beyond my skill set."

"I beg to differ. Just from the little I know about you, I know you are the *only* person who can handle this." He paused and met her defiant gaze. "One hundred thousand dollars."

"Stop trying to throw money at me!" she yelled. "You can't get your way all the time! And throwing piles of cash at me to convince me to help you is just..." She shuddered. "It's awful and does nothing to improve my original thoughts about you. If anything, it just confirms it."

"And what were your original thoughts about me?" he asked, curious.

"That you're the kind of guy who throws money at people to get what you want," she said as if he were an idiot. "I would have thought that was obvious." Then she looked him up and down, her nose wrinkled. "And don't you own any casual clothes? You show up here in your thousand-dollar suit, you showed up at my café in a tuxedo and...by the way, what the hell was that even about?"

Now it was his turn for his eyes to go wide. "Um...I needed a dinner catered."

"Not the food," she said with annoyance. "The tux. Who shows up at a small-town café in the middle of the afternoon in a tuxedo?"

Raking a hand through his hair, he murmured, "I was being photographed for a magazine article right before I got the call that I needed to get dinner, so..."

"And you didn't think it was weird to drive around town in a tuxedo? You couldn't take five minutes to change into... you know...normal clothes?"

Okay, the conversation was getting way off-track and he knew he needed to reel it in.

Fast.

"I don't see what that has to do with anything. As I was saying..."

"But it does," she interrupted. "Don't you get it? You're very off-putting and condescending. And when you add in the throwing money at people thing, it's beyond offensive. Maybe you should think about working on getting a consultant to help you work on *that*."

For a moment, Ryder was too stunned to respond. While he appreciated honesty, he wasn't used to anyone being quite so blunt with him. Most people he approached with a business opportunity were flattered. He would have thought once Peyton got over her disappointment with the property that she'd realize just what an amazing prospect he was presenting her with. And if money wasn't going to convince her...

"One hundred thousand dollars and I build *your* restaurant on the property I just purchased," he stated, and knew immediately that he had her.

"What?!"

Nodding confidently, he explained. "You tell me what it is that you want on that plot of land, and I'll build it. Just like the restaurant at the resort, you can have input on the building, design, décor, and menu."

"Input? Seriously?" she asked, her arms crossed as she struck a somewhat sassy pose.

"Well, it's my money we'll be playing with, so let's say it will be a team effort. Fifty-fifty."

"Eighty-twenty," she countered.

"Sixty-forty." Because he was enjoying the fact that she was considering this.

"Seventy-five twenty-five. Final offer."

If it were anyone else, he would have laughed because ultimately, he had the final say, but...he'd give her this one. Holding out his hand, he said, "We've got a deal."

Peyton gave him a cautious smile, and when she put her hand in his, Ryder felt like he might crush it. It was small and soft, but she had a firm handshake.

He opted to focus on that part before pulling away. "So...I'll have my attorney draw up an agreement for you to look at and sign. It should be to you early next week."

"That works," she said, but he was beginning to notice how she was trying so hard not to smile or show any excitement.

"You mentioned you had dinner plans," he said, taking another step back from her. "I hope you can now add a bottle of champagne to it to celebrate."

"Well...it was really only going to be pizza out on the deck before going for a walk on the beach. Nothing wild. But I will definitely add a glass of wine to it and toast myself."

"Oh, uh...that sounds...wonderful. Good for you."

Shaking her head, she walked to the front door murmuring, "Such a snob."

"I'm not a snob," he replied, trying to hold on to his

temper. When he was standing in front of her, he decided he'd had enough. "You know, I've had more than enough of your insults. What gives you the right to pass judgement on me like this?"

"Like you didn't do the same to me the day you came to the café?"

Dammit, she had him there.

"And I'm mature enough to see and know that I was wrong," he said smoothly, issuing the challenge. "Are you?"

She crossed her arms over her chest and studied him for a long moment. "That depends."

"On?"

"Prove me wrong."

"Excuse me?"

Nodding, she repeated, "Prove me wrong. Show me you're not some pampered rich dude who wears tuxedos and suits all the time because he doesn't know how to relax and get dirty."

It was borderline ridiculous the way she was baiting him, and yet...he took it.

"Fine. Challenge accepted."

A slow smile crossed her face. "Okay, go home and change into something casual and be back here in an hour."

That...wasn't quite what he expected.

"Why?"

"It seems to me we have a lot of work ahead of us and we'll be spending a good amount of time together. No time like the present to start."

"Then why should I leave and come back? I can just take off my jacket and tie..."

"Nope. Nuh-uh. Go home and change and come back in something less...suity." She waved her hand, motioning to all of him. "This. A lot less this."

"Peyton..."

"I'm ordering a pizza. What are your topping choices?"

"I can pick up something..."

"Everyone likes pizza, Ryder, and considering you interrupted my relaxation time, I'm picking the meal."

It was on the tip of his tongue to call the whole thing off, but...

"Fine. Pepperoni, sausage, peppers, and mushrooms are all acceptable. Choose what you want and I'll be back in an hour." With a nod of agreement, she thanked him and opened the door for him.

It wasn't until he was standing next to his car and the front door was closed that he heard her scream with joy.

With a small laugh and a sense of satisfaction, Ryder climbed into his car and tried to figure out who was teaching who right now.

And where he was going to find casual clothes on such short notice.

4

For the life of her, Peyton had no idea why she would invite Ryder to eat with her, but it was too late to take it back.

Although, now that she had some time to think about it, she realized this was potentially a good test to see if they even *could* work together. No contracts were drawn up, nothing was signed, so if she found sitting and having pizza with him to be painful, she could just say thanks but no thanks and move on.

And kiss a lot of money goodbye.

Yeah, she wasn't particularly proud of the fact that she even considered the money, but how could anyone say no to that kind of cash?

Certainly not me...

The initial offer he threw out annoyed her. The second shocked her. But once he mentioned building her restaurant, she was a goner. So it was important for her to test the waters tonight and see how unbearable Ryder was and what he was going to be like to work with. If he didn't listen to her ideas or tried to push aside her contributions, then she'd seriously reconsider this deal.

And then immediately said a prayer that he wasn't as awful as she originally thought.

She ordered the pizza and then grimaced at her wine selection.

"Screw it," she murmured. "We'll consider that our first test."

Under normal circumstances, Peyton wasn't this antagonistic or confrontational. Something about Ryder just seemed to push all her buttons. At first it was his looks that intimidated her, then his presence–he seriously seemed to command attention no matter where he was. With all the ways he had gotten involved with her cousins, he was around more and more and she knew eventually she'd get up the nerve to introduce herself. She just never imagined things would end up going down the way they did.

Or how bold she'd end up being.

Maybe it was a good thing; maybe by asserting herself the way she was, Ryder would take her seriously. It was obvious he had an issue with her age–that "mature enough" comment was definitely a dig at her–but she was going to prove to him that her age wasn't a strike against her. If anything, her friends and family had always said she was sensible and cautious and that she was born old.

Not the most flattering description, but accurate nonetheless.

So maybe now that she and Ryder overcame this first obstacle, she could prove he shouldn't discount her based on her age.

No, but he could certainly do it based on your lack of experience...

Yeah. That.

Peyton knew in her heart that she could do what he was asking for anyone else. It was Ryder personally that was a bit of a stumbling block for her. If any other person in Magnolia Sound had come to her with the offer to consult— much like Tommy Flynn did with The Mystic Magnolia— she wouldn't have even given it a second thought. Of course she could do it. But when the offer came from Ryder, it suddenly seemed far too challenging. The kind of business he was proposing seemed way more out of her league than the places she was familiar with.

Plus, she wasn't sure she'd be able to handle working so closely with him without it becoming obvious that she was attracted to him.

"Please don't let me make an ass out of myself," she muttered as she walked around fluffing pillows and making sure everything was neat and tidy. Considering the house was really more of a bungalow, it didn't take long and the only thing left to do was put out a couple of plates, napkins, and wine glasses. Once that was done, all she could do was wait.

Fortunately, Ryder was prompt, and so was the pizza delivery because they showed up at the same time. Peyton watched as Ryder tipped the driver before walking up to her door. For some reason, she expected him to show up in perfectly creased khakis and a polo shirt carrying a bottle of wine. But he surprised her—pleasantly. Wearing a pair of navy athletic shorts, gray t-shirt, sneakers, and sunglasses, he looked extremely casual. It wasn't until he was closer that she saw he also looked extremely uncomfortable.

And how the clothes were brand new.

Smiling, she took the pizza from him. "Hey, thanks! Perfect timing! Come on in!" He followed with a murmured "thanks" and didn't say anything else.

Weird.

Placing the pizza on her kitchen table, Peyton motioned

for him to have a seat. "I went with sausage and peppers. I hope that's okay."

Nodding, he took off his sunglasses and seemed unsure of where to put them. It was almost comical watching him look around.

"Why don't you just put them on the coffee table," she suggested and was relieved when he did. But once he sat at the table, he squirmed a bit before he finally seemed to settle. "Are you okay?"

He nodded again. "I'm fine. Why?"

"You seem uncomfortable." Then she noticed him tugging on the shorts and then the neck of the t-shirt and decided she'd had enough. "You cannot possibly be this twitchy over dressing casually, Ryder."

The glare he shot her way said otherwise.

"This is absurd. Do you have a change of clothes in your car?"

"Now *that* would be absurd," he replied defensively. "There's nothing wrong with me. I'm perfectly fine." And to prove it, he reached for a slice of pizza and took a bite.

With a shrug, Peyton sat and took a slice for herself. "Can I pour you some wine? It's nothing fancy, but it's not awful either."

"With a glowing recommendation like that, how can I resist?"

Yeah, this wasn't going to work.

Closing the pizza box with a weary sigh, that's exactly what she told him. "This was a stupid idea and I never should have suggested it. You should just...go. Go home and put on a suit or a tux, eat lobster and filet mignon, drink expensive champagne and just...find another consultant."

She watched as he slowly finished chewing and braced herself to watch him get up and go.

But he didn't.

Instead, he stood up and grabbed the bottle of wine before pouring them each a glass. He sat back down and took a sip of his wine before looking at her. "Peyton, one of the most important rules of business is to never be afraid to leave your comfort zone. While this isn't the sort of thing I'd normally put in that category, the fact is it's exactly what you forced me to do." He raised his glass to her. "Thank you."

Now she was thoroughly confused. "I'm not even sure what to say to that."

"You could say 'you're welcome' and eat your dinner. That would be a start." Then he shifted a bit in his seat before taking another bite of his pizza.

"Can I ask you something?"

He nodded.

"How is dressing casually in the same category as taking a business risk?"

Ryder studied her for a long moment before responding. "Work is my life. Even when I'm not in the office, I'm working. I've made a name for myself and created an image and that means that I'm almost always...on."

It was her turn to nod.

"I work long hours and the only time I ever truly relax is at night when I go to bed." With a shrug, he continued. "It's not a bad thing, but basically I am in a suit all day and that's what I'm used to because..."

"Because you're always working," she finished for him. "I get that, but I'm sitting here watching you and it seems like it's completely foreign for you to be in shorts and a t-shirt. How is that possible? You weren't born in a suit. You were obviously a kid at some point, so...why is this so hard for you?"

He blinked at her, but instead of answering, he took another bite of his dinner.

"When was the last time you wore something like this just...because?"

"Maybe...fifteen years," he finally said, and Peyton was fairly certain her jaw hit the floor.

"How is that even possible?"

"It wasn't necessary. I worked all through college and the only time I had to wear anything like this was that semester I needed to get my phys ed credits in." He took a sip of wine before shaking his head. "Other than that, I had no use for them."

"Not even for comfort? I mean...what do you wear around the house? What do you sleep in?" The moment that last one was out of her mouth, Peyton wanted to crawl under the table and hide.

"My suits are very comfortable," he said, completely unfazed by her question. "I do take off my shoes when I get home as well as my jacket and tie if I'm wearing one." He shrugged. "I roll up my sleeves too." Pausing, he took another sip of his wine. "As for sleeping...well...I don't think we know each other well enough to discuss that."

She was pretty sure her face was on fire and she grabbed her glass and downed the rest of her wine just to have something to do.

Big mistake.

Everyone knew Peyton was a lightweight where alcohol was concerned, but never had she felt it more than that moment. She put her glass down with a little too much force and the room began to spin slightly.

"Peyton? Are you okay?"

Rather than speak, she giggled.

Giggled!

Ugh...kill me now...

Out of the corner of her eye, Peyton could see the amusement on his face and rather than call him out on it, she opted to finish her dinner. The sooner they got through this meal, the better.

Turning the tables on her, he asked, "Can I ask you something?"

She desperately wanted to say no, but ultimately shook her head yes.

"Why did you want me to come here dressed like this? I know you mentioned us starting to work together and being casual, but...this was a bit of an odd request."

The groan was out before she could stop it.

"It's not a big deal," she said, unable to look directly at him. "Really. It was a stupid thing for me to ask and I'm sorry."

It was weird how she could actually feel Ryder staring at her, but she did.

"Okay, fine!" she said with a huff, forcing herself to look at him. "You're very intimidating, Ryder! You're this huge, handsome, and sexy presence and I'm not comfortable with that. It's one of the main reasons we'd never been introduced before. I've seen you at several family events and I've gone out of my way to avoid meeting you. So I thought if we could sit and talk tonight with you just looking like...you know...a regular man instead of your Mr. Sexy Suity-Suit persona, I'd be able to relax with you!"

Pushing away from the table, Peyton stood and walked away, feeling completely mortified.

Seriously, if the man didn't leave and immediately start looking for someone else to act as a consultant, then he was crazy. At the sliding glass doors that led out to her deck, she stopped and slid them open and stepped outside, hoping the fresh air would clear her head. It seemed like the thing to do, even as she wondered what had possessed her to do... well...everything tonight.

No wonder he had an issue with your age. You're acting like a child...

As she leaned against the railing and looked out at the ocean, Peyton cursed herself. It was like she was going out of her way to sabotage herself and this deal. Shaking her head, she sighed and then found Ryder standing beside her, mimicking her pose. She glanced at him and found him staring out at the ocean too.

"I think we need to address some things," he said without looking at her. "I can't help if I intimidate you. I realize it's something I strive for in business dealings, but I didn't realize it came across at social events too."

She wanted to call BS on that statement, but kept it to herself.

"But this is business, Peyton," he went on. "I'm not going to jump through hoops and change who I am just to amuse you. Believe it or not, I'm trying to help you."

"Help me? How?"

"I realize I'm hiring you as a consultant, but I'd also like to help you learn a little more about how to grow your business. Sort of like a teacher or a mentor."

While that was a sweet offer, it would be easier for her to handle if he were about twenty years older, six inches shorter, and possibly bald. The man standing beside her was very...tempting. It didn't seem possible, but she found him even more attractive right now than she did in a tuxedo.

I'm in deep, deep trouble...

Ryder turned his head and caught her staring at him. Blushing, Peyton wanted to look away, but his eyes sort of held her right where she was.

It was practically hypnotic.

Peyton had always been shy around boys, and later, men.

And those had just been average-looking guys.

There was nothing average about Ryder and now, as she stood close to him—could smell his cologne and feel the heat radiating off his body—she felt way out of her element. It would be incredibly rude to walk away from him twice, and she realized he was waiting for her to respond.

"Oh."

He arched a dark brow at her. "Oh? That's all you have to say?" Amusement laced his words.

Forcing herself to look away, Peyton let out a long breath and chose to focus on the waves while she spoke. She wanted to say it was odd how he was taking an interest in her and her business, but considering what he'd just done for her cousin Garrett, maybe it wasn't so odd.

Say something!

"I appreciate the offer, Ryder. You certainly don't need to do that. I'm sure you're very busy as it is without adding teaching me to your schedule." She paused, but the confession was out before she could stop it. "I've worked very hard to manage everything. I've only really taken the lead at the café in the last year because the staff had everything under control and I wanted to learn as much as I could before stepping in and being the boss. I doubled up on classes at school when I inherited it and I'm always taking online classes to make sure I'm as up-to-date as possible on everything, but it's exhausting. I've got no one to talk to about it and I keep a smile on my face so no one knows I'm struggling." Then she let out a mirthless laugh before turning and facing him. "Still want to take me on as a consultant?"

Ryder's expression was intense and he was quiet for so

long that she was on the verge of babbling an apology. But then he reached out and took one of her hands in his and her knees went a little weak.

"Thank you for sharing that with me," he said, his voice low and soft. "I know it's not easy to admit to struggling and I'm sorry you don't have some sort of support group of friends or family that you can turn to. But you're not alone. Not anymore." He squeezed her hand as tears stung her eyes. There was a sincerity there that she didn't expect, and it was crazy how much she wanted to lean in and hug him.

But she didn't.

"Part of being good at your job is knowing your strengths and weaknesses and always wanting to learn how to do better. Based on what you just told me, I bet you're doing a better job than you think."

"I don't know about that..."

He gave her hand another gentle squeeze. "Come on. Let's go back inside and start talking about our visions."

"Our?"

Nodding, he explained. "I obviously have a vision for the resort and you have a vision for the restaurant you were going to build. I'd be honored if you shared some of that with me." He gave her a boyish grin that seemed completely out of character for him. "Of course, I'd completely understand if you wanted to keep it to yourself and use on a future restaurant."

"I doubt..."

She never got to finish.

"I told you I'd build your restaurant," he quickly interrupted. "But if you'd rather hold on to your original plans and use them at a later date, that's fine too."

This was all almost too good to be true. She wanted to pinch herself to make sure she wasn't dreaming. But then

Ryder squeezed her hand and she figured that was close enough.

"Let's go inside," he said softly, and Peyton was more than happy to let him lead the way.

———————

As soon as Peyton excused herself to go get her laptop and files, Ryder let out a long, uneven breath.

He wanted her.

When he had followed her out onto the deck and listened to her confession, he'd felt something he'd never felt before—the need to comfort and protect. In his mind, he kept telling himself to treat her like a friend's little sister who was off-limits. When that didn't work, he reminded himself how they were entering into a potentially long-term business arrangement and how he never mixed business with pleasure.

Then he went and touched her and all those thoughts flew right out the window. The rush to get her inside to talk about plans and strategy was less about him actually wanting to do it, but more like he *needed* to. If they had stayed outside any longer, Ryder knew he would have pulled her into his arms to offer her comfort and then...

It didn't matter. He'd taken control of the situation and he knew he would hold onto it while they opened a dialogue on how they saw these two projects going. He'd never had a problem keeping his focus on a task before, and he didn't plan on having one now.

"Why don't we sit in the living room and I'll lay everything out on the coffee table," Peyton said with a smile as she walked back into the room.

Ryder watched as she moved with the grace of a dancer,

and realized he'd also never done business with a beautiful woman wearing yoga pants and a clingy top.

Austin had warned him not to do this, not to show up on her doorstep and try to convince her to work with him. Of course, Austin's reasoning for it being a bad idea had nothing to do with how alluring his cousin was.

She walked by him on her way to the kitchen. "Would you like another glass of wine? A bottle of water?"

"Um..."

"We really didn't finish eating, either," she called out. "Want me to warm the pizza up and we can eat while we work?"

"Um..." For a man who always had something to say, Ryder found himself at a loss for words. Not that it mattered. Peyton was fluttering around putting the pizza in the oven, pouring him another glass of wine and grabbing a bottle of water for herself. Within minutes, she had everything set up on the large coffee table and was sitting with her feet tucked under her. She smiled up at him, and he knew he would need to sit down.

Close to her.

Think business...statistics...financial statements...

He sat putting the most distance he could between them without being obvious and thanked her when she handed him a plate with another slice of pizza on it.

"Okay, I need to apologize for my behavior," Peyton stated. "And not just tonight. I was rude to you at the café, and then again at Austin's office. So...I'm sorry. I swear I'm not usually like that and I promise to be more professional moving forward."

Putting his plate down, he gave her a sympathetic smile. "To be fair, I was a bit of a condescending jackass at the café. Looking back, I realize I must have sounded like an entitled snob."

Her head turned away, but he heard the soft snicker before she composed herself. "Just a little."

"I'd like to say I'm not usually like that, but I have a feeling I am without even realizing it. So, like you, I promise to be more professional and less condescending moving forward."

That made her visibly relax. "Okay then! Where should we start? The resort?"

Nodding, he picked up his pizza and took a bite before he began to explain to her his vision for The Ashford. The property he'd purchased from Austin's father wasn't ocean-front–hell, it wasn't even on the sound or in a prime loca-tion–but it had a lot of potential.

He'd make sure of it.

Because Magnolia Sound was small enough and narrow enough that it was only a block or two in either direction to get to water, Ryder knew he could play up on the views and proximity to the water.

Something he planned to do.

"Okay," he said, wiping his hands. "The Ashford. I envision it being..."

"I'm sorry," Peyton interrupted softly. "The Ashford?"

Nodding, he explained, "The resort. That's what I'm naming it."

"Seriously?"

"You don't like it?"

"It's a little...narcissistic, don't you think? Naming it after yourself."

"That was the point," he replied, and immediately real-ized how that sounded. "Not that I wanted to come off as being a narcissist, but this is my first step into the hospitality industry and the thought of using my family name felt right."

With a small shrug, she murmured, "Oh."

It would have been easy to move on, but for some reason, her reaction annoyed him. Shifting in his seat, he twisted to fully face her. "I thought the name sounded better than the overuse of the word Magnolia on everything here in town. I'm going for originality."

Another shrug. "It's your resort, Ryder. You're allowed to name it whatever you want."

And while that was true, now she had him wondering if other people in town would have a negative reaction to the name, dammit.

"I know I can name it whatever I want," he replied with a small huff or irritation. "And I was fine with it until your little reaction."

"My reaction? All I said was oh."

"Exactly!"

Her gaze narrowed. "You're not making any sense and the name of the resort really isn't the issue here. Tell me about your plans for the resort itself. What is the theme? The style? What kind of clientele are you hoping to attract? What amenities are you planning to offer?"

The smart thing to do was move on and answer her questions, but Ryder knew himself well enough to know he was going to obsess about the name from here on out.

But he'd do it when he was alone.

With a bit of a renewed focus, he decided to give her his entire project pitch and focus on the details. He hoped she'd be able to envision it all with him while not obsessing over her reaction. Of course, this would have been easier if he had brought his laptop with him and showed her the PowerPoint presentation, but for tonight he was going to simply have to rely on doing things the old-fashioned way.

"As you know," he began, "the property we're building on isn't waterfront, and it is right on the border of Magnolia Sound and the town of Laurel Bay. However, my goal is to give the illusion of being right on the water. Imagine a boutique hotel, if you will. The buildings will all be crisp and bright and done with a high level of coastal décor. Spacious guest rooms, spa services, a pool with cabanas around it, a sophisticated and elegant restaurant along with a poolside café, and everyone will have concierge service."

"So this is definitely a high-end resort," Peyton commented.

"Exactly. Like a gated country-club resort–white-glove service all the way," he went on and then stopped when she got that look on her face again. The one that showed she was completely unimpressed. "Now what?"

"What?"

"I can tell I've lost you already. What's wrong with my plans?"

She let out a long sigh and looked mildly uncomfortable. "It's nothing. Really. Go on."

He'd shared his plans with investors who all loved it. He'd shared his plans with several friends who all thought it was great. Why was he letting the fact that Peyton wasn't the least bit impressed with any of it bother him so much?

"Peyton," he began evenly. "If we're going to be working together, then you need to be honest with me. If there's a flaw in the plans–even though I don't believe there is–then you need to tell me about it."

"It doesn't matter what I think of your plans," she countered. "I'm only going to be consulting on the restaurant. The rest of it doesn't have anything to do with me."

It was the perfect and politically correct response and yet...

Resting his arm along the back of the sofa, his annoyance came to the surface.

"The restaurant is part of the resort–an important part of the resort–and as such, you need to have an understanding of the property as a whole. So if there is something you find undesirable about any aspect of it, then you need to share it."

"Need to?"

"Yes. Need to."

In the blink of an eye, her mood seemed to match his.

"Okay, Ryder, here's what I think," she said with a bit of snap to her soft voice. "You've come around here enough to know what kind of town Magnolia is. It's a small, sleepy, coastal town. We're not big on commercial investors coming in changing things. That's not the vision my great-grandfather or any of the founding families had in mind. What you're proposing sounds like a perfectly lovely resort for a city that is much bigger and caters to your snooty clientele."

"Snooty? I never said..."

"And on top of that, your location isn't conducive to what you want to do. Granted, the north end of town has undergone a bit of a revitalization in the last few years, but it's certainly not the gateway to some upscale, snobby resort!"

"Now it's snobby? If you'd just..."

"You're going to exclude the locals, don't you get that? The average person who lives here won't be able to afford a stay at The Ashford," she went on with a serious eye roll, "and the type of guests you'll be courting aren't going to leave the resort property to shop around town because they'll consider it beneath them. Everyone will get their hopes up that this is going to bring revenue to the town, but it's not. Not in the long-term. Have you even thought about that?"

For a moment, Ryder was too stunned to speak. Here he was thinking that he was going to mentor Peyton and teach her about business, and yet she'd clearly hit on something his entire team of researchers hadn't.

Or maybe they had, and he just wasn't listening.

His mind was spinning with all the ways she was wrong and how he could still make things work, but...

"Look, all I'm saying is that maybe tone down the exclusivity of the resort or maybe do a little market research around town to see if this sort of thing is wanted or needed," Peyton said patiently, as if sensing his inner turmoil. "Maybe I'm way off-base here, but other than my parents and some of their friends, you'll find a bigger crowd at places like The Sand Bar than you will at the country club."

"I understand that, but maybe a more upscale clientele would help the town's image," he reasoned. "Perhaps they'll find a certain...charm to Magnolia and won't mind its lack of commercial appeal or lack of some of the creature comforts you'd find in a bigger, more established beach town."

She looked ready to spit nails but didn't respond right away. But when she did...

"Or maybe you can just throw some cash to all the businesses at that end of town and make them do more beautification to match your snobby-snobberson guests!"

Pinching the bridge of his nose, Ryder silently counted to ten, because this was getting them nowhere.

"Who elected you the person to come in and change the town?" she demanded, her voice rising with every word. "If you think so little of Magnolia, why are you even considering building here? Why do you *keep* buying things here?"

"Peyton..."

Jumping to her feet, she stepped in and leaned closer to where he was sitting. "Part of the charm of this town is how it's not a tourist trap! The people who live here have lived here their entire lives! They're the same people who own the businesses and support one another and if you ask me, what you're looking to do will destroy everything that makes Magnolia special!"

He was done. Getting to his feet, Ryder took pleasure in the fact that he towered over her and caused her to take a step back. He wasn't opposed to the debate on the pros and cons of his plan. What he *was* opposed to was the fact that Peyton was getting emotional rather than sitting and having a rational conversation.

"That's enough!" he shouted and immediately regretted it. Her eyes went wide and he had to remind himself that he was in her home. Raking a hand through his hair, he let out a weary breath. "I had really hoped to have a calm and level-headed discussion with you, but that's proving to be impossible. This isn't personal, Peyton; it's business. Surely you can differentiate between the two!"

"Anything that happens in this town is personal! My family built this town, Ryder. Don't you get that? You think you can just come in here and tweak it and turn it into something that will only benefit you! Don't you have enough? Can't you find some other town to play God with? Why don't you move things over to Laurel Bay, huh?"

"I don't see making improvement as playing God and I think it's childish for you to be carrying on like this. Honestly, you haven't let me get through even one-tenth of the presentation before you passed judgement on the project *and* me!" His hand went through his hair again because he was on the verge of physically shaking some sense into her. "Ten minutes ago, you apologized for your behavior and yet here we are dealing with it again!"

"And you promised not to be so condescending and yet," she said snidely, throwing his words back to him. "Here we are." A small growl came next before she looked at him with utter disdain. She crossed her arms over her chest and instead of looking intimidating–which he was fairly certain was what she was going for–he found she looked...sexy.

Uh-oh...

She was a little breathless, her cheeks were flushed, and...yeah. Sexy.

Ryder took one step back and then another because he needed to put the space between them.

A lot of space.

"What's the matter? Is it possible the great Ryder Ashford has nothing to say?" she provoked as she advanced on him. "Or are you just pissed off because I wasn't all wowed by something you're looking to do? You seem the type who surrounds himself with a bunch of yes-men who just ooh and ahh over everything you propose."

It was wrong how much she fascinated him, or the way he found her whole demeanor so arousing. And she wasn't wrong. He did surround himself with people who typically agreed with everything he did or said. Having someone challenge him wasn't exactly new, but it was never quite like this.

"Tell me I'm wrong," she went on. "Tell me I don't know what I'm talking about." With each word, she got closer, and Ryder was pretty sure he must look like a deer caught in the headlights. When she was toe-to-toe with him, she looked up at him with a confident smile. "Aren't you going to say anything?"

It took all of three seconds for his response to come to him, and it wasn't something he was prepared to think about.

And it certainly wasn't something he'd ever done in a meeting before.

He reached out and hauled Peyton into his arms and silenced her with a kiss.

It wasn't a sweet or slow getting-to-know-you kind of kiss either; it was purely about want and need and heat and desire. Her palms flattened against his chest as his own hand anchored the back of her head before tugging the clip holding her hair back and tossing it across the room. Long, silky tresses covered his hand as he heard Peyton's soft gasp.

Then she was kissing him with equal abandon and it was hard to tell who was in control, but...dammit, Ryder wanted it to be him—needed it to be him.

Banding his arm around her waist, he pressed her even closer as his tongue teased hers. She fit perfectly against him and kissed like a damn dream. When her hands smoothed up over his chest and shoulders and then up his neck and into his hair, he thought it was the most erotic thing he'd felt in a long time.

Too long.

His own hands twitched with the need to touch her more—to explore her—but it suddenly hit him how wrong this was. He had come here to talk business with her—to offer to mentor her—and instead he was manhandling her in the middle of her living room. With a mental curse for his lack of control, Ryder broke the kiss and took a step back, swallowing hard.

"Peyton, I'm...I'm sorry. That was incredibly unprofessional of me and I'd completely understand if you didn't want to move forward with our working relationship." He paused and tried to gauge her reaction, but she was simply watching him while her fingers gently rested on her lips.

Lucky fingers...

"You have to know that...this...I mean...it had nothing to do with business and in no way was I implying that it would be," he rambled on. "So please forgive me and...I think I should go." And in a very un-Ryder-like fashion, he practically tripped over his own two feet in his haste to get to the door. Yanking it open, he turned and looked at her one more time and noticed she hadn't moved. "I'm sorry. Have a good evening."

And like a coward, he walked out.

5

If Peyton had ever thought she'd been kissed thoroughly before, she was wrong.

Utterly and completely wrong because...

Holy hell.

Ryder left over an hour ago and she was still trying to wrap her brain around what happened. There had been no hint of him wanting to kiss her. Hell, there hadn't even been a hint that he was attracted to her and then...*BAM!* Kissing!

And she wasn't complaining one bit.

If anything, she wished she had been bold enough to tell him not to leave.

Looking around, she realized all the ways this night went off the rails. She wasn't relaxed, they'd never finished their dinner, she never had the chance to talk about her ideas for the restaurant, and as much as she'd like to blame it all on Ryder, she couldn't.

"I was majorly bitchy," she murmured. "Again."

Yeah, this was a side of herself she wasn't loving.

Her whole life, Peyton always avoided confrontations of any kind. She remained neutral in just about every situation, no matter how frustrated she felt. There was just something about Ryder that just...brought out the worst in her.

And that just cost her the opportunity to get what she wanted most.

Her own restaurant.

Okay, so technically it wouldn't truly be hers, but it was closer than anything she was going to be able to accomplish on her own and she'd blown it.

Or...had she?

Grabbing a slice of cold pizza, she leaned back on the sofa. Everything happened so quickly, but she knew she didn't say anything about *not* wanting to work with him and all Ryder said was how he'd understand if she didn't want to move forward with their working relationship. So...the way she saw it, they were still working together.

But without the kissing.

Which was unfortunate because it had been a long time since she'd been kissed and it had never been like that.

And she would not have minded one bit if Ryder had kissed her some more.

Or carried her off to bed.

"That's *definitely* not going to happen." While she couldn't know for sure, Peyton had a feeling that once Ryder Ashford set his mind to something, he stuck to it. And it was pretty obvious that he was horrified at the thought of kissing her again.

Just thinking about it made her sigh.

"Figures," she said around another bite of pizza. "A sexy guy who happens to be crazy handsome goes and kisses me and he practically leaves skid marks in his haste to get away. Awesome."

Yeah, it definitely didn't do much for her self-esteem.

Which was why she ate another slice of pizza before walking to the kitchen and searching for something sweet to eat that wasn't gourmet chocolate from Ryder. Then she remembered her plan to go walk on the beach and decided to save dessert until she got back.

She made it all of three steps off the back deck before she realized how it wasn't what she wanted. A walk wasn't going to calm her down or help her relax because what she wanted was answers. She wanted to know more about this resort Ryder was planning and made a promise to herself—again—that she would control herself and not react no matter how much she disagreed with what he was envisioning.

Back in the house, she walked to her bedroom and grabbed a hoodie and pulled it on before slipping on a pair of sandals. It wasn't glamorous, but it didn't matter. When she picked up her phone, she quickly tapped out a text to Austin asking for Ryder's address and was surprised when he didn't question it.

"Smart man."

Five minutes later, she was in her car and driving to the southern tip of town. Her nerves were all over the place and she played out at least half a dozen different scenarios in her head in hopes of being prepared for his response to her showing up on his doorstep.

Only one involved him kissing her senseless again and it was the one she was most in favor of.

But when she pulled up to his house a few minutes later, Peyton found herself second-guessing her impulsive decision. His car was there, the lights were on in the house, but suddenly it felt wrong for her to be there.

And completely unprofessional.

If she wanted Ryder to take her seriously, then she

needed to learn to act slightly more reserved, think before she spoke, and not show up at his home after dark and uninvited. Tomorrow was another day, and she'd call him and set up an appointment and go from there.

Pausing, she stared up at the house and sighed wistfully. It figured that his home was big and beautiful and someday she hoped to live in something equally magnificent. It was three stories, right on the beach, and from what she could see, there was a pool around the back. The property was large so the neighbors weren't too close and she had a feeling the inside was just as impressive.

Maybe knocking on his door isn't the worst idea...

She immediately admonished herself because it was just wrong—all of it. Tomorrow she would call him and they'd sit and talk like colleagues and stay on task instead of making snarky comments at each other.

Knowing it was the right thing to do, Peyton pulled out of the driveway and slowly made her way home.

But stopped for some ice cream first.

The next morning, she went to the café and put in a few hours helping out in the kitchen before going into her office to take care of some invoices. When everything was done, she knew it was time to bite the bullet and call Ryder.

Only...she didn't have his phone number.

With a muttered curse, she texted her cousin—again—and asked for it. Her phone rang less than a minute later, and she couldn't help but laugh.

"Hey, Austin!"

"The two of you are taking up way too much of my time," he said instead of a greeting. "What in the world is going on?"

Peyton gave him the super abbreviated version of what went down the previous evening.

Minus the kissing.

"So you see, I'm trying to be respectful and I wanted to reach out to set up a time for us to try talking things through again."

"Honestly, Peyton, are you sure you even want to do this?"

"Why wouldn't I?"

"It just seems like Ryder pushes your buttons..."

You have no idea...

"And I don't know why you'd consider pursuing this," he went on. "If you want, I'll talk to him for you and make it clear that you're not interested and to just leave you alone."

"That's very sweet of you and I do appreciate you wanting to do that—even though you're the one who gave him *my* address—but I'm really curious now about the whole thing. For all we know, it won't work out and we'll discover we can't work together, but I'd like to try."

She also left out the part about Ryder building her restaurant because it would require a much lengthier conversation.

"If that's what you want, I'm not going to stand in your way."

"Thank you, Austin."

"However...I'd rather not be in the middle, either. So... when the two of you talk, get each other's contact information and only involve me when absolutely necessary. Please."

It was said lightly, but she understood what he was getting at.

"No worries. I promise to leave you alone."

"Thanks," he said with a small chuckle. "I know I'm partially responsible, but..."

"Really, Austin. It's okay. From here on out, we've got

this." Then she laughed softly. "Well, I've got this. I really can't speak for Ryder."

"He'll get the same mini-speech if he calls me about anything related to you, so again...you sure you want to work with him?"

Peyton wished the answer were cut-and-dried, but her cousin didn't need to know that. "I'm sure. I think it's going to be a challenge, but it will also be a fantastic learning experience."

"I'm not so sure Ryder's the guy to be teaching you anything about the restaurant business. If anything, you'll be teaching him," he mused. "You've worked wonders with both places, Pey, and he's just dipping his toes into this sort of thing for the first time."

"So what are you saying?"

"I'm just saying...you've got a good head on your shoulders and you've got great instincts. Don't let anyone make you second-guess yourself. I hate the way he beat you out on the property, but...in time, I truly believe you'll do something even better."

It was probably the sweetest thing he'd ever said to her, and if she were in the same room as him, she'd hug him. "Thanks, Austin," she said quietly. "I appreciate that."

In the background, she heard voices before Austin told her he had to go. With another round of thanks and promises to get together soon, they hung up.

Then she stared at Ryder's number for a solid five minutes before she felt bold enough to make the call. Her fingers flew across the phone screen, and she held her breath until he answered.

"Ryder Ashford," he said, his voice was low and a slightly rumbly and almost made Peyton want to hum with appreciation. "Hello?"

Oh, right...

"Ryder, it's Peyton Bishop," she said, feeling positive.

"Peyton...hello. This is...unexpected." His tone was flat and she had a feeling he was frowning.

While his words and tone didn't instill confidence in her, she also didn't let it stop her. "Yes, well...you left before we could finish talking last night, and I'd very much like to continue our discussion. I was hoping you had an actual presentation for the resort and I think having a visual would certainly help me get a feel for what it is you're looking to do."

"Um..."

"Do you have time this afternoon? I'm free after two if that works for you."

"I...I have a call at two, but...are you sure about this? After the way things went last night, I would have thought..."

"That we could both be adults and move past it?" she finished for him. "Because it seems to me like the timing was possibly off and maybe if we move into a more professional setting, we could try again. Would three o'clock work for you?" Her heart was racing with false bravado, and she hoped Ryder didn't see–or hear–through it.

"I'm not sure." He drew the phrase out and she knew he was trying to come up with a reason why they shouldn't do this.

"Ryder, I think we're *both* mature enough to realize what happened yesterday didn't mean anything." Her stomach flipped just thinking about the kiss, but she powered on. "And as for our disagreement over concept, well...maybe I judged things too soon. After all, I never let you finish telling me about it and I'd really appreciate the opportunity to hear the entire presentation. Surely you can spare me an hour for that."

And once again, Peyton found herself holding her breath waiting for his reply.

"Four o'clock would be better," he finally said. "Unless that cuts into your time at the café...?"

She knew what he was doing and did her best to hide her amusement. "Four is perfect. There's plenty of coverage here at the café so they won't miss me."

"Oh, uh...okay. Then I guess I'll see you at four."

"Great!" she said, and then realized there was one bit of information she needed. "One last thing, Ryder."

"Yes?"

"Where's your office?"

"At my home," he replied. "I'd offer the address but considering you were in my driveway last night, I figured you didn't need it."

Crap!

"Um..."

"See you at four, Peyton."

As soon as she hung up the phone, she gently banged her head against the desk out of pure embarrassment. Maybe working with Ryder was a mistake. After all, how many times could she possibly keep making a spectacle of herself with him?

But as soon as the thought entered her head, she pushed it aside.

"As many times as it takes to get the job done."

If there was one thing Ryder excelled at, it was doing his research to make sure he was always prepared.

But right now, he was completely unprepared for seeing Peyton again.

All night long he had cursed himself for his lack of control even as he kept reliving how incredibly satisfying kissing her was.

And how much he wanted to do it again.

Yeah, he was completely unprepared for this.

When he put his personal feelings aside, however, he had to admit that he admired her tenacity and the fact that she even reached out to him. Somewhere in the back of his mind, he figured last night was a one-and-done situation and the only time he'd ever see her again was at some sort of Coleman family event.

Which there were a lot of.

But now not only was he going to have to face her, but face her in his home. Her comment about meeting in a more professional setting wasn't lost on him, and if he had been smart, he would have offered to meet her at the café or maybe some other neutral location. But it hadn't registered with him until it was too late and now he was stuck trying to figure out the best way to handle this.

One of the bedrooms was set up as an office for him, but...the last thing he wanted to do was lead Peyton past any room with a bed. The living room was another option, but considering how that went last night, they should probably avoid that as well. That left the dining room table and if he tried, Ryder knew he could set it up like a conference room table and try really hard not to be hospitable or let the conversation get too personal.

"Surely I can handle that," he murmured as he went about setting up his laptop. It took several minutes, but he printed out some reports before pulling up the PowerPoint presentation. Next, he placed two bottles of water on the table along with a couple of notepads and pens in case either of them wanted to go old-school and take notes.

Stepping back, he was pleased with the setup and knew the last thing he needed to do was grab a tie and his suit jacket. It was a childish thing to do; he knew that, but he was using it as a defense mechanism so she'd go back to seeing him as the uptight workaholic she originally saw him as.

He just hoped she took the same approach and dressed a bit more formally than last night's yoga pants and tank top.

Well, maybe he didn't *hope* she did that, but...he needed her to.

Desperately.

It was insane how he was suddenly so drawn to her and completely unlike him to be so...bold and utterly clumsy about it. He was normally suave and sophisticated; his usual MO was to take a woman out for a romantic dinner–somewhere she'd be noticeably impressed–and at the end of the night, he'd offer a chaste kiss. Thinking back, Ryder was pretty sure the last time he'd been so consumed with lust was when he was seventeen and about to get laid for the first time.

Why did he have to feel this way now? And why did it have to be with Austin's cousin? His *younger* cousin at that!

So he put on a tie and jacket–he'd already been in dress trousers and a button-down shirt–and walked out to the living room to pace and try to figure out what he needed to do to not look at Peyton Bishop as a desirable woman.

Unfortunately, when he opened the door to her ten minutes later, he had his answer.

Nothing. There was nothing he could do because he'd seen her dressed in business casual at the café, and he'd seen her in yoga pants with her hair up in a ponytail. Today she was wearing a black pencil skirt, a coral sleeveless blouse, and stilettos with her hair down; he was fairly certain he was staring at her in an inappropriate way.

Practically drooling.

I'm so screwed...

Taking a step back, he forced himself to smile. "It's good to see you, Peyton," he said and groaned at how lame that sounded.

"Hey, Ryder," she said with a smile as she stepped into the house. Then she paused in the entryway and looked around in mild confusion. "Oh, this is one of those reversed floor plans, isn't it? The living area is upstairs, right?"

Nodding, he motioned for her to head up the stairs ahead of him.

And then immediately realized his mistake again.

Walking behind Peyton while she wore a figure-hugging skirt was a new form of torture.

So screwed...

They stepped out onto the third floor–houses on the beach were notoriously tall–and she walked right over to the dining room table to put her satchel down before walking over to the sliding glass doors. "Wow! This is quite the view!"

A small chuckle was out before he could stop it. Stepping up beside her, he asked, "Don't you have the same view? You're right on the beach too."

"My little bungalow is ground level. But up like this you really have a much better view. And at this end of the town there are fewer houses so it's just more breathtaking, don't you think?" She smiled up at him, and he felt his heart kick hard in his chest.

"Yes," he murmured. "Breathtaking."

He couldn't care less about the view outside. The woman standing beside him truly took his breath away and there wasn't a damn thing he could do about it.

For a moment, he thought he saw something there–a hint of heat and need–but it was gone before he could be sure and figured it was just wishful thinking. Her smile faltered and she quickly moved away and sat down at the table. "It looks like you've got everything ready to go here. I'm sure you're very busy, so why don't we get started?"

With a curt nod, he joined her and started up the official presentation.

For the next fifteen minutes, Ryder went through everything he had planned for The Ashford and read through and explained all the bullet points, and was pleased that Peyton was taking notes. The final slide was a rough property map that he left up on the screen to show her where he planned to place all the buildings.

Leaning back in his seat, he smiled at her. "And there you have it. The Ashford." As soon as he said it, he wondered if she was going to comment on it again.

But she didn't.

"So, what did you think? Do you have any questions?"

She started scanning her notes and didn't respond right away. Placing the pad down on the table, she straightened and folded her hands on top of it before clearing her throat. "Okay, I think your design for the buildings and the grounds are very appealing," she began. "The property is closer to the sound side of the island so I would suggest possibly maximizing on that view rather than trying to capture both the sound and the ocean."

Nodding, he noted it on his pad. "May I ask why?"

"It's just...it feels like by trying to do too much, you're pulling guests in opposite directions. The sound side offers a more tranquil experience whereas the ocean side tends to be a little more crowded and busier. So if your goal is to be offering this peaceful resort stay, then focus on one side and merely mention the other as a secondary offering."

"Noted. What else?" he asked, genuinely interested.

"I know I was a bit snarky about it last night, but you really should reach out to the businesses that are closer to the property. We've made great strides in cleaning up and revitalizing that part of town, but it's nowhere near as eye-catching as one would expect–especially near the entrance to the resort."

"Okay. But reach out...how?"

"Well...I'm no marketing expert, but maybe by throwing some business their way as an incentive to... polish their property a bit?" With a nervous laugh, she shook her head. "I'm not saying that properly, but I'm thinking start the incentive before you even break ground. Ask the Mystic Magnolia to cater lunch to the construction crew or talk to Jones Automotive about servicing the resort vehicles you purchase." Pausing, she seemed to be collecting her thoughts. "Talk to my cousin Sam about what else can be done on the properties nearby. He owns a landscaping company and did a lot of the work there during the initial revitalization. He might be able to work with you on the transition property leading up to where the entrance to the resort will be. Do you know who owns it?"

"Um..." Leaning over, he reached for his laptop and began searching through his research on the town.

"We don't need to know that right now," Peyton inter-rupted. "It was just a thought. If the property isn't being used or built on, maybe the owner will work with you on beautifying it. Maybe lease it from them or something." She shrugged. "Like I said, that's not really my area of expertise so..."

"No, no...it's a good point for sure," he murmured and made a note to look into it further. Then he looked up at her. "Okay, let's talk about the restaurant. What kind of equipment should I be looking into ordering?"

A slow smile played at her lips. "Well...there's a big restaurant trade show in Denver at the end of the month. I had bought a ticket and planned on going when I thought I was getting the property."

"Peyton..."

Holding up a hand to stop him, she went on. "I wasn't going there, so please don't either." With a small huff, she continued. "There are still tickets available and as much as I can point you to websites and offer suggestions, you seem the type who might enjoy going and seeing everything in person and being able to ask questions of the suppliers."

She was right, he realized. "How long is the show?"

"Five days. There are around fifteen hundred exhibitors and tons of workshops. I've gone to events like these before and they're a little overwhelming but very informative. So if you're interested..."

"I am," he replied firmly. "What do I need to do?"

"Um...here. Let me have your laptop," she said, reaching for it and turning it toward her. Ryder watched as her perfectly-manicured fingers flew over the keyboard and in less than a minute she turned it back toward him. "There's the site. You can look it over and have your assistant fill everything out and pay and they'll send a packet to you. There's a link on there for local hotels. I'm sure a lot of them are booked, but..."

"Not a problem," he assured her as he began filling out the info.

"What are you doing?"

"Filling out the registration. Why?"

"I just thought..."

With a grin, he looked up as he continued to type. "Peyton, believe it or not, I can handle registering for an event on my own. That would be a waste of my assistant's time. Plus, why wait? Besides, it looks like registration closes tomorrow."

Wordlessly, she nodded.

Once he finished, he looked up at her again. "Where are you flying out from and where are you staying?"

"Oh, um..." She glanced down at her hands, and Ryder had a feeling she was hesitating for a reason.

"You're still going, aren't you?"

She shrugged. "I mean...I still have my registration packet and passes, but...I canceled my hotel and never booked my flight to begin with, so..."

Waving her off, he shut his laptop. "Not a problem. I'll fly us out and I'll handle our hotel reservations."

"But..." Her eyes were wide and she didn't look convinced, but that didn't deter him.

"Peyton, do you want to go to the show?"

"Of course I do! I just don't need you to do all of that. I'm perfectly fine flying out on my own and making reservations for myself. I'm sure you're used to staying at the kind of places I can't even afford."

"The trip is on me because we're going together for the sake of my resort," he explained. "Consider this all part of the whole consultation package. Besides, I have a company plane for this exact reason. Why not utilize it?"

That seemed to make her relax. "Well, okay. If you're sure. Just know I have no problem making my own arrangements and..."

"Peyton?" he interrupted.

"Yes?"

"Just say 'thank you' and let's move on," he said with a smile.

She blushed prettily as she smiled back at him. "Thank you, Ryder." After a small pause, she added, "And for what it's worth, I think you're going to really enjoy the show and learn a lot about everything we're going to be working toward."

"I'm counting on it."

After that, they started talking about concepts for the resort restaurant and potential menu ideas before moving on to discuss the poolside café and what that would entail. The entire vibe was different from the night before and rather than snarking back and forth at each other, they had a very interesting and informational conversation that he was enjoying immensely. It seemed like she was as well, which was why he was surprised when she stood and began gathering her things.

"Is something wrong?" he asked as he came to his feet.

Peyton smiled at him as she adjusted the satchel strap over her shoulder. "It's getting late and I need to get going."

Glancing at his watch, Ryder was shocked to see it was after six.

"I think we accomplished a lot here today," she told him. "We're off to a good start and I'm going to think a bit on a couple of different ideas for both resort eateries."

"We can keep talking," he offered. "Can I take you to dinner?" It was an attempt to prolong their time together under the guise of business, but deep down, Ryder knew he was doing it because he was enjoying her company.

"I appreciate the offer, but I have plans tonight." Reaching out, she shook his hand. "You have my number and I'll text you my email address. If you have any questions, please feel free to reach out."

"O-kay..." He kept her hand in his, unwilling to let it go just yet.

"And if you wouldn't mind letting me know about the travel arrangements, I'd appreciate it. I'm a stickler about itineraries," she said with a small laugh. "I love to know where I need to be and when."

"I get that," he replied and appreciated her honesty, and realized he was still holding her hand. "I'll get all of that to you once the reservations are made."

"Thank you," she said softly as she gently pulled her hand from his. "I look forward to hearing from you."

He walked her to the door and wished her a good night, and then stood by the door and watched as she drove away.

"I am in big trouble," he murmured as he shut the door.

Going to the trade show made perfect business sense.

Being away with Peyton for a week could only wreak havoc on him and test his self-control in ways it hadn't been tested before.

He just wasn't sure he was up for the challenge.

And that scared him more than anything.

6

Two weeks later, Peyton stood on the tarmac of the local airport in disbelief.

"I don't understand," she said, staring at the small plane in front of her.

"I told you I had a company plane..."

"You didn't mention how small it was, Ryder!" she cried, nearing hysteria. "It doesn't look safe!"

Beside her, he chuckled softly as he kept walking. "Believe me, it's very safe." When he noticed she wasn't following, he paused. "Peyton, are you afraid of flying?"

"No," she replied defensively. "Not on a normal plane. But this is...it's just not what I expected." Silently, she willed herself to calm down because she knew it had to be safe. There was no way someone like Ryder would have a subpar jet. It wasn't possible. Letting out a steadying breath, she nodded. "Okay. I'm fine. I'm good. I promise."

If only she truly believed it...

"Come on," he said softly. "I think you'll be very impressed." Then, leading them up the airstairs. "It's a six-passenger–including pilot and crew–and has a restroom.

Our flight time is four hours and I can guarantee you'll be very comfortable."

Peyton wasn't quite so sure. Right now she felt a little like she was going to be sick, so all she did was nod.

"Our luggage is being loaded and we'll be taking off in about twenty minutes."

Looking around the small and luxurious interior did not make her feel any better. "Um...where's the pilot?"

"You're looking at him."

A nervous laugh was out before she could stop it. "Um... no. No, no, no. You are *not* flying us. Just...no."

Frowning, he stared down at her like she was crazy. "Why not?"

"Because you're not a pilot, Ryder! It's bad enough I'm flying in this teeny-tiny plane! I can't do this with you as the pilot! It's crazy!"

"I can assure you that I have my pilot's license. I'm completely certified." His tone was calm and soothing, but it wasn't working on her at all. If anything, it annoyed her. "You need to trust me on this, Peyton."

It was on the tip of her tongue to counter that she couldn't, but...she'd be lying. After their initial falling out over her property, she'd come to realize that Ryder was a man of his word. Over the last two weeks he'd reached out to get her input on numerous things and always took her suggestions into consideration. And on top of that, it seemed like everyone in her family couldn't say enough nice things about him. That meant no matter how uncomfortable she was right now, she owed it to him to trust him.

With a curt nod, she walked over and took one of the seats, closing all the window shades as she went. She immediately buckled her seatbelt and pulled out her phone.

And began to search for flights to Denver.

Okay, so maybe she didn't truly trust him with just this one thing.

Looking up, she saw him in the cockpit with his headset on as he quietly talked to someone on the other end.

This is wrong, this is wrong, this is wrong...

Her words only amped up her anxiety, which then doubled when she saw there were no available local flights to Denver today. If she got off the plane and didn't fly out until tomorrow, she'd miss the first day of the show and potentially cause Ryder to miss out on seeing things as well.

Dammit, I hate being empathetic.

But right now, she hated Ryder more.

They had talked on the phone just about every day since their meeting at his house. She had sent him several menu ideas, and they talked décor and theming and even about the show, and not once did he mention that he was going to be the one flying them to Denver. It was something they were going to have to discuss because she did not appreciate being blindsided like this. If they were going to work together, then he was going to have to be way more transparent about the things he planned–especially when they involved her.

Of course, that wasn't going to happen right now. There was no way she was going to argue with him or distract him when she needed him to fully focus on flying them safely across the country.

"Just take some deep, cleansing breaths," she murmured to herself. Doing her best to get comfortable, she pulled out her tablet and figured she could settle in with a good book and do her best to pretend she was on a 747, except...

"Ryder?"

"Hmm?"

"Is there anything to drink?"

"One moment," he replied before standing and stepping out of the cockpit. Peyton watched as he walked over to a small cabinet and pulled out two bottles of water and then a small basket. "I had this made for you. Hopefully there's something in there you'll like." He handed her the basket before placing one of the waters in the cupholder beside her. "Enjoy." And with a confident smile, he went back to his position in the cockpit.

For a minute she felt like a kid on Christmas morning. The basket had all of her favorites, and she didn't know what to touch first. There were fresh strawberries, mini chocolate chip muffins, pretzels, and a small assortment of chocolate truffles. It literally had everything she could want for a trip–sweet and savory. She had to hand it to him. The man thought of everything.

Except to tell her they were traveling in a plane equivalent to a VW Bug.

Within minutes the airplane door was shut and locked, and Ryder checked on her one more time. "Do you have everything you need? It's going to be a little while before I can do anything. There are more beverages in the cooler, the lavatory is behind you, there's Wi-Fi, and outlets for any electronics you want to use. Just wait until I give you the okay to use them."

Mutely, she nodded.

This is it. I'm going to fly in the tiny plane...

"You are welcome to join me in the cockpit at any time..."

"Yeah, no. I'll just sit right here," she told him, and he must have sensed her discomfort because he didn't push. And with a nod of his own, he took his seat in the cockpit.

As soon as they started to move, Peyton's hands gripped the armrests hard. Her knuckles were white as her nails dug into the soft leather. Her eyes slammed shut as she immediately began to pray and hated the fact that she hadn't reached out to her family to tell them she loved them. The plane picked up speed and her stomach clenched as she felt them take off. Part of her wished Ryder would talk to her, but she heard him talking softly to someone. She knew nothing about pilots or flying a plane, but she assumed he was talking to someone in air traffic control.

And prayed they knew what they were doing, too.

Time passed. She knew it did, but she had no idea how long it was until Ryder told her she could use the Wi-Fi and could stand up if she wanted to.

Um...no thank you.

Still, she forced herself to relax and breathe. She turned on her tablet and pulled up the new book she had just started—a cute rom-com about a cheery baker and an uptight CEO. Taking a sip of her water, Peyton opted to try the mini muffins and before she knew it, she was on chapter three of the book.

"You're awful quiet back there," Ryder called out. "Everything okay?"

"Just reading," she replied, hating the interruption. Out of the corner of her eye she could see he was turned around and looking at her. "Shouldn't you...you know...be watching the sky?"

His laugh was low and deep, and at any other time, Peyton knew she'd appreciate it.

Just not right now.

"Seriously, Ryder, can you please just watch the sky?" her voice shook slightly and she could tell he was torn between doing what she asked and being what she needed.

Ultimately, he turned around and focused on flying.

They were two hours into their flight when the first real

bout of turbulence hit. Ryder called back to her to stay seated and buckled, and she quickly tightened her seatbelt. After that, things didn't get better.

The turbulence was awful and because the plane was so small, she knew it probably felt worse than it actually was. But it was powerful enough that her basket fell over, her purse spilled, and her bottle of water went flying. There was no way she was going to call out to Ryder and disturb him, but if things didn't settle down soon, she knew she was going to freak out.

She was back to having her white-knuckled grip on the armrests, with her eyes shut and praying. Right now she'd give anything to be on the ground. Hell, if they lived through this, she was never going to fly again. She'd drive from Denver all the way back to Magnolia Sound before she got back on a plane!

Please let me live...please keep us safe...please stop the turbulence...

It was bizarre how it felt like they were on the ground, off-roading, rather than in the sky. It felt like hours, but she was sure it was only minutes. Either way, whatever the problem was, it wasn't easing up.

"Peyton!" Ryder called out authoritatively. "Things are about to get even bumpier! We're going to make an emergency landing!"

She nodded, unable to speak.

There was a loud booming sound and suddenly things got quieter. She heard him curse, but didn't dare ask what was going on. If she was going to die, she didn't want to know how.

Well...it was obvious how considering their current situation, but the less she knew, the better.

The plane lurched to the side drastically, and this time she did scream.

"Almost there! Just hold on!"

The plane shook and sounded like it was going to come apart, and tears began to stream down her cheeks. This wasn't supposed to happen. This wasn't the way things were supposed to end for her.

Compartments opened and she could hear things falling down all around her, but she didn't dare open her eyes to see any of it.

I love you, Mom...I love you, Dad...I love you, Parker...I love you, Mason...

She went through every family member, every friend, and wondered how everyone was going to get along without her. There was another loud boom and more shaking before everything went quiet–eerily quiet. The only sound she heard were her own sobs. There was no point in trying to subdue them. She wanted the universe to know how devastated she was and just wished there were someone she could scream at right now–someone she could shake and demand they make things right.

"Peyton? Peyton, can you hear me?"

Was that God? Was He talking to her?

"Hey," the voice said softly. "I've got you. It's okay. We're okay."

It was Ryder's arms that went around her. She knew it without opening her eyes. With shaking hands, she undid her seatbelt and wrapped herself around him as she continued to cry. And she had zero intentions of letting him go anytime soon.

They were alive and on the ground and as much as she had what felt like a million questions to ask–like where they were–there was no way she could speak right now. So she held him and was thankful he was holding her right back.

———

Right now, Ryder had no idea which of them was shaking more. As soon as the plane came to a stop, he jumped from his seat to go to her. The sound of her sobbing was more than he could bear.

Of all the egotistical things he'd done in his life, this was by far the worst.

There had been no reason for him to pilot this flight. He had a pilot who worked for him who could have flown them, but Ryder had wanted to show off a bit.

And look where it got them.

His arms banded tightly around her and Peyton's limbs held on to him like a vice. Her arms and legs were wrapped round him and there was no way he was going to try to pry her off just yet. She needed this.

And so do I...

One hand reached up and anchored into her hair as he felt her calming down. She wasn't shaking nearly as much as she was a minute ago. Not that it mattered. She was entitled to cry, and Ryder would do his best to comfort her for as long as she needed.

Or so he thought...

There was a banging on the aircraft door and even with the blinds closed he could see the flashing lights of emergency vehicles. Pulling back slightly, he cupped Peyton's face in his hands. Big, dark eyes stared up at him and in that instant, he saw the same heat and need he was feeling. More than anything, he wanted to close the distance between them–to claim her lips and kiss her until all the fear and trauma were wiped away.

The banging continued and Ryder knew their time was up. "I need to handle this," he said quietly. She was pale and her lips were quivering, but she nodded. Slowly, he got to his feet and went to release the door and stairs, stepping outside rather than allowing anyone on board.

There were easily a dozen rescue responders waiting for him along with people from the tiny airport he had managed to get them to. The only thing Ryder remembered was that they were in Missouri. All the other details did not register with him in his desperate attempt to land the plane safely.

He shook hands with some and agreed to let the paramedics board the plane to check on Peyton. Other than his nerves, Ryder knew he was uninjured. Questions came at him from every direction and he did his best to answer them all. Bottom line was that he'd never flown through such strong turbulence and he panicked. It was a rookie mistake and one that could have cost both him and Peyton their lives. There had been no engine failure, no storms; it was 100% pilot error.

He was the only one to blame.

It took almost two hours for interviews to be done and paperwork to be filled out. The plane was being towed to a hangar to be inspected. During it all, Ryder managed to arrange for a ride to a local motel where he and Peyton would spend the night. In all the commotion, he hadn't had a chance to talk directly to her but from what he'd been told, they were in a fairly remote location with very few options for lodging and none of them sounded particularly appealing. Still, he made the decision for them to stay rather than finding another flight to Denver today. And when she was beside him with his hand resting on the small of her back as he guided them to their car, it appeared she was on the same page.

"I'm not flying to Denver, Ryder," she said in a rush of words.

"Don't worry," he told her. "We're not going anywhere today. We're going to go rest and just try to recover." Looking around, he saw all of their luggage was with them and was relieved to see it being loaded into the trunk of the car.

Carefully, he helped her into the back seat. "We're staying at a place not too far from here and we'll talk about travel arrangements once we've both had a chance to calm down, okay?"

She nodded, but immediately reached for his hand and pulled him in beside her as if she needed the connection to him. "That's fine. It's fine," she said quietly. "Just...no flying."

There was no way he was going to get into how long of a drive it would be for them to get to Denver so he just nodded.

When they pulled away from the airport, the list of things he still had to do ran through his head. There were arrangements to be made for the plane and any repairs it was going to need, getting his pilot here, finding a way to get to Denver, and getting settled for the night. As they drove, Ryder noticed the lack of...everything. It was like they were literally in the middle of nowhere and he had to wonder how they were going to get through the night.

It took twenty minutes to get to the motel, and the only place he spotted to eat was a diner. Fortunately, it was directly across the street from the motel, but neither looked promising.

Before they got out of the car, Ryder looked over at Peyton and asked, "If you're not comfortable with any of this, I can get us on a flight out of here tonight."

"Ryder!" she cried with indignation.

"I know, I know," he quickly interrupted. "Believe me, it's not ideal for me either, but this...I'm not sure staying here is the lesser of two evils."

"I realize it's not the Ritz, but...how bad can it be for one night?"

Famous last words...

Not five minutes later, Ryder knew exactly how bad it could be for one night.

"What do you mean you only have one room available? There's no one here!" he yelled.

The young kid behind the desk didn't look the least bit offended. "Sorry, but...the motel's under renovations and we only have two rooms that are finished. One of them already has a guest staying in it." Then he smiled. "Lucky for you, you'll get to be the first ones to use the other room!"

He wasn't feeling the least bit lucky right now and when he glanced at Peyton, he saw she was taking the news much better than he was.

"I'm sorry, Lucas," Peyton said sweetly as she stepped up to the desk. "We've had a rough morning. Our plane almost crashed on our way to Denver and we're kind of stuck here in town for the night."

The kid–Lucas–who had to be about eighteen, leaned forward and looked like he was about to take Peyton's hand in his. "Oh, man, that sounds scary! What are you going to do? How are you getting to Denver?"

"We're not sure yet," she replied. "All I know is that my nerves are a little frazzled and I'd love to get settled in our room."

Lucas turned and grabbed a key–an actual key–from a peg on the wall behind him and handed it to Peyton. "It's room 110. You step out the door and go to your right and it's all the way at the end."

"You are a lifesaver, Lucas." Taking the key from him, she smiled. "Oh, one more thing. I'm starving. Is the diner the only place close by to eat or is there maybe someplace that delivers...?"

"The diner is your best bet. Their burgers are legendary! Jimmy's Pizza will deliver but they don't open until five so..."

"Got it. The diner for lunch and maybe pizza for dinner. Thanks, Lucas." Turning toward him, Peyton smiled. "You want to put this on your card or mine?"

What he wanted was to find somewhere else to stay, but clearly that wasn't happening, so he paid for the room and followed Peyton out the door.

Neither spoke as they walked down the sidewalk to the end of the building. In his mind, Ryder tried to imagine what a small town in the middle of nowhere considered renovated. He pictured perhaps fresh paint on the walls and maybe new bedding, but for everything else to remain woefully outdated. Standing behind Peyton as she opened the door, he braced himself for disappointment.

"Oh my God," Peyton murmured, and Ryder knew this was possibly the final straw for them today. "This is amazing!"

Wait...what?

Following her into the room, he had to admit he was... pleasantly surprised.

There was a king-sized bed with floating night stands on either side and the wall behind it was covered in a bold geometric wallpaper in blue and gold. The furnishings were mid-century modern and the room had an overall vintage vibe.

It wasn't nearly as offensive as he would have imagined.

The room still smelled like paint, drywall, and cleaning products, and it instantly had him relaxing. The carpet was new and as he walked around the room, he spotted the smart TV and minibar. Seriously, he couldn't find a thing wrong with it.

"This is very retro-chic," Peyton said as she put her purse down. "I can't believe I'm going to say this, but this is seriously the highlight of the day!" Looking over at him, she laughed. "The way things were going, I was expecting to walk into a room that hadn't been touched since the seventies, but this is amazing!"

Then she sat on the edge of the bed and bounced, and Ryder had to force himself to look away.

"Memory foam!" she said happily. "Oh my goodness! It's so comfortable!"

"Um..." Rather than focus on her sprawled out on the bed, he set their luggage down in the corner of the room. "So, uh...are you hungry? Want to go across to the diner?"

She fell back on the bed and Ryder stifled a groan. "I know I'll feel better once I eat something, but I feel like my limbs are made of lead right now." Turning her head, she looked over at him. "Any chance you'd be willing to go over and bring some food back here?"

After what he'd put her through today, he'd go out and hunt for food if she wanted him to.

"Of course," he told her. "I'm not sure what they have, but..."

"Bacon cheeseburger, fries, and a Coke, please," she said, kicking off her ankle boots. "Thank you!"

Ryder envied how relaxed she looked and wished he

could feel the same, but he knew this tension was going to be with him for a while.

Walking across to the diner, he was again surprised by how neat and tidy and retro it all looked. He was greeted by three different waitresses and when he glanced at the menu, he saw plenty of items that appealed to him—far too many for just lunch and considered talking Peyton out of pizza delivery for dinner and simply coming back here.

"What can I get for you?"

Looking up, he noticed her nametag said Janet and smiled. "Hey, Janet. Can I please get two bacon cheese-burger deluxe platters to go with two Cokes, a slice of apple pie, and one of those giant chocolate chip cookies?"

"You got it!" she said, smiling warmly at him.

While he waited for their food, his mind raced with the events of the day.

Reckless. Egotistical. Stupid. Yeah, that pretty much summed up his thoughts about himself. It had been a long time since he did something like this, something to impress a woman that went so horribly wrong. Not only could he have killed them both, but he was never going to forget the look of sheer panic on Peyton's face even before they stepped foot on the plane. Looking back, he knew he should have changed plans right then and there. At the very least, he should have called his pilot and had him come and take over just to put Peyton's mind at ease. Instead, he'd charged forward because he believed he was in the right.

And he'd never been so wrong.

Groaning softly, he sat at the counter and tried to think of how he was going to get them to Denver with the least amount of trauma. Driving was the obvious answer, but it truly was a long drive and he was not a road trip kind of guy. However, if that was what it took, then he was going to have to do it. They were still going to miss the first day of the show no matter what, so he supposed it was the way it was going to go. Deep down, Ryder knew he could get on a commercial flight–or even on a larger chartered plane–and be okay, but he didn't think the same could be said for Peyton.

And then they were still going to have to figure out how to get back to Magnolia Sound when the show was over. There was no way he was going to waste two or three extra days driving, so...they were going to have to figure something out.

But as he went to open their motel room door fifteen minutes later, he still had no idea about any of it.

"Here, let me help you," Peyton said when she spotted him. She had changed into an outfit similar to the one she'd worn at her home that night–yoga pants and a tank top with tiny straps.

It's like she's trying to torture me...

"This little table and chair set might make a tight fit for all this food, but the thought of eating on the bed just seemed wrong." She went about setting up their food, completely oblivious to the fact that he was uncomfortable. Then she smiled up at him. "I think you can lose the jacket and tie, don't you?"

"Um...sure," he muttered, slipping his jacket off as he walked over to the closet to hang it up. His tie followed before he unbuttoned his cuffs and rolled up his sleeves. It didn't do much to help him relax, but it definitely would have looked ridiculous for him to stay so formally dressed.

Peyton was already seated and munching on a fry when he sat down. "So?" she asked. "How was it? Did you hate it? Should I be leery of the food? Although...I have to admit, it smells so damn good that maybe I don't want to know."

"Trust me, you're safe," he said with a small laugh, reaching for a fry for himself.

"Well, you told me that this morning and look what happened."

She wasn't looking at him as she said it, and her tone was light, but it pretty much gutted him.

Reaching across the table, he took one of her hands in his. "You have to know how sorry I am," he began gruffly. "In all the chaos once we were on the ground, I realize I never apologized to you. I should have taken your concerns seriously before we even left the ground. There's no way I can ever make it up to you or even apologize enough, but... you have to know how awful I feel about the entire thing. I never should have put you in that position." Pulling his hand back, he raked it through his hair as he let out a long breath. "Hell, I realize now just how unprepared I was, and it would be one thing if it were just me on the flight. I had no right to bring you along."

The whole time he spoke, she slowly ate another fry.

Damn. This was harder than he thought it would be.

"I don't know what happens from here," he went on. "Not just with our transportation, but between you and me with our working relationship. If I were in your shoes, I know I wouldn't trust me. I've never endangered anyone before and I can't believe I was foolish enough to do something like this now."

"Ryder, did you intentionally fly into the turbulence?"

Was she crazy? "It doesn't work like that."

"Exactly," she said plainly. "I'll admit that I was terrified when I saw the plane this morning and even more terrified when you told me you were the one flying it."

"Oh God..."

"But," she quickly interrupted. "It was my decision to

stay on board. Granted, I did search for other flights before we took off and there weren't any, but I could have left if I wanted to." With a patient smile, she reached over and took his hand again. "It was the scariest thing that's ever happened to me in my life and if I keep thinking about it, I know I'll freak out, so...can we just...not talk about it?"

If only it were that simple...

"Peyton, you have to realize that it's going to come up. We still have to get to Denver and then all the way back to Magnolia. The topic of transportation can't be avoided forever."

With a shrug, she picked up her burger and took a bite, moaning with pleasure.

Yeah, she was going to be the death of him. Rather than obsess about it, Ryder opted to pick up his own lunch and try it. They ate in companionable silence because the food was that good. Other than random comments about just how good it was, they were both focused on their burgers and fries. It wasn't until they were done that he mentioned the dessert.

"I'm not saying we have to eat it now, but there's a slice of pie and a giant cookie in that white bag."

"Ooh...what kind of cookie?"

"Chocolate chip."

Her smile was radiant. "I'm beginning to think my cousin gave away all my favorites to you. That basket this morning was absolutely amazing. I'm kind of bummed that it spilled all over the floor. I only had the muffins before everything happened."

"I promise to send you a replica of it when we're back in Magnolia."

Standing, Peyton stretched and cleaned up their mess. There was a trash pail outside their room and she took everything out there before coming back in and sitting on the bed. "So...do you think we should have looked into getting a rental car and starting the drive today?"

His bark of laughter was the first response, and when she looked offended, he instantly sobered. "Peyton, after the morning we had, I didn't think it was smart to try to drive anywhere. I realize this is going to cost us the first day of the show because it's an eleven-hour drive to Denver from here, but..." He shrugged.

Collapsing back on the bed, she sighed loudly. "Damn. I didn't realize it was that long. Then again, geography really isn't my thing." Turning her head, she looked over at him. "So what can we do?"

Ryder was still sitting at the small dining set by the window and tried to think of a reasonable response. "I...I guess we go online and see about renting a car for tomorrow and getting as early of a start as possible."

"And what about the plane? You know, your plane?"

"I've got some calls to make about it. Someone's going to inspect it today to make sure there's no damage and then my pilot will come and fly it back to North Carolina."

"Oh."

"As a matter of fact, why don't I get started on that," he said, pulling his phone from his pocket. "I'll just be outside and..."

"You don't need to leave the room. I'm going to pull out my laptop and do some work too so I promise not to disturb you."

"I was actually afraid I was going to disturb you," he said with small laugh.

"Well...you do you and I'll just be over here doing my thing."

For an hour, Ryder made one call after another. He set

up his laptop on the table and made notes about the mechanic who was going to look at the plane and made arrangements for his pilot to fly in to take it home. It killed him to do it, but...he couldn't put the full blame on Peyton. The thought of getting back on the small jet didn't sit well with him, either.

There weren't many car rental locations nearby. He studied their options and then the route and he thought maybe this was the universe's way of saying they shouldn't go to the trade show. He had no idea why, but...it seemed like an awful lot of bad luck was following them.

Turning, he saw Peyton climb from the bed and stretch before she padded over toward him, smiling. "I can't concentrate on anything," she told him.

"How come?"

"It seems my mind can only focus on one thing and... I'm not proud of it."

His mind instantly went to the night they kissed, and he secretly hoped that's what she was referring to. She was a living, breathing temptation, and that clingy little outfit had been driving him mad for weeks now.

As she got closer, her smile turned a little...impish. "It's probably going to sound naughty, but..."

"But...?" he croaked, starting to sweat.

"The temptation is too much. It's crazy and I know I shouldn't, but..."

"Peyton, I...I feel the same way," he admitted as he stood.

"Oh thank God," she said with a laugh. "I kept telling myself I should wait to eat the cookie because lunch was so filling, but that bag is just sitting there mocking me!" Stepping around him, she grabbed it and pulled the cookie from it.

Food? She was thinking about *food?* Was that all she thought about?

"Do you want the pie?" she asked, holding it out to him.

Taking it from her hand, he tossed it on the table, much to her wide-eyed dismay. "No."

"But...you just said..."

Ryder took one step toward her and then another until they were practically toe to toe. "I didn't realize you were talking about food."

Frowning, she stared up at him. "What did you think I was talking about then?"

It would have been easy to simply grab her and kiss her like he had that night at her house, but that wasn't how he wanted it to be with them. It was important for him to know that Peyton wanted him as much as he wanted her.

Slowly, Ryder reached up and caressed her cheek. "I thought you were talking about...this. Us." Swallowing hard, he never realized how awkward this could be. If she wasn't interested–or worse, was offended–then the rest of this trip was going to be hell. But he needed to know if he was alone in this, if he was the only one fixated on this attraction that was growing stronger by the damn day.

"Ryder, I..." she began softly, pausing briefly to bite her lip. "I'm not sure what to say."

So he *was* alone in this. He misread all the signs.

Peyton Bishop was hell on his ego and making him second guess every instinct he had. But when he went to move his hand away, he felt Peyton grab onto it tighter and hold it against her skin.

"I thought you regretted kissing me that night," she said quietly, beautiful eyes scanning his face. "You said it was a mistake."

"At the time, I thought it was, but...I can't seem to be in

a room with you without wanting you." His admission earned him a soft gasp from her and it made him bold. "When you pulled into my driveway later that night, I stood waiting by the door but...you never got out of the car."

"I was afraid, but I hated the thought of you regretting what happened. If you hadn't left so quickly, I would have told you that I wanted it too." Then she pressed closer until they were touching everywhere. "I wanted more."

Thank God.

"Peyton," he warned gruffly. "I'm hanging on by a thread here. Be sure because as much as I want to kiss you, I want more, too."

A slow smile spread across her face as she tossed the giant cookie back onto the table. "Then we're on the same page," she whispered before going up on her toes and pressing her lips to his.

7

For two weeks, Peyton had regretted not going after what she wanted with Ryder and she wasn't going to make the same mistake twice. The moment her lips touched his was one of the most exciting of her life.

Strong arms banded around her just as her hands smoothed up over his chest, along his throat and stubbled jaw on their way up into his hair.

And Ryder had really great hair.

The man certainly knew how to kiss, and it was even better than their first one, which she didn't think was possible. He smelled good, he felt great, and he kissed her with a thoroughness that made her want to climb him and hold on tight. Instead, she gripped his hair and gave it a little tug, causing a sexy-as-hell throaty moan from Ryder.

I want to hear that again...

With another tug, he broke the kiss and breathlessly stared down at her. "Am I doing something you don't like?"

She shook her head. "No. Why?"

"It felt like you were trying to get me to stop."

So much for me being some sort of sexy vixen...

"I...you made a sound, and it was kind of a turn-on and I wanted to hear it again," she blurted out and knew her face was on fire from sheer embarrassment.

A slow, wolfish smile crossed his lips and it made her heart skip a beat. There had never been a man who made her feel so wholly out of control and needy. And there'd certainly never been one who made her want to drop into bed with them after a few kisses.

There's a first time for everything...

Swallowing hard, Peyton forced herself to look up at him. "Okay, I need to say something." First, she let out a long breath and then decided to just go for it. "There's probably a million reasons why this isn't a good idea. We work together, you're friends with my family, and from what I can tell, you're not the kind of guy who does relationships."

"Well, I..."

"Please," she quickly cut him off. "I need to get this one last embarrassing thing out." One dark brow arched at her and it made butterflies take flight in her belly. "I'm always overly cautious with every aspect of my life. The risks I allow myself to take have only been where business is concerned, never in my personal life. But I know if I don't do this—if *we* don't do this—I'm always going to regret it."

One hand came up and gently caressed her jaw. "First of all, there is nothing embarrassing about anything you just said. If anything, it was incredibly brave." He paused and simply looked down at her with a heat and hunger she'd only read about in romance novels. "You never have to be embarrassed with me. Ever. I always considered myself a risk taker," he went on with a low laugh. "Or someone who just takes."

No argument there...

"But with you...I feel completely out of my element."

Ryder slowly leaned down and rested his forehead against hers. "I've been telling myself for weeks to leave you alone, but...I can't."

His words made her feel sexier and more powerful than she'd ever felt. To know that a man like Ryder Ashford wanted her was the headiest sensation and she was greedy for more of it.

"I don't want you to leave me alone," she whispered. Taking a step away from him, she gave him what she hoped was a sexy smile. Then, with trembling hands, she slipped her cami up and over her head before letting it fall to the floor and then slowly slid her yoga pants down her legs, kicking them aside. Getting naked for the first time was always anxiety-inducing, but the way Ryder was watching her put her at ease.

Even as it excited her.

He closed the distance between them and reverently touched her breast, causing her to sigh. His hand was so warm and so large and felt so good that she slowly arched into his touch.

"You're so beautiful," he murmured before lowering his head and kissing her. This kiss was different from the one before. Where it was so hungry and wet and wild, this one was almost agonizingly chaste.

His hands, however, were doing some pretty wicked things to her nipples, causing Peyton to gasp as she reached for him. This time when Ryder lifted his head and smiled at her, his words took her by surprise. "I've fantasized about having your hands on me. I need you, Peyton. Please."

This man had done nothing but surprise her from the first time she laid eyes on him, and it was clear he wasn't through yet.

Meeting his gaze, she slowly unbuttoned his shirt and,

as expected, his chest was spectacular. Running her hands over it—feeling his warm skin—was more erotic than it should have been. If she was getting this turned on already, she couldn't wait to see what it was like to lie in bed naked under him.

Boldly, she pushed his shirt over his shoulders, never breaking eye contact with him. Ryder was the one to remove his belt and trousers, and when he stood before her in nothing more than dark and snug boxer briefs, she didn't know where to touch first.

Before she could decide, Ryder scooped her up into his arms and made the short walk to the bed. As he lay her down and covered her body with his, Peyton forced herself to savor the moment. They might only have this day and night before they had to go back to what they had before. And when he leaned down and claimed her lips in another hungry kiss, she told herself not to think about tomorrow. For now, she wanted to make this one night last a lifetime.

The room was starting to get dark, but Peyton was feeling too boneless to move to turn on a light. She was thoroughly exhausted and far too comfortable naked in Ryder's arms. He placed a soft kiss on her shoulder and she hummed with pleasure.

If she'd thought his kisses had ruined her for other men, they were nothing compared to the way he'd made love to her. It was like riding a roller coaster—frenzied and out of control one minute and then soft and tender the next. Glancing at the clock, she saw it was her usual dinner time but didn't want to ruin the moment by asking about what they were going to eat.

Even though she had worked up an appetite...

Ryder continued to kiss along her shoulder and neck, and Peyton couldn't believe his stamina. They'd made love twice and in her own limited experience, that was impressive enough. Hell, when he'd pinned her under him the second time, she was pretty sure the shocked look on her face was almost comical. Not that Ryder had commented; no, he was pretty much focused on making her feel good.

Mission accomplished.

The slight sting of a bite made her jump, and she glanced over her shoulder at him. "Hey, what was that for?" she teased.

"Well, you were very quiet and I thought I should do something to get a response out of you."

"You could have just said something. No need to go biting."

"You didn't seem to mind my biting earlier so..." Carefully, he rolled her over so she was facing him. "And I certainly hope to see where else I can taste you later."

Now she knew her eyes went wide. "Later?"

"I have big plans for the rest of the night and they all involve you being naked and willing," he told her, making her shiver with delight.

Before she could answer, her stomach had a little something to say. Loudly. Peyton ducked her head and groaned. "Um..."

Ryder's arms tightened around her before placing a kiss on the top of her head. "I think that means I need to feed you first."

She burrowed down under the blankets, which really just put her at eye level with his chest. "You can just throw the cookie at me and I'll eat it down here before I die of embarrassment."

To her surprise, Ryder joined her under the blankets. "I thought we already covered the part where you don't need to be embarrassed with me."

"Ryder..."

"If it makes you feel any better, I'm hungry too."

"Well...maybe I feel a little better..."

"And I think we should go across to the diner and eat there. The menu was a little impressive."

Tossing the blanket off so she could see him, she smiled. "Really?"

"I've learned several things about you, Peyton. And one of them is that food is very important to you."

"Does that mean you won't judge me if I eat some of that cookie before we go to dinner?"

"Only if you're unwilling to share it," he teased before leaning in and kissing her thoroughly.

Yeah, she'd share the cookie and anything else he wanted for more of this.

It took several minutes, but they reluctantly got out of the bed. Peyton knew she had to shower before they went anywhere, and was about to ask Ryder if he wanted to join her when his phone rang.

A weary sigh was his response when he looked at the screen.

"Who is it?"

"The mechanic from the airport. I need to take this."

"Go ahead. I'm going to grab a quick shower," she told him, but he was already answering the phone.

As much as she wanted to linger under the hot water, she wanted to eat more. So it was super quick, and she was out and drying off in less than ten minutes. There was a knock on the bathroom door before Ryder peeked in with a bashful grin.

"Damn. You're out already," he said. "I didn't think I was on the phone for that long."

"You weren't," she assured him, walking over and giving him a quick kiss. "The water pressure was amazing, but I didn't want to spend too much time in there." Then, with a soft laugh, she added, "Plus, I'm that hungry."

Fortunately, he laughed with her and pulled her to him. "Any chance I can take a quick shower, too?"

"Absolutely!"

"What if I'm not as fast as you?"

"Then you'll just have to meet me over at the diner," she said with a sassy wink before pulling out of his arms and heading for her suitcase.

But she never made it.

Ryder came up behind her and hauled her into his arms before depositing her on the bed and covering her body with his.

"Ryder!" she cried out with laughter. "What in the world?" This was a side of him she'd never seen, and if anything, it made him even more appealing. He had her hands pinned above her head and as she squirmed beneath him, the only thing she accomplished was having her towel unwrap.

"What if I told you dinner was being delivered in thirty minutes?" he murmured, kissing his way from her jaw to her shoulder.

"I...I thought..." she panted, as his mouth captured her nipple. "I thought we were...oh that feels so good...going out...and...and..." The moment she gave up trying to speak and bucked beneath him, Ryder released her hands. Peyton immediately raked them through his hair, holding him to her.

"I took a chance and ordered in," he told her before

moving to her other breast. "I couldn't stand the thought of leaving the room." When he lifted his head and gave her that heated gaze she was already addicted to, she didn't care if they never left this room.

Or ate dinner.

"Are you disappointed?" he asked.

Shaking her head, she guided him back to her. "Just promise we'll make good use of our time before dinner arrives."

His smile was slow and seductive. "Duchess, I promise you'll be very satisfied with how we spend our time."

And when his head lowered again, Peyton was pretty sure Ryder Ashford was never wrong.

The room was pitch black and Ryder hated the fact that he was awake.

Beside him, Peyton was sound asleep and would occasionally let out a soft snore that was kind of adorable. His arm was around her and their legs were tangled together and it was a contentment that felt slightly foreign to him. All he knew was that he wanted more of it–not just for a night or for a weekend, either–more as in...indefinitely more.

Peyton brought out a side of him that Ryder thought simply didn't exist.

He came from a rather serious family–there wasn't a lot of laughter in his life. Responsibility and the importance of an education had been drilled into him since he was a young boy. And while he loved what he did for a living and found it satisfying, he never felt a sense of...joy in it. Working with Peyton these last few weeks showed him he could have heated debates and deep discussions and conversation as well as laugh and learn new things. He'd always been inquisitive, but he felt like this was the first time he was truly enjoying what he was discovering.

And it was all thanks to the woman in his arms.

Softly, he kissed her forehead and she hummed sleepily.

Today had been...well, it had been both terrifying and exhilarating. After the way things happened with their flight, he'd been certain there was no way to turn the day around. And he certainly never imagined he'd find himself naked and thoroughly worn out in bed with Peyton. If they ignored what brought them to this room, then the day could best be described as perfect. Everything, from the moment they'd stepped into this room had been faultless.

It was a shame he was going to have to ruin it in just a few hours.

Yeah, he'd sort of put some things in motion earlier in the day—as in right after lunch—that he opted to keep to himself.

Namely, booking a flight for them to Denver.

Honestly, Ryder had no idea how Peyton was going to take the news, but he had a feeling she wasn't going to be thrilled. Maybe after a good night's sleep she'd feel better about the prospect of getting on a plane.

At least...he hoped she would.

And he hadn't gotten them seats on a major airline either because there were no direct flights and it almost wasn't worth the effort since they could drive it in almost the same amount of time.

No, he'd gone and...chartered them a plane. A larger one than his, but still not anything particularly large. The one he secured could hold fifteen passengers and was considered large by the charter companies. But he had no idea how one skittish young woman would see it.

Glancing at the clock, he saw it was a little after four. Their flight was at ten. The last he and Peyton talked about their route to Denver, he had told her they'd go back to the airport around eight because it was where the car rental agency was.

He just hadn't mentioned that they wouldn't be utilizing it.

Letting out a long breath, he wondered if he was making a mistake.

Another mistake.

If she really wanted to drive, then...

His thoughts were interrupted when one of Peyton's hands started to smooth over his chest. Then his abdomen. And then lower.

Oh, God...

The feel of her soft lips following that same trail made him moan. With his hands going to her hair, he whispered her name like a plea. They needed to sleep. She needed to sleep, but...God help him, he didn't want to stop her.

Not now.

Not ever.

———

A little over four hours later, they were standing in the airport hangar.

"I don't understand," she said, giving Ryder a strong sense of déjà vu.

Stepping in front of her, he took one of her hands in his. "Okay, hear me out."

"Do you expect me to get on a plane?" she asked, interrupting him with barely-contained fury.

"I just think an eleven-hour drive is a bit excessive and will cause us to miss the entire first day of the show," he reasoned, amazed at how calm he sounded. "You know things don't kick off until noon and if we take a plane, we can be in Denver by eleven and at the hotel by noon. If you think about it, it just makes sense."

Then he held his breath because he could tell she was gearing up to give him a piece of her mind.

"Are you out of your mind?" she hissed, aware of all the people walking around the hangar. "Do you remember what nearly happened to us yesterday? Are you *that* insensitive that you would force me back on a plane after being traumatized like that?" Pulling her hand from his, she paced a few feet away. "Unbelievable. You are unbelievable!" Pausing, she faced him. "You told me we were driving!"

"Technically, all I did was mention where the car rental agency was," he said quietly, realizing how bad this made him look.

"Ryder, you cannot keep doing these things! You make these plans and then spring them on me and they never work out!"

"One time!" he reminded her. "It was *one* thing I sprung on you that didn't turn out so great and it wasn't my fault! I don't control the *air*, Peyton!" He knew losing his temper wasn't helping his cause, but...

"Look, if we're going to work together, you can't keep pulling this shit, Ryder," she snapped as she went toe to toe with him. "I refuse to work for someone who treats me like I'm not entitled to an opinion!"

"That's not what I said, and it's not what I implied!" Ryder forced himself to take a step back and calm down because things were spiraling out of control. When he looked at her, he almost laughed at her defiant pose–arms crossed, hip cocked, foot tapping, and an angry glare. She'd checked all the boxes of how to look pissed off, but he wasn't going to let it get to him.

"Peyton," he began.

"Not flying," she countered quickly.

Of all the ridiculous...

"You know what?" he yelled. "Fine! We'll do it your way. We'll drive the eleven hours to Denver and miss the first day of the show and probably lose our rooms. Again!" Then he leaned in close and figured two could play at this game. "You know, for someone who claims to want to be taken seriously and have her own business, you seem more than willing to pass up an opportunity to hit those workshops and demonstrations you've been rambling on and on about for weeks!" With a final look of disgust, he added, "I expect a higher level of professionalism from my colleagues. I guess that was my mistake in thinking you could handle it."

Her shoulders sagged and he felt like the world's biggest ass, but she seriously aggravated the crap out of him.

"And if you're going to toss out your expectations of people you work for and how they're failing you, then you need to be prepared for them to tell you all the ways you're lacking." There wasn't anything else he wanted to say because he was already choking on his heated words. Now he had to deal with getting them over to the car rental agency, canceling their charter flight, and getting his assistant on the phone to try to see what could be done about the hotel because he just didn't have it in him to do it himself.

After everything he and Peyton shared last night–and

again this morning–it hurt him more than he thought it would that she would immediately slip back into work mode. Didn't she get it? What happened between them had nothing to do with work and business. It wasn't just about last night. He thought it was obvious it wasn't a one-night stand.

Clearly, it wasn't.

And it stung that not only did she think like that, but that it didn't seem to bother her that it's all it was.

Raking a hand through his hair, he looked over at her. "Wait here while I go make arrangements to get us over to rent a car." He made it all of five feet before Peyton called out to him. Hanging his head, he let out a long breath before facing her. "Yes?"

Walking over, she shook her head. "Do you even understand why I'm upset?"

He nodded.

"I don't appreciate you making light of my fear, Ryder. If you don't respect me enough..."

Reaching out, he grasped her shoulders and gave her a small shake. "I do respect you! I think it's the other way around here and you don't respect me!"

"How...?"

Dropping his hands in exasperation, he struggled to find the right words. "I don't give a damn about this trade show! Do you know why I'm going?"

She shook her head.

"Because it's important to you! No matter what we saw or which vendors we talked to, I was always going to defer to you on what we put in the kitchens. Don't you get that? I would have been fine looking at a catalog or even if you just gave me a list of what you wanted me to buy!" Her expression never changed, and he had to wonder why he was even trying. With a helpless shrug, he said, "I wanted to experience it through your eyes. You were so excited about it and I guess...I just wanted to know what that was like. That's why I'm pushing so hard to get us there."

"Oh," she said quietly.

"If you'll excuse me, I just need about five minutes to let everyone know the change of plans. Could you possibly see about reserving a car for us while I handle this?" Turning, he started to walk away, and again, she called out and stopped him.

This time he didn't turn around.

"No," she said.

Slowly, he glanced over his shoulder. "What?"

"No," she repeated. "I'm not going to see about reserving a car."

His initial impression of her being an immature brat flashed through his mind, but Ryder quickly pushed it away. "Fine. I'll take care of it. Travel arrangements weren't in your job description. Now, if you'll excuse me, I really need to let everyone know what's going on."

"I'm not making the arrangements, Ryder, because... you're right," she said, and he heard a hint of annoyance in her voice and did his best to hide a smile.

"About...?"

This time she rolled her eyes. "This show is important to me and I really *do* want to get there. I just...I can't help being scared. If we were getting on a 747, I'd like to think I'd feel better, but...I don't know!"

There was no way he couldn't go to her. She might just want a working relationship with him from now on, but he wasn't going to think about that right now. Walking over, he pulled her into his arms and hated how she stiffened against him.

"I hate that you're afraid," he whispered, relieved when she started to relax in his embrace. "And I hate that I'm the one who caused that fear. Nothing's going to happen this time, Peyton. We have a pilot and a co-pilot who have over thirty years of experience between them. The plane is more than twice the size of mine." Then he pulled back and looked down at her with what he hoped was a reassuring smile. "And you won't be sitting alone. I'll be right there beside you and I promise to do anything you need to distract you."

Her own smile was reluctant. "You promise?"

He nodded. "I promise."

With a weary sigh, she met his gaze. "Okay. Let's do this."

Ryder was afraid to hesitate for even a minute because he didn't want her to change her mind. "Can we get some help with our luggage, please?" he called out as he led Peyton over to the plane. "If there's anything you want before we take off, just let me know and we'll get it."

Walking up the steps ahead of him, she murmured, "Any chance you have a tranquilizer dart? I'm pretty sure that would be helpful."

The thing was, he knew she was only partly kidding.

On board, they took their seats and Ryder figured the best way to keep her distracted–and stay in the business zone like she wanted–was to focus on work. Booting up his laptop, he pulled up the site for the trade show and spent the next two and a half hours letting her talk about which vendors they were going to see and why they were the best of what they were looking for. She'd held his hand in a vice grip during takeoff and landing, but other than that, it was business as usual.

And he hated every second of it.

A town car picked them up at the airport and took them to their hotel. He'd booked them at the Four Seasons because it was his usual hotel of choice and the look on Peyton's face when they checked in was almost comical. She'd made a few comments on how she would have been fine at a "normal" hotel, but he simply shrugged.

"We have one deluxe mountain-view room with a king bed and then the one-bedroom presidential suite," the clerk confirmed.

"Correct," Ryder replied and signed where he was directed and thanked him when he got the keys. It wasn't until he and Peyton were in the elevator with the bell hop that she spoke again.

"A deluxe mountain-view room?"

"I thought you'd enjoy it. The view truly is spectacular."

She made a non-committal sound. "And...you're in the presidential suite?"

He nodded. "Probably just down the hall." Glancing at his watch, he frowned. "I figure we can spare about thirty minutes to get settled in our rooms and then we'll meet up and head over to the convention center. Will that work for you?"

Another quiet sound and nod were her only response and for the life of him, Ryder didn't understand what was wrong. The flight had been flawless, the trip to the airport had been equally pleasant, and they were staying at one of the most luxurious hotels in the city before going to the big trade show. He might not know Peyton that well, but he figured she'd be a little more excited than this.

"Peyton, is everything alright?" he forced himself to ask.

She was staring at the elevator doors. "Fine. Why?" she responded listlessly.

O-kay...

"It's just...you seem a little...underwhelmed. I thought you were looking forward to this?"

"I am."

Something was definitely bothering her and for the life of him, he had no idea what it could possibly be.

"You're not still upset because we flew, are you?"

"No." Turning her head, she gave him a smile that didn't quite reach her eyes. "I'm not upset, Ryder." Then she resumed staring at the elevator doors. Their rooms were on the sixteenth floor and when they stepped out a minute later, she thanked him and promised to meet him in the lobby in thirty minutes.

All without looking at him.

There were at least a dozen things he wanted to say to her–to force her to look at him and tell him why she was acting like this–but...he didn't want to make a scene. The bellhop took care of her luggage before stepping back into the hall to lead Ryder to his room. So with nothing more than a curt nod, he turned and strode down the hall to his suite.

Inside, he tipped the bellhop and waited for him to leave before growling with frustration. It was going to be damn difficult to deal with walking around a trade show with Peyton being in this mood and being so...indifferent to him. And really, how dare she? She was the one who decided they needed to go back to a work-only relationship as soon as they'd left the hotel this morning. So why was he being punished?

The last thing he wanted to do was unpack, so instead he simply prowled around the suite. It was magnificent, just like he knew it would be, and he couldn't help but wish Peyton was staying in it with him. The look on her face yesterday when she explored their ridiculously small motel room came to mind, and he wondered if she'd look around at all this luxury with the same expression. Walking over to the wall of windows, Ryder studied the view of the mountains and wondered if Peyton was looking out her window and impressed by what she saw.

"I'm seriously losing my mind," he muttered before turning away. The bar was fully stocked and it was beyond tempting to have a drink. Picking up a bottle of Patrón, he was about to pour himself a glass when there was a knock at the door. It wasn't unusual for the concierge to come up and make sure everything was to his liking, so he figured he'd just tell them yes and ask to be alone.

But when he opened the door, it wasn't the concierge.

It was Peyton.

And she looked ready to spit nails.

"Peyton, is everything...?"

Her hand in his face stopped him. "Not a word!" she snapped before stepping around him and walking into the room. "I've got something to say to you!" By the time he shut the door and turned, she was already out of his sight. The suite was huge and he found her in the middle of the living room, slowly turning in a circle as she looked around. When she spotted him, she paused and frowned. "Why does one person need all this space?"

"Um..."

"You know what? It's not important," she muttered before walking over to him. "What the *hell*, Ryder?"

Honestly, he wasn't sure what he was supposed to do or say, so he just waited for her to keep going.

And she did.

"You know, I knew I had you pegged from the get-go– the uptight, haughty rich dude who didn't do relationships.

I knew it and yet I threw caution to the wind anyway. And just when I thought that maybe I'd been wrong about you, you go and prove me right!"

"I'm sorry, but...what?"

She nodded and then began to walk in a slow circle around him. "Yeah, you go and prove me right! We had this amazing night last night–at least, it was amazing to *me*–and as soon as we left the hotel, you acted as if nothing happened! I mean...how is that possible?" she demanded, even though she didn't wait for an answer. "Don't you have any feelings? Isn't it even a little awkward for you to have us working this closely together after seeing each other naked?"

"Peyton, I..."

"Or is this just the norm for you? Do you usually sleep with the women you're working with? Schmooze them and impress them with your private plane and fancy dinners before sleeping with them and walking away? Huh? Is that your MO? Do you..."

He never let her finish and honestly, he hated that this was how he was continually having to break her train of thought but...he stepped in close, cupped her face and silenced her with a kiss. He didn't give her a chance to say another word; he simply conquered and claimed and practically sagged against her when she kissed him back with just as much eagerness.

Glad I'm not alone...

On and on it went–hot and vicious and all-consuming– and if Ryder had his way, they'd stay like this until she believed he wasn't that guy. It was important that she understand that...

Wait a minute...

Abruptly, he broke the kiss and stared down at her as he

caught his breath. Her expression was a little dazed and confused and he had a feeling he looked the same way.

"Peyton," he began and immediately had to stop and clear his throat. "I'm not the one who wanted to go back to a work relationship. That was you."

"What? No, it wasn't! You were all about talking business on the plane," she countered.

"But that was only after you had started throwing back at me what you expected of our working relationship!"

Her eyes went wide, and she went to say something but seemed to instantly reconsider, her mouth opening and closing as she stared up at him.

It galled him how this girl had completely knocked him on his ass time and time again with her boldness. For all his years of wheeling and dealing and believing he had all the confidence in the world, Peyton Bishop had been doing nothing but proving to him just how wrong he was about himself for the past month.

Stepping in close again, he repeated his pose of cupping her face. He didn't kiss her this time, though. Now it was his turn to say a few things.

"You have no idea how much you destroyed me yesterday," he began gruffly. "You are bold and sexy and exciting and I want more of that. More of you. I don't want last night to be all we have." He felt her relax against him. "Do you want more with me? To see where this can go?"

"I do, Ryder," she agreed softly. "But I need to know that you're truly all in with me, that you're not just killing time while we're working together."

"That's not it at all. This has nothing to do with our business relationship. I want to spend time with you, get to know you, laugh with you, and make love with you. Are you willing to give me a chance?"

She nodded. "More than anything," she said, her tone more than a little breathless.

"Thank God," he murmured before sealing it with a kiss.

Peyton's body molded to his, and it was all he could do to stop from picking her up and carrying her into the bedroom. The way she hummed and rubbed against him told Ryder she'd be open to that idea, but he didn't want to take away from why they were here and how important it had been to her.

So for the second time today, he reluctantly broke their kiss. "Trade show," he panted, swallowing hard. "You mentioned a demonstration you wanted to see today."

Biting her bottom lip, she looked up at him. She was a mix of sweet and sexy, vixen and virgin and he wanted her with a ferocity that scared him.

"Would it be terribly irresponsible if I said I don't want to go?" she asked.

Ryder's hands were firmly gripping her waist. With a gentle squeeze, he gave her a wolfish grin. "Not at all." Leaning forward and resting his forehead against hers as he held on to the final threads of control, he added one last thing to reassure her. "If it makes you feel any better, I never shirk my responsibilities or play hooky, but for you, Duchess, I am more than ready, willing, and able to skip it all and take you to bed."

She went limp in his arms with a soft moan. "That was the most perfect thing to say ever." Her tongue teased at his lips. "What are you waiting for? Take me to bed, Ryder."

So he did.

Neither regretted missing the first day of the show.

8

For two weeks, it was like they lived in their own bubble.

The trade show had been amazing and Peyton not only learned a lot, but got to design her dream kitchen for both restaurants *and* the resort café. Ryder didn't spare any expense when it came to these projects and as much as she had tried to reason that just because something cost the most didn't necessarily mean it was the best, he tended to go with what cost the most.

It was both interesting and exasperating.

Back in Magnolia, she had gone back to work at the café and kept her normal schedule, but every night she and Ryder would collapse into bed together as if they had been apart for weeks rather than hours.

It was the best kind of exhaustion imaginable.

The man made love like he did everything else—with a commanding presence and take-charge attitude.

And she loved every minute of it.

Today was going to be their first foray out of their bubble, and she was more than a little nervous about it; although, any interaction with her mother tended to bring her anxiety to the surface. Georgia Bishop made her crazy on a good day and was known for being hypercritical. Seeing her daughter with Ryder was certainly going to have her either questioning why someone like him was dating her or she was going to start planning their wedding.

Neither were good options.

Then there was Austin. Even though he was only a cousin, she knew he was going to have some opinions about this relationship. The last time they talked, he expressed how he didn't think they should be working together, so she couldn't imagine him being agreeable to finding out they were now dating.

Why are we going to this party then?

Oh, right. It was her brother's birthday so...she really needed to be there.

"You're frowning again," Ryder said as he walked over and kissed her. "If you don't want me to go with you..."

They'd been talking about the party and all the things Peyton feared would happen. It was still a bit mind-boggling how comfortable she was with telling him things–like...everything–but at the same time, it felt completely natural.

"You know I want you there with me," she told him, kissing him softly on the cheek before sitting down on the sofa. "You were invited even though no one knows we're dating. Plus, my sister is finally home for a visit and I really want you to meet her."

"Peyton, you know I like your family and normally I'd go and make an appearance without giving it a second thought, but this is going to be different. I can see how stressed it's making you and maybe...maybe we should just wait for another time. Maybe we could just get together with your siblings for dinner and then–when you're ready–

go out with your parents. It's not a big deal. I won't be offended if you don't want me there."

It would be the easy way out; she knew that. Her entire extended family knew Ryder and genuinely liked him, but no one would think twice if he didn't show up for a family birthday party.

But she would.

Actually, she'd obsess about it.

And even though he didn't come right out and say it, Peyton had a feeling he enjoyed those gatherings more than he was letting on. Besides the fact that he had already gone to a lot of them, he already forged friendships with almost everyone she was related to—and not just to be nice. Besides his friendship with Austin and the way he helped Garrett with the veterinary clinic, it turns out he'd gone to lunch with her brother several times after deciding to build the resort here in town. Then he told her he'd shopped in her cousin Mallory's place and purchased several pieces of furniture from her for the house Austin and Mia were currently living in. He'd stayed at her aunt's B&B, and had hired Mallory's husband Jake as the general contractor for the resort. She had joked that the only one he hadn't worked with was her cousin Sam, and the next thing she knew, the two of them were working together on landscape design for the resort! Honestly, he spent more time with her relatives than she did.

Which was a little weird.

"I'm being crazy and overthinking it, that's all. I'm sure everyone is going to be great except my mom who...you know...never is," she admitted. While it was true her mother was definitely getting better about her snobbish ways, she seemed to target in on Peyton more than her other children lately. It was probably because normally she was the meekest of the three and for as much as she was coming into her own as an adult, Georgia Bishop hadn't quite gotten the memo on it yet.

And probably never would.

"No," she finally said, remembering that he was waiting for a response. "We're going to go and do this. If anyone has an issue with our relationship, then that's on them. Besides, we've had more than our share of unexpected couples in my family."

Brows furrowed, he sat beside her. "What does that even mean?"

"Well...let's see. My brother and his wife? My mother nearly had a stroke when she found out Mason and Scarlett were dating. Scarlett is not part of the country club sect and she rides motorcycles. It was wild when they first got together. Then my cousin Sam was a major hell-raiser in his youth and he ended up marrying the preacher's daughter. And you know Austin and Mia's story."

"Do you really think we're like them? That we're so unexpected?" he asked casually, resting his arm along the back of the sofa.

"Don't you?" she asked with a small laugh. "Ryder, you're older and much more worldly than I am. I'm someone who enjoys living a quiet life here in Magnolia in my little bungalow, and you're someone who owns a jet and buys million-dollar properties around the world. We're about as odd as they come."

It was something Peyton tried not to think about because she knew if she did, she'd just freak herself out. Then, once she started freaking out, she'd spiral and start questioning why Ryder was with her and how long it was going be before he got bored and moved on. So far, he didn't seem the least bit bored, but it had only been a few weeks.

There was no way she was going to get her hopes up and think this was the be-all and end-all relationship that was going to end with a trip up the aisle.

At least...she tried not to think like that.

On a few rare occasions, she not only imagined herself walking down the aisle with Ryder, but even started planning what their wedding would look like.

She wanted to partly blame it on the fact that he looked so damn good in a tuxedo, but the truth was that she was seriously falling hard for him. It was hard to keep from saying she was in love, but...that would definitely be courting trouble. Men like Ryder Ashford did not fall in love with girls like her. They were worlds apart no matter how much he might not want to see it. As much as she knew she grew up in a very privileged home, it was nothing compared to Ryder's upbringing. The wealth of the Ashfords made the Bishops look as if they were the hired help.

"I disagree," he said, pulling her out of her reverie. "I don't see us as odd at all, and I'm surprised you do. We have more in common than anyone you mentioned."

"Seriously?" she asked in disbelief. "How do you figure that?"

"Peyton, you're a beautiful, intelligent woman. No one could doubt for a minute why I'm attracted to you. Besides that, we're both very business-minded and share a lot of common interests. Throw in the fact that we're working together on projects that are near and dear to both of us, we just make sense." Smiling, he took her hand and placed a gentle kiss on her palm.

His words were sweet, just not particularly romantic.

Forcing herself to smile, she squeezed his hand. "I'm sure it's all going to be fine. Like I said, it's just me obsessing and overthinking everything. It's going to be fun."

"What time do we need to be there?"

"Um...Scarlett said three. Normally I go early to help set up, but I'm not the caterer this time so I can relax."

"You cater family parties?" he asked incredulously.

"Occasionally. I did Courtney and Dean's wedding–Dean is Scarlett's brother–and then I catered for her other brother Hunter's wedding. For birthday parties, I usually bring a couple of dishes. This time, Scarlett told me she wanted me there as a guest and to relax so...I'm relaxing."

Ryder glanced at his watch and then at her. "It's barely noon. Seems to me we have a couple of hours to ourselves." One long finger traced lazy circles on her palm. "How about we go inside and I help you relax a whole lot more?"

She could feel her cheeks heat. "Ryder, there is no way you can call what we do in bed relaxing. If anything, you'll exhaust me and I'll be too tired to move."

"Relaxed," he countered as his fingers moved to gently caress her from wrist to elbow. "You'd be too relaxed."

"Hmm...you might have a point," she teased, more than willing to do whatever he wanted when he got that sexy look in his eyes. Wordlessly, Peyton rose and held out her hand to him. It was crazy how much she wanted him. The way Ryder made her feel wasn't like anything she'd ever known before, and for the first time in her life, she felt like she was actually enjoying her life.

Which was crazy.

Beside her bed, Ryder dipped his head and claimed her lips with his. That's all it took for her to go from mildly aroused to feeling a wild and urgent need. Dropping her hand, he pulled back just so he could tug his polo shirt over his head. Peyton took the opportunity to do the same with her own top and tossed it to the floor. After that, it was a slow, choreographed dance as they kissed while undressing, and by the time they were on the bed, she was thrilled to be the one straddling his magnificent body.

Her hands gently roamed over his chest before she leaned forward to kiss it. Large hands anchored into her long hair, keeping it away from her face, and it made her look up and smile mischievously at him. The heated gaze he leveled at her told her he was enjoying her touch and it made her feel powerful. It didn't seem to matter how many times they'd made love, she still marveled at that feeling. Ryder was a very generous lover and it seemed to turn him on the most when she took the reins.

"You're so beautiful, Peyton. So sexy," he groaned as she licked and kissed her way across his chest and then lower. She loved the heat of him, the saltiness of his skin. There was a part of her that kept waiting for him to be tired of her and tell her they were through, but if anything, the neediness she felt seemed to go both ways.

And right now, hearing Ryder's breath quicken, she knew he needed her.

And it thrilled her.

The first time Ryder was invited to a Coleman family event, he'd considered begging off. He knew it was a token invitation sort of thing, but...he went and, surprisingly, enjoyed himself.

The second time, he not only accepted the invite, but had looked forward to it.

Now he downright loved them.

They were filled with laughter, good food, and great conversation.

And the complete opposite of any Ashford family gathering.

Ryder knew he'd never admit it out loud, but...the Colemans were the kind of family he always wanted but never believed existed. The fact that he now found himself involved with them on so many levels—his business dealing with both Austin and Garrett, and now his relationship with Peyton—felt like he was dealing with family rather than friends. The best part was how they embraced and welcomed him. They were definitely more kind and loving than anyone he was related to.

He meant what he said earlier to Peyton, though. He would have stayed behind if it would cause her less stress, but...he was really happy he didn't have to. Now, with her hand in his, they walked around to her brother's backyard. If a vinyl record had been playing, it would have screeched to a halt.

At least, that's what it felt like.

There were dozens of eyes on them and it was as if all conversation stopped.

Scanning the crowd, Ryder immediately spotted Austin and couldn't miss the scowl on his face. Then he simply shook his head and turned away.

Well, that's not a good sign...

The rest just stared at them curiously until Parker came jogging toward them with a big smile on her face.

Thank God at least one person was happy to see them.

"Oh my goodness! I'm so happy you're finally here!" she cried as she gave Peyton a fierce hug. Ryder had seen tons of pictures of the two of them, but it wasn't until the sisters were right there beside him that he realized just how much they looked alike. Pulling back, Parker smiled up at him. "Hey, I'm Parker and FYI, I love gourmet chocolate too!" She laughed before adding, "I am so excited to meet you!" Then she hugged him.

It felt weird to hug her with everyone watching him, but...obviously no one was planning on looking away any time soon.

With a glance over at Peyton, he saw how uncomfortable she looked and figured the faster he hugged her sister, the faster they could possibly move out of the spotlight.

"It's nice to finally meet you, Parker," he said quietly. When he straightened, he did his best to smile at everyone and gave a quick wave.

Parker looked over her shoulder and groaned. "Ugh... this is worse than I thought."

"You and me both," Peyton murmured.

It took less than a minute for him to realize what they had to do. "Okay, this is a little like going into a hostile negotiation," he said for only their ears. "We need to smile and put on a united front and act like this is all no big deal. We'll just..."

"It shouldn't be a big deal," Parker interrupted, loud enough for anyone standing close by to hear. "You'd think people would simply be happy for the two of you rather than making stinky fish faces."

O-kay...not quite as eloquently stated as he was going for, but...it seemed to work. Conversations resumed and almost everyone turned away.

Except for the few who were walking toward them.

Ryder refused to be intimidated. This was a social gathering—a birthday party for crying out loud—he couldn't quite fathom why everyone was freaking out. They liked him and they loved Peyton, so...

"A word," Austin said quietly when he was beside him.

"Good to see you, too," he replied with an easy smile. When Austin's expression didn't change, Ryder knew they needed to get this over with. He gave Peyton's hand a quick squeeze, but she started to walk with them. "It's okay. I've got this."

"But..."

"I've got her," Parker assured him and he silently vowed to buy her some of the gourmet chocolates she apparently loved when all this was over.

They were on the side of the house and away from prying eyes and ears before Austin said a word. He let out a weary sigh before asking, "What in the world, Ryder? I thought we talked about this."

Yeah, the conversation from so many weeks ago came to mind and how Austin had gently but firmly told him he wasn't the guy for Peyton. But that was then and...things changed. Which was exactly what he replied. "We did, but...it just sort of happened. We've been working together and got to know each other and...things just sort of progressed from there."

"Progressed? Seriously?" Austin questioned.

"Believe me, we were both as surprised as you are, but..." He struggled to find the right words. "She's brilliant and vibrant and a genuinely good person. I'd have to be an idiot not to be attracted to her."

Austin's only response was to shake his head.

"Austin, you know me. I'm not someone who just gets involved or even does relationships. So for me to feel this connection to Peyton..."

"Yeah, I know. Just...don't hurt her."

"Never," Ryder said fiercely.

For a moment, all Austin did was study him. Then his

shoulders sagged and he looked miserable. "You could have given me a heads-up."

"I didn't really think I needed to. You know me, we're friends, and I've never done anything to make you question my actions on anything. I don't want this to be an issue between us, Austin. So...are we good?"

"Yeah," Austin said, holding out his hand. "We're good."

Shaking his friend's hand, Ryder gave him a curt nod before he strode back to the yard to find Peyton. Turning the corner, he found her surrounded by her parents, her sister, her brother, and sister-in-law.

Great.

With a weary sigh, he walked over.

"Honestly, Peyton, you could have at least told us you were dating Ryder Ashford," her mother was saying quietly, but firmly. "Everyone's staring and wanting to know what in the world is going on. We shouldn't be the last to know. It's very irresponsible of you."

"How is it irresponsible?" she replied with a hint of annoyance.

That's my girl...

"I'm dating Ryder," she went on. "Everyone knows him. He's not a stranger and he's not some slacker you can find fault with!"

"Peyton!" Georgia said dramatically–hand on her chest and everything.

"Mom, please," Peyton said, rolling her eyes. "We're here to celebrate Mason's birthday and I think you and everyone are being a tad bit overdramatic."

"Overdramatic? Now you listen here, young lady..."

That was it. Ryder had heard enough. He'd gone all of three steps, however, before Scarlett walked over with her hand up. It was tempting to ignore her because Peyton needed him, but she took him by the hand and all but dragged him into the house.

"I really need to..." he began, but she cut him off.

"No, you really don't," Scarlett countered. Pointing to one of the stools at her breakfast bar, she stared at him until he sat. The last thing he needed was someone to lecture him about his relationship with Peyton, but...she surprised him. "I get that you want to swoop in and tell them to leave her alone, but you need to let her do this."

"Why? She was already freaking out about this exact thing for the past week. I don't see why making her face them on her own could possibly be good."

Leaning against the marble countertop, Scarlett smiled at him. "As someone who has been in your exact position, you need to trust me on this." When he went to comment, she stopped him. "Don't get me wrong, there's probably going to come a time when you'll need to step in, but today isn't that day. Plus, this is good for Peyton because Georgia seems to give her the most grief."

That...didn't sound like a good thing at all. Raking a hand through his hair, he asked, "And why is that?"

Shrugging, she explained, "Probably because she's still here in Magnolia. Parker's like a moving target–hard to pin down and critique. On top of that, Peyton's the classic middle child. She's the one always trying to keep the peace and afraid to make waves. You have no idea how thrilled I am that she's finally making some!"

Was this woman crazy? "Um...I don't see how dating me is making waves."

Scarlett reached over and gently pat his arm. "Oh, you poor, sweet, clueless man. Trust me. Dating you is most definitely wave-making material."

"How...?"

"You're older, you're wealthier than the Bishops–and you just know that chaps Georgia's ass–and you're not someone her mother's been trying to fix her up with."

"Who has she been trying to fix her up with?" he demanded, suddenly ready to go back out into the yard to make sure everyone knew she was with him.

"First of all, relax. I hate saying it, but...Peyton's been the family pushover. Everyone knew how to get her to do what they wanted because she didn't argue. Mason was the first to give her a chance to prove herself when he asked for her help with The Mystic Magnolia. Granted, she already owned the café, but she was content to let other people manage it. Mason pushed her to take a chance on herself and it's been amazing to watch her really come into her own."

"But...?" Because there was always a but.

"But...she's bold and confident with her business and not with her family. You're her first big defiance, first act of rebellion!"

Ryder stood because he'd had enough. "How is dating me defiant now?"

"Haven't you been listening at all?" she asked with an eye roll. "You weren't on Georgia Bishop's approved list! You're not a friend's son! You're not..."

Stepping away from the bar, he stared down at her. "No, I'm better than anyone on any damn list, and I'm certainly better than some spoiled country club crony's son! Peyton's not with me to spite her parents or as an act of rebellion! She's with me because she wants to be!" He let out a long breath before turning and stalking toward the sliding glass doors. "Now if you'll excuse me, I'm going to make sure she's okay."

Fortunately, Scarlett didn't stop him.

Walking across the deck, Ryder slid in beside Peyton, his arm banding around her waist as he smiled at her family. "It's delightful to see you, Georgia. You're looking lovely as always." Then he held out a hand to Peyton's father. "Beau, it's good to see you." And finally, he turned to Mason. "And happy birthday, Mason." Her brother shook his hand and started to smile, but Ryder's attention went back to Peyton. "Everything okay?"

"Everything's fine," she told him with a small smile. He knew better than to second-guess her in front of her parents, so he simply smiled back.

Scarlett rejoined them and hooked her arm through Mason's. "The caterer just told me the food is ready, so..."

"I still can't believe you hired someone for this," Peyton murmured with a small pout.

"We wanted you to enjoy yourself," Mason explained. "You tend to run around checking on things and then no one gets to visit with you and you don't relax."

"Plus, I kind of put my foot down on it," Parker said with an impish grin. "Whenever you cater and I'm home, you drag me along to help out so...now we *all* can enjoy ourselves!"

Some of the tension seemed to ease and Ryder told himself to relax.

Scarlett announced that lunch was ready and everyone should go and help themselves, and Ryder simply followed Peyton's lead. He was dying to know if she was really okay, but her sister never left their sides and when they sat down to eat, they were at the table with both siblings. Mason kept eyeing him, but not with open hostility. There was enough of a question there, however, that Ryder knew the two of them were going to have to talk.

Had it really only been less than an hour ago when he was thinking how much he enjoyed these get-togethers?

"So, when are you coming home for good?" Peyton asked her sister. "I get that you've been house-sitting and all that, but wouldn't it be nice to be back in Magnolia for more than a weekend?"

"And what, move back in with Mom and Dad? Um...no thank you."

"You can stay with me!" Peyton offered, and Ryder did his best to hide his surprise. Her place only had one bedroom and they tended to utilize it a lot, so...

"Oh, stop. Your place isn't big enough," Parker responded, and yeah, he was seriously buying her as much chocolate as she wanted now. "And I'm not sure this is where I want to be when all is said and done."

"All what is said and done?" Mason asked. "You've traveled, you've done college remotely, I mean...what is your endgame here, Parks? Eventually you are going to have to settle down and do something. At least here in Magnolia, you know you have family to help out and support you."

She huffed even as she shook her head. "There's nothing here for me anymore. I don't want to be in the restaurant business and I don't want to work for the town or in an office, so..." She shrugged.

"What is it you want to do?" Ryder couldn't help but ask.

"I don't know," she said quietly, moving her food around on her plate with her fork.

While Ryder realized he didn't know much about her, he was fairly good at reading people. There was more to Parker's hesitation than simple indecision. There was something keeping her away, and she didn't want to talk about it.

Yet.

"Parker," Mason went on. "There are endless opportunities for you here! We all have connections and can help you! You don't have to move back into your childhood room; there are plenty of places to rent."

"Not if I don't have a job," she volleyed, and Ryder saw the frustration on her brother's face.

A change of subject was in order.

"So, Mason," he began, "I'm thinking about getting a boat. How do you like yours?"

Luckily, he took the hint and smiled with gratitude. "We actually love it. Want to check it out?"

"Sure, why not?" As much as he wanted to stay next to Peyton where it had the potential to be safe, Ryder believed in dealing with the opposition as swiftly as possible. So if a talk about boats led to a heart-to-heart with her brother, so be it. He kissed Peyton on the cheek before excusing himself to walk across the yard.

"We started out with a bowrider," Mason said as they began walking toward his dock. "But with a toddler and another on the way, we thought we'd upgrade." He let out a low laugh. "Granted, I only had the opportunity to enjoy the bowrider for a year, but I sold it to Scarlett's brother Kyle. Every once in a while, I get to go out fishing with him on it, so..."

"And what's this one called?" Shaking his head, he laughed too. "As you can tell, I know nothing about boats."

They walked along the dock and Mason glanced at him. "And I'm guessing you really aren't that interested and this was a chance for you and I to talk privately."

"Smart man."

Shrugging, Mason stepped up to the boat and motioned for Ryder to climb on. "This is a forty-foot cabin cruiser. We were going to go a little smaller because it's not like we take it out on overnight trips, but with the way the family is growing and all the nieces and nephews, it's nice to have enough space to put little ones down for naps."

Ryder wasn't sure what to do with that information so he simply nodded.

They sat down on one of the benches and Mason looked out at the sound for a moment. "My great-grandfather left me this property in his will. Scarlett and I designed the house, Jake built it, my cousin Sam helped design the yard, and we enjoy hosting parties here. We're fortunate that it's big enough with our extended families." Then he faced Ryder. "I'm not going to lie to you, seeing you show up here today with my sister was a little...unnerving."

Not this again...

"I don't see why everyone's making such a big deal out of this. I'm not some random guy she met on the street. I'm wealthy and successful and not looking to latch on to her success! It's not like..."

Mason held up a hand to stop him. "It's not about you, Ryder. I don't have an issue with you. We've hung out enough times that I feel like I know what kind of man you are. And just so you know, it doesn't matter how wealthy and successful you are. If I didn't think you were a decent human being, you wouldn't be here right now."

"Oh."

"What has everyone a little...curious–for lack of a better word–is Peyton." He shook his head. "She's always dated guys who are either quiet, socially awkward types or one of the spoiled douches my mother sets her up with. Her showing up here today with you was just...unexpected. But not in a bad way."

"Are you sure about that?" he asked with a mirthless laugh.

"Absolutely."

"Oh. Okay. Um...thanks."

"I do have to ask you one thing," Mason said, his tone going mildly somber.

"Sure."

"Are you just passing the time with her?"

Ryder's temper flew to the surface, but he managed to keep it under control. "I find it appalling and offensive that you even ask that."

"You have to understand..."

"Not to me," Ryder quickly went on. "But to Peyton. Do you all think so little of her that you believe no one would be interested in her for real? That she can't hold the interest of someone and only be useful as a temporary distraction?" With a growl of frustration, he cursed the fact that they were on this stupid boat because he wanted to pace and rant and rave. Instead, he forced himself to calm down. "You know what I like most about your sister? Her mind. She's freaking brilliant in ways that I don't think anyone gives her credit for. She's spent her entire life trying to blend into the background and now that she's finally becoming the person she was always meant to be, no one knows what to do with her. I love her intellect and listening to her ideas. I love how fearless she is and how she stands up for herself–except here."

"Well, my wife dragged you away before you got the earful Peyton gave us all, so..."

"Really? Because when I joined all of you, it seemed like your mother was still poking at her."

"I think you've been around my mother enough to know that's just the way she is," Mason said with a small shrug. "The important thing is that she got her point across. It's just going to take some time for my parents to learn how to deal with it. And believe me, I've been there, and she's got a long battle ahead of her." Then he smiled. "If you really care about her, you'll know when it's time to step in."

"I was ready to step in earlier but your wife talked me out of it."

Mason's smile grew. "She's been dying to see Peyton put her foot down. For her to step in like that and lead you away means she knew how important that moment was. I hope you don't fault her for it."

"As long as she's looking out for Peyton, then that's all I can ask for." Slowly, Ryder stood and looked down at Mason. "I care very deeply for your sister. We're not messing around or passing the time. This is still new and we're figuring it all out, but...I'm in."

Standing, Mason shook his hand. "Thank you for being honest with me."

"I don't see the point in lying."

"That's good to know."

"So...are we good here?" he asked for the second time today.

"Absolutely." Together, they climbed from the boat and slowly made their way up the dock.

"Can I ask you a question?"

"Sure."

"Do you truly believe Parker doesn't know what she wants to do with her life?"

"Not even for a minute. There's a reason why she doesn't want to come home, but...she's not ready to share that with anyone and I'm not going to force her. She needs to work it all out on her own, but know that we're all here for her if she needs us."

For a moment, Ryder was almost overcome with emotion because this was the exact reason he was drawn to this family–the unconditional love and support. He was like a moth to a flame with it because he had spent a lifetime looking for it and trying to earn it with his own family. Hearing Mason's words...well...he hoped Parker realized just how lucky she was and secretly hoped that someday they all found him equally worthy.

And for a man who prided himself on being confident and making it look like he didn't need anyone, he was finding he needed far more than he ever dreamed.

9

"I hate that you're leaving already," Peyton said as she hugged her sister for the tenth time in so many minutes. "Please consider staying a little longer."

"We've been over this, Pey. I need to go." Pulling back, her sister smiled at her. "You know, you could come to Florida for a few days. There's a guest room just waiting for you."

"You know I can't just pack up and take time off. I did that last month for the trade show."

"And look how great that worked out!" she said with a sassy wink.

Peyton felt herself blush. "Anyway..."

"Anyway, I am so happy for you. I don't think I've ever seen you smile so much. Ryder's a great guy and it's obvious he's crazy about you."

She nodded because she refused to agree out loud for fear of jinxing herself. But...she really did think Ryder was serious about her. It wasn't about sex and chemistry–although those were off the charts–but there was a connection there on so many levels that it sometimes scared her.

There was a time not so long ago that she hated him–like seriously hated him–so being where they are right now was nothing short of a miracle.

Taking her hands, Parker smiled at her. "You have no idea how happy and jealous I am right now. Everything is falling into place for you and you deserve all of it. You've worked hard and were so patient and...I just love you."

Now she was going to cry.

Pulling her sister in for yet another hug, she squeezed extra hard this time. "I love you too."

Outside, a horn blasted. "That's my ride," Parker said as she pulled away.

"You know I would have driven you. You didn't need to call an Uber."

"It's just easier this way. Besides, I already forced Ryder to sleep alone last night so you and I could have our sleep-over, so..."

"We're adults and can handle a night away from each other. We don't always have to be together, you know."

"Peyton, if I were lucky enough to be sleeping with a man who looked like Ryder, I'd be pissed if anyone kept me away from that." She kissed her on the cheek. "Just something for you to keep in mind should I ever have the opportunity to have a sex life."

"Oh, stop. I'm sure you..."

The horn sounded again and they both pouted. "I need to go."

"Call me when you land so I know you're okay."

With a dramatic eye roll, Parker promised as she walked out the door. Maybe it was silly, but she still walked over to the window and watched as the car pulled away. Tears stung her eyes and rather than fight the tears, she let them fall. It was such a cliché, but her sister truly was her best friend and she hated living so far away.

But what she hated more was the way Parker was keeping a part of herself a secret. Peyton didn't believe for a minute that her sister didn't know what she wanted to do with her life or that she didn't want to move back to Magnolia. They'd always talked about living here and the things they were going to do once they didn't live at home anymore. Parker used to talk about opening her own spa where they offered massages, facials, body wraps, the type of things that offered a day of total relaxation. They always used to go for pedicures together, and Parker used to say how she'd never offer nail services at her spa because she loved the local businesses who already offered them too much.

Peyton couldn't imagine why her sister would give up on that dream or why she wouldn't talk about it anymore, but they were definitely going to be having a conversation about it.

Soon.

Glancing at the clock, she saw it was almost noon. She'd taken the day off from the café so she and Parker could have breakfast together, and just in case she got to be the one to drive her to the airport. Now she didn't know what to do with herself. Ryder was working and the last thing she wanted to do was disturb him. And, unfortunately, she wasn't in the mood to do any work herself.

So now what?

Walking over to the sofa, she sat down with a sigh. She and Parker had stayed up most of the night talking. Well, Peyton did most of the talking, answering the dozens of questions her sister asked about Ryder.

Their relationship was good—really good—and not just

their personal one. Their professional relationship was exciting and interesting. He'd given her some advice on how to make some improvements on a few matters with the café and she was already seeing results. Next week, they were supposed to get the first set of plans for the resort and her restaurant. She had given in and trusted him with all the notes and specifications she'd been working on for the last year and trusted that he and Austin were going to come up with something amazing.

Yawning, she got comfortable and considered taking a nap. There wasn't anything else she wanted to do and there was no place she had to be, but...

Glancing toward the kitchen, she considered making something. She was sad and tired and was seriously considering making some comfort food–something like mac and cheese or meatloaf. For a minute, she tried to think of what ingredients she had in the house without having to get up and look.

So tired...

Somewhere in the distance, she heard her phone ding with an incoming text and because she was curious and knew she could use it as an excuse to check her pantry, she got up to see who it was.

Ryder: Are you taking Parker to the airport?

Peyton: No. She took an Uber ☹

Ryder: Why don't you come over? I've got something to show you.

Part of her thought he was teasing and being sexy. Not that it mattered. She'd much rather be with him than sitting here alone.

Peyton: I'll be over in a few minutes

Ryder: See you soon, Duchess

The nickname made her smile, even though she had no idea why he chose it for her. It was different and unique and...totally Ryder.

She was already dressed and didn't have anything she needed to do to get ready, so she grabbed her keys and purse and headed out the door. The drive was short and as soon as she climbed out of her car, she spotted Ryder in the doorway, holding the door open for her.

"Hey, you," she said softly when she reached him. He kissed her softly before gently ushering her into the house. Together they walked up the stairs and then Ryder steered her toward the kitchen, where it looked like he had lunch all set up for them. "What's all this?"

"Wishful thinking," he said, holding out a chair for her.

"I don't understand. It looks like..."

He silenced her with a kiss and just as she melted against him, he lifted his head and smiled sweetly down at her. "I didn't want to push or interrupt your time with your sister, and I had no idea if you were going to the airport, so I ordered lunch for two just in case you were free." They both sat before he reached out and took her hand in his. "I missed you last night."

It still blew her away that this big, strong, confident man would want her–need her–and be so open and honest about it.

"I hardly slept," he told her. "The bed was too empty."

"I missed you too," she told him. "But it was nice having the time with Parker. Normally she comes and goes like a whirlwind. This was the first time in a while that we spent any quality time just the two of us so...thank you."

"Nothing to thank me for. You're entitled to time to yourself, Peyton." He squeezed her hand before motioning to the food. "I was going to go to the café and pick stuff up, but wasn't sure you wanted your own food, so I went for sushi. I hope that's okay."

"Okay?" she asked with a laugh. "Ryder, this is incredibly sweet of you. I'm feeling a little spoiled. I would have been happy with grilled cheese sandwiches!" Then she let out a soft sigh. "I was thinking of making some comfort food when you texted."

"Comfort food?"

She nodded.

"What does that even mean?"

The look on his face and the question itself were enough to make her laugh a little. "Oh, Ryder, come on! You have to know what comfort food is!"

His blank expression said otherwise.

"Okay, comfort food is...exactly what it implies–food that brings you comfort. Things like macaroni and cheese, meatloaf and mashed potatoes, pot roast, soup and grilled cheese, um...spaghetti and meatballs..." With a smile, she reached out and rested her hand on his. "It's different for everyone, but usually it's food from your childhood that makes you feel good. Don't you have something that you make when you're tired of eating out?"

He shrugged. "I don't cook. At all. PB&J, I can handle. Basic sandwiches of any kind, I can do. Once you get the stove or oven involved, all bets are off."

That just made her laugh again. "I can't imagine having to get takeout for every meal!"

"Haven't you noticed that in the last month? You've looked in my refrigerator. Has there been anything in there that indicates that I can cook?"

She had to think about it for a minute before realizing he was right.

"Is there a meal from when you were a kid that you still

enjoy? Something maybe you ask for when you get together with your family?"

Now it was his turn to laugh. "The Ashfords don't take food requests. Although, my mother really enjoyed all the food I ordered from the café. If she ever comes back to Magnolia, I'm sure she'd have a few requests. But other than that, I can't think of a single meal we had as a family that I'd ask for."

"Well that's just sad."

Another shrug. "There are meals I've had while traveling that I'd gladly hop on a plane for, but..."

"Please...I still don't want to think about planes."

Picking up her hand, he kissed it. "Sorry."

She was just about to comment when she yawned. "Sorry! We didn't sleep much last night either. We talked and watched TV and it was a good night, but...I'm definitely a girl who needs her sleep."

"Good to know." He motioned to the food. "Come on, let's eat."

Peyton helped herself to a bit of a variety and they talked about everything and nothing while they ate. An hour later, she was still yawning and very full. Ryder stood and held out his hand to her. "How about this—we take a nap. I think we both can use it."

She didn't even argue. She simply let him lead her to the bedroom where he helped her undress before taking his own clothes off. As soon as they were under the sheets and in each other's arms, sleep was suddenly the last thing she wanted.

"Ryder?"

"Hmm?"

"How sleepy are you?"

He chuckled softly. "Peyton, you were half asleep at the

table."

"I know, but..." Her hand gently roamed over his chest as she tangled her legs with his. "I was just thinking..."

Slowly, Ryder rolled them over until she was beneath him. His heated gaze told her he was on the same page. "There is never a time when I don't want you," he said gruffly. "All day, every day. Last night was torture and I kept telling myself to relax because it was just one night, but...I don't sleep when you're not here. It's crazy and completely unlike me, but..." His dark eyes scanned her face. "I need you."

If the look in his eyes and the heat and hardness of his body didn't do it for her, his words definitely did. She raked her hand through his hair. "I need you, too." Then he guided his head closer and kissed him. It was warm and possessive and so full of promise. He maneuvered above her until she wrapped her legs around his waist. She loved the feel of him on top of her, loved the weight of him. It was such a simple thing, and yet it turned her on more than she thought possible. "Make love to me, Ryder."

And he did.

Slowly, tenderly, and thoroughly until they both fell asleep, exhausted and sated in each other's arms.

"Thanks for agreeing to meet with me."

Ryder fought hard to keep a neutral expression on his face as he slid into the booth at The Mystic Magnolia on Friday afternoon. He was here because Austin was a good friend and colleague, but that didn't mean he wasn't still a little annoyed with him.

"I was a complete ass to you at Mason's party and...I never should have reacted the way that I did."

All Ryder could do was arch a brow at him.

"Mason told me the two of you talked and..." With a growl, Austin shifted in his seat. "You have to see where I'm coming from here. You and Peyton had me in the middle of everything not that long ago, and all I knew was that she hated you. Then you show up hand in hand and it just freaked me out. I'm sorry."

He instantly relaxed. "Apology accepted."

"Okay. Whew," Austin said with a smile. "I'm just looking out for Peyton, that's all."

"And while I appreciate that and respect it, you have to know I wouldn't do anything to hurt her."

"You already did hurt her and I was there to see it."

"That was different," he argued lightly. "And we've come to an understanding about it and we're moving forward."

"Just know, that if you do anything..."

"Austin, enough," he said firmly. "You're not her brother and it's none of your business, okay?"

"Fine." Crossing his arms, it seemed like he was trying to intimidate Ryder a little more, but eventually, he relaxed.

"So, how are the resort plans coming?"

"They're all set and back at my office."

"Why didn't you just bring them to lunch?"

"There's not enough room to spread them out here and I figured now would be a good time for us to sort of...you know...talk and straighten things out."

Nodding, Ryder agreed. "We're good, Austin." And because there could be no misunderstanding, he added, "I wasn't expecting this. Her. But now that it's happened, I... she makes everything better." Shaking his head, he let out a mirthless laugh. "I thought I had everything, but being with Peyton has shown me how much I was missing. I can't imagine my life without her."

"Well...shit."

"What? Now what's the matter?"

Groaning, Austin's head fell back for a moment before looking at him again. "Now I feel even worse about the way I acted."

"Yeah, well...you should." Before they could banter about it anymore, their waitress came over and took their orders. After that, they chose to talk about other things–how the house Austin was building was coming along, how Mia's books were doing, and then about the plans for the resort and restaurant.

"I have to admit, I was a little shocked to see you building a restaurant on the site that Peyton wanted. Are you sure that's a good idea?"

For the life of him, Ryder didn't know why he didn't share all the details about his arrangement with Peyton regarding the property and the restaurant, but...he didn't. "It's fine," he said instead. "We talked about it and it's all good. She helped me design the kitchen and we picked out all the equipment and appliances already, so..."

"Okay, I just don't want to get in the middle when she gets pissed off about this again."

A small smile crossed his face because he remembered how much he actually loved arguing with her in the beginning. It was the hottest and weirdest form of foreplay he'd ever experienced and he'd never been happier to have followed his instincts that night by going to her house. "She won't get pissed. Trust me."

When they were done eating, Ryder followed Austin to his office and then felt a bit giddy when he saw all his plans for The Ashford laid out. It was happening. This was going to be the most personal project he'd ever created and there was something uniquely satisfying about building something from the ground up like this–something that he'd designed.

Now he understood a little about how Peyton felt when she began planning for her restaurant. Part of him felt bad that she wasn't doing it, but...wasn't she? Ultimately, she was still getting the place that she wanted and she didn't have to pay for it. So really, she was coming out the winner here and he was happy to make that happen for her.

For two hours they talked about the resort and about permitting and Austin recommended setting up the meeting with Jake Summerford to get the ball rolling. With that done, Austin pulled out the restaurant plans.

"You didn't have a name for this one, so I called it Magnolia on Main," Austin said as he laid out the blueprints.

"What is it with this town and that word?!" he asked, laughing.

"Not really sure, but it's just always been that way," Austin explained. "My great-grandfather started it and I think it was probably a lot cuter when the town was about a quarter the size of what it is now. Either way, feel free to name your stuff whatever you want."

"Gee, thanks."

"Okay, there were a few concerns with the initial designs you gave to me, so I tweaked things and I believe it still gives you everything you want," Austin explained.

"So what changed?"

"The kitchen seemed to take up a lot of space and I figured you wanted it that way for a reason so I left that alone. The property, however, wouldn't allow for the amount of parking you would need while letting you have the large outdoor dining. So I recommend you go with cutting the outdoor seating in half, making this side of the building the bar with the sliding glass wall that leads to the outdoor area, and moving this wall here to give you more space in the dining room. The hallway to the restrooms will be shortened by six feet, but I think table space is more important than a hallway."

Ryder studied the plans and had to agree. "What about this tree here? If we remove it, that opens up more parking spaces, correct?"

"Absolutely. Or..." Austin paused and scanned the paper for a moment. "If we turn everything ninety degrees *and* remove the tree, then you can get back your outdoor dining area. It will mean eating closer to the road, but..."

"That's the side road, so traffic won't be an issue. Let's go with that. It makes the most sense to get everything as close to the original plans as possible."

"I agree. Now that everything's finalized, I can get copies of these made and have them to you on Friday when we meet with Jake. Will that work?"

"That's fine. Thanks, Austin." They shook hands and Ryder glanced at his watch and couldn't believe how late it was getting. He had a four o'clock call and then Peyton was coming over and making them dinner because she decided his kitchen was a dream and deserved to have someone cook in it. So if it made her happy, he was more than willing to let her do it. "I'll see you Friday," he said on his way out the door.

No sooner was he in the car than his scheduled call came in early. It wasn't a problem to talk while he drove, but he preferred to be home with his tablet or laptop in front of him when discussing financial reports. So he made do while he drove home and once there, he went directly to his office and settled in. When he came up the stairs two hours later, he found Peyton in the kitchen unloading groceries.

He'd given her a key to the house a week ago, and this was the first time she'd used it. She hadn't offered to return the favor with a key to her place and Ryder swore he didn't take it personally, but...he did. But rather than mention it, he simply walked over, rested his hands on her shoulders, and kissed her.

"Hey," she said softly. "I hope you don't mind that I used the key. When you didn't answer..."

"That's why I gave it to you," he interrupted with a low laugh. "So what are we making tonight?"

"We?" she teased.

"Okay, fine. What are you making for us?"

"I thought about our conversation the other day about comfort food and I decided that's what I wanted to make tonight. So brace yourself. I'm making a meatloaf and home-made macaroni and cheese."

"I thought you said mashed potatoes with the meatloaf?"

Peyton shook her head as she laughed. "It was just an example. Besides, I've kind of been jonesing for both of these so I figured...why not?"

"I'm sure it's all going to be delicious." Stepping away, he went to pour them each a glass of wine before taking a seat and watching her work. He considered asking if she needed help, but Ryder knew his strengths and cooking was not one of them. "So tell me about your day."

It was completely mundane–this whole scenario where they came together after work and talked while Peyton cooked. Ryder never imagined himself as the kind of man who found this appealing, and yet...he did. Actually, he was finding there were a lot of aspects of his relationship with Peyton that he never thought he'd find appealing that he now did. Other than their trip to Denver, he hadn't traveled anywhere since their relationship started. All of his business had been done via phone and Zoom calls. He always imagined he'd be antsy by now and anxious to hit the road–or the air–just for a change of scenery, but he was very content exactly where he was.

"So then he starts boasting about this fantastic property on the edge of town and how much commission he'll make from the sale," she was saying before looking at him and rolling her eyes. "The thing is, I know that property, and it's kind of a legend in town because the guy who built it was a total recluse. I can't imagine that it's in the kind of shape Shawn was talking about or that it will fetch the kind of money he thinks it will." Then she turned back and was putting some sort of ingredients in a pan.

"Wait...who are you talking about?"

"Shawn Markle. He's a local real estate agent–we went to high school together and now works with Jenna who..." Pausing, she shook her head. "He works here in town and primarily does smaller home sales. Anyway, he's a regular at the café and today he came in and was pretty much bubbling with excitement over this listing."

"And it's...just property?" And yeah, he hated how he clearly wasn't paying attention to what she said the first time.

"No, it's an estate. Massive. It's on the sound side of the island. Not far from here at all. It looked more like a resort than a home when it was being built, but then the owner did some massive landscaping for privacy and you really can't see much of anything if you drive by it. Plus, there are more houses built around it so it's even more hidden."

Ryder watched as she flipped whatever was sautéing in the pan before removing it from the burner. She moved around the kitchen without missing a beat. She knew where everything was and didn't ask him for anything.

"And now this house is for sale?"

Nodding, she filled a large pot with water. "It's on two acres and the house is almost seven thousand square feet." Shaking her head, she let out a snort. "I mean, who needs that much space?"

The Ashfords always did, he thought.

"You can go online and check out the listing," she told him. "Shawn said it went live last night and then bragged about the amazing pictures he took."

Pulling out his phone, Ryder did just that. Just from Peyton's brief description, he was intrigued. And really, how much could the property possibly be worth? He'd been doing his research all over Magnolia and thought he'd seen the best of the best with residential real estate. There was no way his realtor wouldn't have mentioned a property that was...

"Three point nine million?!" he cried. "Seriously?"

Peyton laughed as she mixed up whatever it was that went into a meatloaf. "Yeah, crazy, right?"

"Why would someone build something like that here and then let it go?" he wondered. Although, as he scrolled through the pictures, he saw how the place needed a lot of work due to neglect. It had a lot of potential. The grounds consisted of a saltwater infinity pool with swim-up bar and dry seating under a pergola, three golf greens, landscape and hardscape on a triple waterfront lot with five outdoor fire features. "Peyton, did you see these?"

"What? No. I was dealing with a luncheon we were catering and trying to get it out the door. Why? Is it nice?"

"Nice?" he asked incredulously. "Property at that price point isn't normally labeled as nice. This place is just...it has everything. It just needs to be updated."

She was busy putting the meatloaf into the oven and then washing her hands, but as soon as she was done, she came and stood beside him to look at the pictures.

"Damn...look at the size of that kitchen," she commented in awe.

"And that's one of three," he told her. "There's a full outdoor kitchen as well as one on the ground floor and then one on the main floor."

"Holy crap! Who needs three kitchens?" Then she laughed. "Although, I would probably find a use for all of them! Especially during the holidays!"

Ryder knew his family probably would have utilized them for entertaining and then never touch them for the rest of the year.

"Look at that pool! I can't even imagine living in a place like that. And honestly, it was a single guy who built it. Older guy." She shrugged. "I guess if you have the money, you can have whatever you want, huh?"

He had no idea how to respond to that because...yeah, basically that was how he had lived his life.

Was still living it that way, if he were honest.

"Well, hopefully Shawn finds a buyer for it. He's a decent guy and he and his wife are having their first baby. It would be nice for him to make this deal and get a little ahead financially." Smiling at him, she asked, "You have any rich friends who want to live in a small coastal town?" Without waiting for an answer, she walked back over to the stove and poured some pasta into the pot of boiling water.

But Ryder continued to scroll through the pictures with interest. If he hadn't already purchased a house on the beach and renovated it, he'd be seriously tempted to buy this property and turn it into something great. But with the resort and the restaurant, did he really need another project? Especially one that he didn't particularly need?

"No, I do not," he murmured, closing out of the site.

"So what about you?" Peyton asked. "How was your day?"

"I had lunch with Austin."

Glancing over at him, she looked surprised. "Oh? And how did that go?"

"He apologized for his shitty behavior Saturday. I wanted to stay mad a little longer, but...I get where he was coming from. He's concerned about you, that's all."

She snorted again. "Please. Even my brother didn't react that way."

"Your brother seems way more laid back than Austin."

"Everyone is more laid back than Austin," she said with a small laugh. "So...you guys are good now?"

He nodded.

"Come on," she urged. "I can tell you're not fully okay with it."

It was petty, he knew that, but...

"It just bothers me that he treated me that way. I've always been fair with him and I've never given him any reason to doubt me. And yet..."

Sitting down beside him, Peyton wrapped her hands around his and smiled. "Ryder, sometimes people speak without thinking. And trust me when I say that it happens in this family more often than not. Don't let it bother you. The two of you have been friends for a long time and I'm sure he feels bad about the whole thing." Pausing, she gave his hand a gentle squeeze. "Besides, the two of you are going to be working together for a good long while." Straightening, her smile grew. "Did he say when we can see the plans for everything?"

For the first time ever, business was the last thing Ryder wanted to talk about. He was simply enjoying her company and didn't want to get into all the stuff he and Austin discussed about the plans. It made him feel good just talking about her. "He's tweaking some things, so...sometime next week," he said vaguely. Right now, he needed a distraction. So he turned the conversation toward food and knew immediately it was the right thing to do.

"So this meatloaf," he said. "Is this something you offer at the café?"

"It is!" Standing, she walked over to the stove to stir the pasta. "You want to know something funny?"

"Absolutely."

"As much as I am looking forward to my restaurant and having it be more upscale than the café, there's a part of me that..." She stopped and shook her head. "It's stupid."

If there was one thing he was learning about Peyton, it was that she had a lot of genuinely great ideas but lacked the confidence in herself to express them. But when she did, he was always blown away. So he stood and walked over to her and gently turned her to face him. "Tell me."

He felt her relax under his grasp. "I kind of love the idea of a retro diner–a little like the place across from the motel we stayed at on our way to Denver. I'd love to have a total comfort food menu, a jukebox, and lots of stainless steel with red accents."

"That does sound interesting."

"I think about that motel we stayed at and the diner and...I don't know...how cool would something like that be? Bright colors and family-friendly...a place that says fun and comfort." Then she shook her head. "I don't think it will happen here in Magnolia though."

"Why not?"

The look she gave him was part frustration and part sadness. "Ryder, come on. Where the diner is concerned, I couldn't even get it together to purchase the property I wanted for my restaurant and missed out."

"You didn't..."

"You know what I'm saying!" she stated with a huff and stepped out of his grasp. "And you've looked around town so you know there isn't any more vacant land that would work for a diner." He was about to interrupt again, but she beat him to it. "And none of the existing buildings would work and I don't want to demo something so...it won't work here so just...don't, okay?"

He nodded.

"Magnolia could use another hotel that's more budget friendly than what you're planning for the resort, but...I don't think it will happen. I guess there's something to be said for a little less tourist traffic, right?"

There wasn't anything he could say, so he simply sat back down and sipped his wine and watched her cook.

But his mind was already working on ways to make her dream a reality.

Whether she believed in it or not.

10

It was a lovely Thursday morning and Peyton was having a meeting with her staff to discuss the changes that always came with the end of the summer season. Labor Day was two weeks ago and with the lack of tourists, it meant less business and shorter hours at the café. It was part of her job that she hated–letting the seasonal help go–but it couldn't be helped. It had been a spectacular summer–one of the best in the café's history–and she wished it could go on like that year-round. Sadly, that was out of her control.

The summer was also spectacular on a personal front. She and Ryder were still going strong, and it was the happiest she'd ever been in her life. After almost three months together, Peyton knew for certain that she was in love.

She just wished Ryder felt the same and would say it first.

Honestly, she truly believed they were on the same page, but...neither said it.

Maybe I have to be the brave one to say it first...

Yeah. Maybe.

He'd been so busy lately that by the time they did have time alone together, she didn't want to do anything to rock the boat. They had broken ground on the resort and apparently this was the first time Ryder had been on hand for a project at this stage. So every day he came home and would tell her about everything going on, and she loved listening to his enthusiasm and plans. Then they'd run into some issues with permits as well as problems with the land itself. Apparently it was a thing because it was the same issue that had stalled her restaurant before they even broke ground there. Ryder assured her they were working on it, but she still hadn't even seen the plans. Part of her worried that there was more to it than what he was telling her, but she knew he wouldn't lie to her.

Still...she was starting to consider reaching out to Austin just to confirm what was going on because so much time had passed.

After her meeting, she hugged every member of her staff and was thankful for how gracious they all were. She kept a file on who would like to return in the spring when the season started up again and when she looked at the clock and saw it was almost eleven, she quickly made her way back to the kitchen to see if there was anything she could do to help prep for the lunch crowd. Slipping on an apron, she began prepping chicken for their chicken salad.

Ten minutes later, Dana came looking for her. "Sorry to bother you, Peyton, but there's someone here asking for you."

Wiping her hands, she asked, "Who is it?"

"Helen Ashford." Making a face, Dana nodded toward the dining room. "I put her at a table near the window."

Helen Ashford? Ryder's mother? What in the world was she doing here? Panicking, she walked over and quickly washed her hands before pulling her phone out and calling Ryder. It went to voicemail and that freaked her out even more.

"Hey, it's me," she said quietly into the phone. "Um... your mom is here in the café and asking for me. I'm not sure why or why you didn't tell me she was coming in, but...I really wish you picked up the phone. Please call me back as soon as possible. I'm going out to talk to her so...call me back!"

There was no way she could run to her office to check her hair or makeup, so after letting out a long breath, she smiled and walked out to the dining room.

Ryder's mother reminded her so much of her own mother—so much so that it was almost scary. They shared the same air of sophistication and snobbery that Peyton feared she'd make a fool out of herself.

You can do this...

"Mrs. Ashford," she said pleasantly as she approached. "I'm Peyton Bishop. How can I help you?"

Ugh...way to sound like a business colleague instead of the woman dating her son...

The woman didn't rise, she simply smiled as she greeted her. Motioning to the chair beside her, she asked, "Won't you join me?"

Do I have a choice?

"Thank you," she said instead. "So...um..."

"Miss Bishop, my son ordered dinner from you the last time we were in town and we enjoyed it very much. I would like to order from you again for dinner tonight."

"Oh, um..."

"He doesn't know I'm here and I thought I'd surprise him and bring dinner. I'm afraid he's going to be a bit put-out with me showing up unannounced so I thought I'd cushion the blow by bringing food I know he'll enjoy." She smiled at Peyton again—but not as a woman talking to her son's girlfriend would, but more like how one would smile at an...employee.

Seriously?

"Of course, Mrs. Ashford," she forced herself to say because there was no way she was going to out herself like this. "Why don't you tell me what it is you'd like to order and what time you'd like it delivered?"

"Wonderful! What would you recommend? We thoroughly enjoyed everything we had the last time, but I'd be open to trying something new."

For the next thirty minutes they discussed the menu and Peyton was torn between genuinely liking the woman while getting angrier at Ryder. Apparently talking about food loosened Helen up a bit and she went from snooty to almost pleasant for a bit.

It didn't last long.

Once the menu was set and they stood, Helen handed her a credit card and a twenty-dollar bill.

"Um..."

"Please charge everything on the card and that's a tip for you for being so helpful. I appreciate the owner coming and sitting with me. I'm sure you don't just do that for everyone."

Peyton's smile froze on her face and she had no idea how to respond.

"Honestly, I don't know what my son loves so much about this sleepy little town, but hopefully once he gets his resort up and running, he'll be able to improve things around here." She smiled a little like one of those Disney villains from the old movies. "And I'm sure you'll benefit from it as well, my dear. The Ashford name will certainly help bring a wealthier clientele to the area."

If Peyton closed her eyes, she would swear she was listening to her own mother, and it made her feel a little sick to her stomach. Ryder rarely talked about his family–and definitely nothing specific–but this woman was seriously awful.

As if on cue, her phone rang and she excused herself. A quick glance at the screen showed Ryder's name, but she was too upset to answer. Right now, she just wanted to get his mother out of here and she definitely didn't want anyone to hear her conversation with Ryder.

Or the primal scream she desperately needed to get out.

So she rang up the order, gave Mrs. Ashford her receipt and confirmed all the arrangements to have dinner delivered later.

She simply left out that she was going to be the one delivering it.

And possibly dumping it all in Ryder's lap.

Once the woman was gone, Peyton did her best to help in the kitchen, but within a span of five minutes she'd dropped a bowl of chopped celery and cut herself with a knife so...whipping off her apron, she stalked to her office and slammed the door.

She had barely gotten a breath out when the door pushed open and Ryder was standing in the doorway. His hair was mussed and he looked a little frantic. It shouldn't have looked sexy, but it did and she had to tell her hormones to shut the hell up and not react.

"I tried calling you," he said, mildly breathless. Then he glanced around the office and then out toward the dining room. "Is she still here?"

"No. She's gone."

"Oh, um...so what did she want?" Stepping further into the office, he shut the door. But the closer he got to her, the more Peyton moved away until she was safely seated behind her desk.

"She came in to order dinner," she replied blandly. "Apparently she enjoyed my dishes the last time that she thought she'd surprise you and order from me again. Oh, and after she placed her order, she handed me her credit card and a twenty. You know, to tip the poor working folks." Leaning back in her chair, she crossed her arms. "So obviously she has no idea we're dating."

The muttered curse came first before he raked a hand through his hair.

But other than that, he offered no excuses or explanation, and that pissed her off.

"What the hell, Ryder?" she cried, coming to her feet again. "I get that you're not close to your family, but in the three months we've been together, you never once thought to mention me to them?"

"In my defense, we're not a family who shares... anything. It wasn't intentional and it certainly isn't personal, Peyton."

"It is to me! I just had to sit here with your mother for thirty minutes being treated like the hired help! How do you think she's going to react when I'm the one who shows up not only with the food tonight but then sits down to eat it with you?" He glanced away and her stomach clenched. "Oh my God...you don't want me to come to dinner, do you?"

It wasn't a question.

Raking a hand through his hair again, he paced a few feet away and back. "Again, it's not personal. I just think you wouldn't be comfortable around them. Especially not after your meeting with my mother."

She couldn't believe what she was hearing. "Are you kidding me right now?" There was no way to hide the sarcasm or accusation and she loved the fact that he winced at her tone.

"Peyton, you don't understand. My family isn't like yours. We're..."

"Oh, I believe they're more alike than you realize. For a few minutes there I could have sworn I was having a conversation with my own mother!" Walking around her desk, she approached him and poked him in the chest as she went on. "Do you remember how nervous I was to bring you to my brother's party? I agonized over that for a week, but we went and we handled it. I stood up for you and myself and you're going to stand here and tell me you can't do the same for me? For us?"

"It's not the same, Peyton!" he countered, his frustration showing. "Just...let me have dinner with them tonight and talk to them. Then tomorrow night we'll all go out together, okay?"

The old Peyton—the one who was always a pushover—almost caved and agreed. But she found that persona didn't work for her anymore, especially where Ryder was concerned. "No, it's not okay. Actually, it's insulting that you're even asking it of me."

His eyes went wide, as if he couldn't believe she was disagreeing with him.

"If you'll recall," he said calmly, his voice low and rumbly. "I offered not to go to Mason's party because I knew how uncomfortable you were. Are you going to stand here and tell me you won't offer me the same courtesy?"

She stepped in even closer and glared up at him. "I

didn't forget, Ryder. You did, and I appreciated it, but ultimately I refused to insult you by telling you not to go. I was willing to handle the fallout because you mean that much to me. But if I'm alone in this, if I'm the only one with deep feelings, then..."

His arms were around her in the blink of an eye, pulling her in close. "You're not the only one with deep feelings, Peyton," he said fiercely, his gaze scanning her face. "I have never felt for anyone what I feel for you."

Her heart hammered hard in her chest. The last thing she wanted to do was beg him to say the words—to tell her how he felt—but she couldn't seem to stop herself.

"What do you feel?" she whispered, her voice shaking.

One large hand reached up and gently caressed her cheek, her jaw. "Everything. I feel everything for you."

That...was vague...

"I've never been in love, Peyton," he went on quietly. "Honestly, I don't even know what it is, but I think about you all the time and hate whenever we're not together. All I want in this world is to make you happy and give you everything you want. I want to take you on trips and buy you things and..."

Reaching up, she placed a finger over his lips to stop the flow of words. "You don't have to give me anything or buy me anything, Ryder. Don't you get that? Our business relationship may have started out like that, but...everything changed. I don't want you to feel like you have to buy me to make me happy. All I want is you. You are all I need." And then, because she had to, she added, "You. Not the money and not the things you can offer me." She caressed his jaw. "Just you."

And then he kissed her. She was still a little mad and disappointed in him, but...they'd get through this situation with his family just like they'd gotten through the one with hers.

So for right now, she relished the feel of his arms around her, how good he felt and tasted, and the fact that he was hers.

Later, Ryder was back at his home and awaiting his parents' arrival. His mother texted only minutes ago that they were on their way and he knew they had an hour before Peyton would be arriving with dinner. He groaned just thinking about how this was all going to go. Besides the fact that Peyton was offended by his mother's behavior–and rightfully so–he wondered if his mother would even realize just how rude she'd been.

It didn't escape him how he now realized how stressed out Peyton had been not that long ago when she was in this exact situation. The only difference was that she had a week of it to deal with while he had a handful of hours.

He imagined it was much worse for her and felt guilty about how he'd made light of it.

Talk about karma...

When the doorbell rang, Ryder took a moment to simply breathe before shaking out his body, as if getting ready to go into a boxing ring with an opponent.

And how awful was it that his parents were the ones he was preparing to do battle with?

Pulling open the door, he forced himself to smile. "Mom, Dad, it's good to see you." He kissed his mother on the cheek and shook his father's hand before leading them up the stairs. "So, what brings you back to Magnolia?" He noticed their lack of luggage. "Where are you staying?"

"I thought we were going to stay here," his father began as they climbed the stairs, "but your mother wanted to stay at some bed and breakfast." He shuddered. "The room is small and it lacks any real privacy and amenities."

"I think it's charming," his mother countered. "And I thought it would be a nice change from our usual hotel stays."

In the kitchen, he poured them each a glass of wine and then motioned for everyone to have a seat in the living room. His butt barely hit the cushion when his father blurted out, "Your mother has breast cancer."

"What?!" Ryder cried, staring wide-eyed at his mother.

She nodded, her expression cool. "Yes. I have breast cancer. Unfortunately, I didn't go for my annual mammography like I should have. Maybe if I had they would have found it earlier." She took a sip of her wine. "I'm going to have a bilateral mastectomy—which means both breasts will be removed."

Shock held him still for several moments. When he glanced over at his father, Ryder saw him reading something on his phone and Ryder snorted with disgust before returning his attention to his mother.

"So...when did you find out about this? When is the surgery? What hospital will it be done at?"

"We knew when we were here the last time," she told him. "But I was going for a second and then third opinion before moving forward. Unfortunately, every diagnosis was the same and all the specialists recommended the same form of treatment so..." She shrugged and took another sip of wine.

"Mom, I...I don't even know what to say. What can I do?"

This time his father was the one to snort. "Honestly,

Ryder, what a ridiculous thing to say. You're not a doctor or a magician. There's nothing you can do. Your mother just felt like you should know. She's going to be fine."

But when Ryder looked at his mother, he saw her staring down into her glass, and she didn't look like she was fine.

Suddenly, he wished he could talk to Peyton, because she'd know what to do in this situation. She was a lot more compassionate, and he had a feeling she'd be able to keep this stilted conversation from turning morose.

"How are you feeling, Mom?" he carefully asked.

"I feel fine. Honestly, if I hadn't gone for the test, I would have never known anything was wrong. Now I'm a little stressed and find myself fretting over every little ache and pain, wondering if something is spreading. It's a dreadful way to live."

Another snort came from his father. "The doctors have all been monitoring you, Helen. Nothing has spread. You're turning into a hypochondriac."

His mother looked ready to say something else, but didn't. Instead, she smiled at Ryder. "I hope you don't mind that I ordered dinner for us. I went to that café you used the last time. The owner helped me plan the menu."

"Yeah...about that," he began, and even though he hated dumping this on her after her big revelation, he figured it would be better to get this out now before Peyton arrived. "Peyton and I are dating."

She blinked at him as if she didn't quite grasp what he was saying.

"The owner of the café–Peyton Bishop? We've been dating now for several months," he went on. "So...she's going to be joining us for dinner."

Leaning forward, Helen put her glass down on the

coffee table before glaring at him. "Honestly, Ryder," she said with a hint of annoyance. "You're dating the owner of a small-town café? You could easily have your pick of any number of women who are better suited for you! And then you let me embarrass myself by going in there without knowing about your relationship! How could you?"

He wasn't sure which part of that statement to address first.

"I..."

"Not that it makes any difference, of course," she went on. "It's not like you're serious about this girl. You never are." Her gaze narrowed. "Although...she's not like any of the women you usually date."

Now he seriously wished Peyton wasn't coming because he had a feeling it was only going to lead to disaster.

"You're right. She's not like anyone I've ever dated before. She's better." Pausing, he straightened and mentally braced himself. "This is the best relationship I've ever had and...I'm in love with her."

"Love?" his father murmured with more than a little disgust. "Ryder, a man in your position needs to be a bit more practical. You may think you're in love, but trust me, this girl...this...café owner...sees you as meal ticket." He laughed softly. "Excuse the play on words. Be careful. Have your fun with her but don't think for a moment this is real."

Again, Ryder glanced toward his mother and saw a sadness there.

And possibly disappointment.

"Thanks for the advice, Dad, but I don't agree with it. I don't need your approval on this." He stood and looked down and hoped he appeared menacing. "And I expect you to treat Peyton with respect when she gets here while you keep your opinions to yourself!" He stalked away, but...

there wasn't anywhere for him to go. Then he looked over at his mother. "I'd appreciate it if you did the same. She's nervous enough about joining us for dinner and I don't want either of you upsetting her."

All she did was nod.

After that, conversation leaned toward the mundane in typical Ashford fashion. By the time Peyton arrived, it was as if a lifeline had finally been thrown. Ryder jumped to his feet and ran down to help her carry everything in. He stepped out onto the front porch and pulled her in close, and realized he was shaking.

"Ryder, are you okay?" she asked, pulling back to look up at him. "What's going on?"

Where did he even begin? "It's been...it's been a bit rough in there." He hugged her tightly again. "If you want to run, now's the time to do it."

She laughed softly before kissing him. "Nonsense. There isn't anything they can throw at me that I'm not prepared for."

"Don't count on it."

She grinned before leading him over to her car to grab all the food. "You may not believe this, but my mother has mellowed in the last few years."

His bark of laughter was out before he could stop it. "Good grief! That's mellowed?"

Fortunately, she laughed with him. "I know, right?" They slowly made their way back to the door. "Anyway, I'm just saying that I know how to deal with snobbery. I can't say I won't have my feelings hurt, but...they'll never know."

"Peyton..."

But she wasn't listening and was already walking into the house. He caught up with her in the kitchen where she began unpacking everything.

"Mr. Ashford," she said to his father as she shook his hand. "It's a pleasure to meet you." Then she smiled at his mother. "It's nice to see you again, Mrs. Ashford. I hope everyone's hungry because we have a ton of food here."

She never stopped moving–setting out trays of food and then grabbing plates and silverware and setting the table. Ryder helped before pouring her some wine.

"I picked up dessert from Henderson's Bakery," she said to no one in particular. "Their cupcakes are truly decadent, but I also opted for some of their fresh fruit tarts." Once everything was set, she sat down like she was the queen, and Ryder had never been more impressed with her.

"Mom, Dad, please..." He motioned to the chairs but stopped to kiss Peyton on the cheek before he took his own seat. "Everything looks and smells as spectacular as usual."

"Thank you." Everyone helped themselves and Peyton did her best to engage in conversation. "So, Mr. and Mrs. Ashford, will you be staying here with Ryder while you visit?"

"No," his mother said politely. "We're staying at Magnolia on the Sound. It's the bed and breakfast."

Then, Ryder simply took a forkful of the Southern loaded sweet potato and enjoyed what was about to happen.

"Oh, that's an excellent choice!" Peyton said enthusiastically. "That house is one of the oldest in Magnolia Sound and was built by my great-grandfather, Ezekiel Coleman! The Colemans are one of the founding families of the area. When he passed away several years ago, the house was given to my Aunt Susannah, and she turned it into the bed and breakfast. It's been wonderful to see the old house refurbished and brought back to its former glory where people can learn about the history of the town!" She smiled at Ryder before continuing. "My great-grandfather firmly believed in keeping Magnolia's charm and not letting it be overrun with too many outside commercial interests. He owned many of the businesses in town and passed a lot of them on to his family. That's how I came to own the café."

"That's very interesting," his mother replied, and Ryder thought she was being genuine. "What other businesses does your family own?"

"Oh my goodness, let's see...my cousin Mallory owns a home décor shop in town, her brother Sam now runs the landscape architecture firm, um...Mallory's husband Jake is now the owner of Coleman Construction, my cousin Austin works with Jake but also has his own architecture firm here as well."

"Austin's the one who did the renovations on my place on the beach," Ryder chimed in.

"My brother Mason works for the town but owns a restaurant up on the north end of town and my parents own the marina and yacht club. My father's an attorney and my mother is involved with many local charities. They stay very busy but we all enjoy knowing we're preserving the very things my great-grandfather built."

"My...that's impressive," his mother said, smiling.

"It is," Peyton agreed. "Family had always been my great-grandfather's main priority and he wanted nothing more than for us to carry on in his footsteps. I'm proud to be able to do that."

Ryder noticed his father's silence and refused to let it bother him. Instead, he and Peyton talked about the town and all the perks of it and what they loved most about it, and he was surprised when his mother engaged and shared some of the things she was finding charming about it as well.

Color me surprised...

They worked together to clean up and opted to have

dessert out on the deck. The sun was setting and it was a little cool, but not uncomfortable. "So what brought you in for a visit?" Peyton asked and Ryder inwardly groaned because he probably should have given her a heads-up when she first arrived.

"My wife has breast cancer and wanted to tell Ryder in person. Privately," his father said without even looking at Peyton. "At least, we assumed it would be just the three of us."

"Dad!" Ryder hissed, but rather than apologize or say anything, his father simply stood and walked back into the house. "Peyton, I...I'm sorry. Maybe I should go talk to him."

"Don't," Helen said before taking a forkful of her tart. "You'll be wasting your breath. Let him go pout." Then she looked over at Peyton apologetically. "Although I am sorry he was so rude."

At that point, Ryder was pretty sure his jaw was on the ground.

"It's okay," Peyton told her. "But I am sorry to hear about your diagnosis. Have you started treatment yet?"

His mother looked at Peyton in confusion for a moment before talking more about her diagnosis and her plan to have the bilateral mastectomy.

"Oh my goodness. I can't even imagine how scary this all must be for you." Reaching over, Peyton placed her hand over Helen's. "Is everything scheduled already?"

"It is. I'm going to the Mayo Clinic in Phoenix. We'll be staying in the area for a while so we've been looking for a house there. I want to be as close to the hospital as possible."

"That makes sense. Plus, being able to sleep in your own bed makes all the difference," Peyton commented. "You're already going to be uncomfortable so I'm sure it will help your recovery to be surrounded by familiar things."

She offered a warm smile. "I know luxury hotels are wonderful, but there's something to be said about being home, right?"

"I, um..." his mother began before looking away. "I don't know how much of a home it will be. A rental is hardly the same as my actual home." Her words were quiet and sad, and Ryder realized how much of a burden she was carrying.

"Mom, I realize the Mayo Clinic is one of the best hospitals, but...isn't there something closer to home for you?"

Her laugh was equally quiet and sad as she looked at him. "Where even is home anymore?"

Peyton looked between the two of them. "You know, I imagine even if you rent a place that is furnished, you could ship some of the things from home that you want with you–like your bed and a favorite chair. It's not much but maybe that would help?" Before she could say anything else, her cell phone rang. "Drat. It's the café. Please excuse me for a moment." She stepped away and walked into the house, leaving Ryder and his mother alone.

There was an awkward silence that he wasn't sure how to fill. Luckily, he didn't have to.

"She's lovely, Ryder," she said softly. "And you really didn't do her justice when you said how different she was from the women you've dated in the past."

"Mom..."

"She's far better than any of them," she interrupted with a small smile. "I don't think I've ever met anyone who showed as much compassion and grace as she has tonight."

All he could do was nod.

"Even after the way I treated her at the café, she showed up here and was friendly to me. That takes real class."

"She pretty much knocked me off my feet since the day

I met her," he admitted. "I don't know what I did to deserve her, but I know I can't live without her."

Reaching over, she took his hand in hers, an uncommon gesture. "I'm tempted to say she's too good for you."

He laughed. "You'd be right. But I don't plan on letting her go."

"Good for you." She squeezed his hand. "I like seeing you happy, Ryder. I'm glad you have Peyton in your life. I think she's exactly what you need."

"That she is." Behind them, the sliding doors opened and Peyton stepped back out with a smile that made his heart race. She was so beautiful and just...everything.

"So I was thinking," she began as she sat back down. "When you feel up to traveling after the surgery, you should spend some time here in Magnolia. I think it would be a wonderful and healing atmosphere. You can sit out on the deck and listen to the waves and just focus on healing." Looking over at Ryder, she added, "Of course I don't know what your timeline is with the lease here, but even another house on the beach would work as long as it had an elevator and a view, right?"

Ryder didn't confirm if it was a good idea or not, mainly because they'd never done anything like this—offered to spend an extended period of time together.

"I'll think about it," his mother said after a moment. "But it does sound wonderful."

"Helen! I think it's time to head back to the hotel," his father called out from the house. He didn't offer a word of thanks for dinner or dessert, nor did he say goodbye. Part of Ryder wasn't the least bit surprised, but when he saw the sadness on his mother's face again, he knew he needed to say something.

"Mom, is everything okay with the two of you?"

As she slowly got to her feet, she waved him off. "You know how your father is. I think he's just concerned about me not overdoing things."

"That's not what I mean," he corrected.

Instead of answering him, she walked over and kissed him on the cheek before doing the same to Peyton. "Thank you for a wonderful dinner. Everything was delicious."

Together, they all walked back into the house and to the door. His father was already out in the car, and Ryder chose to ignore it. Once his parents were gone and he and Peyton were alone again, he cupped her face and kissed her thoroughly.

"You're amazing, you know that, right?" he asked gruffly.

"Me? What did I do?"

"Everything," he told her. "You do everything and make everything better. Thank you for persisting and being here tonight. I wish things had gone better..."

"I think your father is hurting, Ryder. And scared."

That made him laugh. "Somehow I doubt that."

"Well...think about it. His wife is facing something he can't fix or control and it has to be hard for him."

He still wasn't so sure, but...it sort of made sense.

"I don't want to think about him right now. All I want is for us to clean up the dessert dishes and go inside where I plan on thanking you properly."

"Ooh...I like the sound of that."

Looking around, an idea formed in his mind. "Actually, change of plans," he murmured before picking her up and placing her on the cool marble countertop.

"Ryder!" she shrieked with a laugh. "What in the world?"

"I don't want to go inside," he growled against her throat

before lightly biting and kissing her. "I want you right here. Right now."

Her nails gently grazed his scalp as she held him close. "I definitely like that even more." And with a throaty moan, Peyton arched against him. "Touch me," she begged. "Please."

And he did.

Everywhere.

Everywhere he touched made her breathless and he loved it. Peeling the clothes from her body took longer than either of them liked and when they heard fabric tear, neither seemed to care. Only when he had her gloriously naked did he step back to take care of his own clothes. When he was just as bare as she was, Ryder stopped and looked at her.

"Peyton Bishop," he murmured darkly. "You look like a total goddess right now." Reaching out, he went to touch her and noticed his hand was shaking. Her hair was tousled, her eyes were slightly glazed with passion, and her skin was flushed. "So sexy." Moving in close again, he kissed her cheek. "So beautiful." He kissed her shoulder. "And all mine," he growled before claiming her lips in a brutally raw kiss.

This need for her only grew every day.

The sight of her left him breathless.

And the feel of her was more intoxicating than the best champagne.

Ryder knew he'd never have enough of her—never. And the way she was wrapped around him and begging for more, he had a feeling it was mutual.

It was late. The room was dark and they were tangled together under the blankets. Ryder knew he should be asleep–they both should–but his mind wouldn't shut down.

"I can hear you thinking," she said sleepily, her head on his shoulder. "What's going on?"

After letting out a long breath, he kissed the top of her head. "I'm still trying to process everything that happened with my parents. I can't believe my mother has cancer and I'm horrified by my father's behavior."

"So that's never happened before?"

"Not like that. My father has always been rather aloof, but that was flat out rude tonight and I'm embarrassed that you had to witness it."

"I'd like to say it's not a big deal but...it wasn't fun being on the receiving end of his mood." She kissed his shoulder. "What was he like when you were growing up?"

"He had less gray hair."

"Ryder..."

Running his fingers through her hair, he decided to confess a little. "One of the reasons I'm so drawn to Magnolia Sound is because of your family."

Lifting her head, she stared down at him. His eyes had adjusted enough to the dark to see the shocked expression on her face. "Seriously? My family? Why? Because they remind you of yours?"

That made him laugh softly as he guided her head back to his shoulder. "No. And I'm talking about your extended family. The first time Austin invited me to some family get-together, I went to just sort of appease him and thought I'd stop in for a few minutes and then leave. Then I started talking to people and ended up staying for the entire time. There was no angle, no one was asking anything of me, I was there and people were just genuinely nice. So, naturally, I thought it was just a one-time thing. But the next event I went to, it was the same and...people seemed happy that I was there."

She nodded.

"As crazy as it sounds, I never knew families could be like that. It didn't matter what the occasion, everyone laughed and smiled and got along. I can't even remember the last Ashford family get-together where anyone smiled," he said with disgust. "Now I find myself thinking of the extended Coleman family as...well...family."

Beside him, she didn't move, didn't make a sound, and he wondered if she'd fallen asleep.

"Peyton?"

"Is that why you're with me? What attracted you to me? The fact that I'm part of the whole Coleman family package?" she asked quietly and Ryder could hear the insecurity in her voice.

Gently, he maneuvered them so he could look at her face. "It wouldn't matter who your family was...I'd be drawn to you. Even when you hated me, I was drawn to you. Never doubt how I feel, Duchess."

He heard and felt her shaky breath. "No one could believe that someone like you would want to date someone like me. So hearing you say all this about my family..."

Caressing her cheek, Ryder leaned in and kissed her softly. "They have nothing to do with us. I swear. It was important for me to share with you this...this part of how I feel. My family was dysfunctional and I didn't realize it until I came to Magnolia." He paused before deciding on one more confession. "And I owe you an apology."

"Ryder, we've already discussed this. You don't need to apologize for your parents..."

"No, not that. I didn't truly understand just how

stressed you were before Mason's party. But earlier today when I was waiting for my parents to get here and then waiting for you? It occurred to me just how much I didn't take what you were feeling seriously. So...I'm sorry."

She snuggled close. "Thank you."

He kissed her again just because.

"What a pair we are, huh?" she whispered. "All this time I kept thinking how we didn't have a whole lot in common besides our business interests and then it turns out we both have nightmares for parents."

That made him laugh. "I guess that's one way to look at it."

"I hope I didn't overstep about your mom coming here to recover. She just seemed so lost and the thought of only having your father around to support her was just...ugh."

"I'll admit the thought never occurred to me, but once you said it, I was kind of ashamed that I hadn't considered it before."

"Well...it sounds like there's a good reason for it." A yawn cut off her words and she hummed softly. "I think I need to get some sleep."

Hugging her gently, he placed a kiss on her forehead. "Good night," he whispered.

And then, when her breathing slowed and he knew she was asleep, he added, "I love you."

11

For the better part of a week, Peyton couldn't get Ryder's mother off her mind. Not only because of her cancer diagnosis, but because of all the similarities she saw between Helen and her own mother. What were the odds that she and Ryder would have that in common?

It was something the two of them talked about over the last few days, and she wasn't sure what broke her heart more–the fact that he wasn't more concerned about his mother's health or how Helen seemed so indifferent to her own son.

And that's how Peyton found herself pulling up to her childhood home on a Wednesday afternoon.

When she knocked as she let herself into the house, the look of shock on her mother's face almost made her laugh.

"Peyton! This is unexpected. Shouldn't you be at work?"

"It's good to see you too, Mom," she murmured as she kissed her on the cheek. Dropping her purse on the entryway table, she walked over to the living room and sat down.

"Is everything okay? You look like there's something on your mind," Georgia said as she sat down.

The thought of confronting her mother really hadn't come to her until earlier today and there wasn't anything that ultimately pushed her to do it. It was like suddenly she just knew this was a conversation that they needed to have.

Studying her hands in her lap, she carefully began. "I need to ask you something."

"Of course. You know you can ask me anything."

That statement was almost laughable, but she held it in. "Why are you so critical of everyone?" she asked, and immediately braced herself for the response.

Georgia didn't immediately reply. "May I ask what brought this on?"

Now she looked up. "I met Ryder's mother and...I noticed a lot of similarities and it made me sad."

"Similarities...how?"

Ugh...how could she explain it? "The way she spoke, the way she criticized, the way she talked to Ryder more like a stranger than a son."

"I don't believe I've ever treated you like a stranger, Peyton."

"No, but you certainly haven't been remotely supportive of me or my dreams," she explained. "You're constantly talking down to me like I'm too stupid to make my own decisions—even though I've always been the one to follow all the rules and haven't failed at anything I've tried." With a sigh, she added, "I just don't understand why it's so hard for you to acknowledge my successes or for you to show any motherly affection."

And there it was—dropped like a lead balloon between them.

The harsh truth.

Every time she ever envisioned confronting her mother in her mind, it always ended with Georgia weeping loudly and begging for forgiveness.

The reality was slightly different.

Georgia primly cleared her throat, folding her own hands in her lap. "You know, the Coleman name always carried weight here in Magnolia Sound," she began, "but we weren't always the wealthy family you know us to be."

That was...new.

"My grandfather–may he rest in peace–always worked so hard and he expected that of his children and grandchildren as well. So while the name had clout, out bank accounts weren't overly impressive." She picked at an imaginary piece of lint on her pants before continuing. "Anyway, my mother–your grandmother–always hated working. She despised it, really. She used to tell me the only way to survive was to marry a wealthy man so I'd never have to work a day in my life. She drilled that into me from the time I was a little girl and told me it was my right–that I was entitled to it."

Peyton thought of her grandmother Betty and remembered she wasn't particularly warm either. Why hadn't she put two and two together before?

"Anyway, I'd like to think if my mother would have spent the time just loving me instead of grooming me for the role as wife to a wealthy man, maybe I would be different." She looked up with a sad smile. "But it was all she could talk about. She used to criticize my weight, my hair, my wardrobe...it got to the point where I just gave up and let her just control every aspect of my life. When she introduced me to your father...well..."

"Oh my God," Peyton interrupted, horrified. "You and Dad were set up by Grandma?"

She nodded. "Fortunately, he was someone I had been secretly crushing on. I never let her know those sorts of things because I used to fear she'd hold it against me."

"But...how?"

Georgia seemed to ponder that for a moment. "I felt like if I said I had a crush on a boy, she'd find fault with them and do something to ruin any hopes I might have had with them. For the longest time she had her eye on Mayor Thompson's son Lyle." She shuddered. "He was awful. Beautiful to look at, but he had a reputation for having an awful temper. Naturally, when she set me up with your father, I was relieved. It turned out we had a lot in common and once we had gone out a few times, he confided in me how he was under a lot of the same pressure that I was and...we bonded."

Bonded. That didn't sound overly romantic, which is what she said to her mother.

"Oh, Peyton...romance is highly overrated," she replied wearily. "We genuinely like and respect each other and made a good life together."

"Yes, but it's a little cold and emotionless, Mom! Didn't you think about trying to break the cycle you obviously hated?"

"I did, but...I couldn't. Things would come out of my mouth of their own accord and after a while...I just accepted that this was who I was. Your father has been much better about it, but..."

"Has he? Because from where I'm sitting it seems like he just opts to say nothing most of the time rather than call you out on your bad behavior."

Her mother frowned at her. "You know, I don't think I like this newfound sassiness from you, Peyton Eleanor. I'm still your mother."

"I know that, Mom, but...I hate the relationship we have! I don't want to dread seeing you or talking to you. I want...I want the kind of relationship Aunt Susannah has with Mallory! I want us to *want* to do things together!"

Georgia's shoulders sagged. "When Susannah moved back here to Magnolia and she was temporarily estranged from Colton, I said those exact words to her."

Peyton's eyes went wide. "You did?"

She nodded. "You were in college and always so busy and Parker was off gallivanting I don't even remember where and...I thought it was too late. I didn't realize you might want the same thing."

"Well, I do," she told her firmly. "I have for a long time, but every time I think we're making progress, you...you talk down to me and make me feel like a disappointing child rather than the successful woman I am."

"You're always going to be my child, Peyton. I can't help that."

"I know, but...maybe don't talk down to me. Maybe just...smile and say you're proud of me."

Her mother's expression softened as her eyes shone with unshed tears. "I've always been proud of you, Peyton. Always. You...you're far braver than I ever was. Both you and your sister. I don't know how I ended up with two such independent daughters."

It would be wrong to tell her it was primarily because they were trying to escape her...

"I'd really like for us to work on this, Mom. Not just talk about it right now and then tomorrow have things go back to the way they were."

She nodded. "I'd like that very much." Reaching over, she awkwardly hugged Peyton.

Baby steps.

When she pulled back, she studied Peyton's face. "So, you met Ryder's mother and felt like we should talk about our relationship."

"Yup. Ryder and I talked about it for days, and I realized he felt the same way about her as I felt about you. Sitting back and witnessing someone else dealing with all the same disappointment was very hard and it broke my heart for him. For the both of them. His mother just found out she has cancer and it was as if she were talking to a stranger about it and he didn't have any particular reaction to it. I thought it was sad."

"It sounds very sad." She paused. "I'd hate to think if I were sick or dying that my children wouldn't care."

"I'd hate that too. Things need to change. I know you've been trying ever since Mason and Scarlett got together, but..."

"Yes, your sister-in-law does tend to call me out every chance she gets..."

"There's a reason for that," Peyton murmured.

"I know. I know." Placing her hand over Peyton's, she asked, "So where do we go from here?"

"Well...for starters, we should have lunch together sometime."

"Peyton, we often have lunch together. That's not anything new."

"Then how about next time we go and you don't comment on my hair or my clothes?" she suggested. "Nothing drastic."

Georgia's mouth was nothing more than a thin line before she sighed. "Fine."

"Thank you."

"May I ask you something now?"

"Absolutely," she replied, bracing herself.

"Are things getting serious with you and Ryder?"

Peyton felt herself blush as she nodded. "Yes. I'm...I'm in love with him and I still can't believe it's true–that someone like him would even be interested in someone like me."

"Why wouldn't he be interested in someone like you? What's wrong with you?"

"Really? You want to pull at that thread?" She paused. "Mom, you've pretty much destroyed my self-esteem! You put down every guy I ever dated or was interested in and then reminded me how I should be thankful for the men you found for me!"

"Oh...that."

"Yes, that! Now do you understand why I find it hard to believe that a man who can have anyone he wants, could possibly want me?"

Then Georgia did start to cry.

And not the genteel weeping Peyton figured she'd do, but full-on sobbing and wailing.

Oh Lord...

"Mom...Mom...it's okay," she said carefully. "Really. I'm...I'm sorry. I never should have said that."

"Yes, you should have because it's true! I should have realized how my words were affecting you! I know how my mother's words hurt me and now hearing you say these things makes me realize just how awful I am! Why would you even want a relationship with me?" she said before sobbing even louder.

For a solid five minutes, Georgia cried. Peyton got up and grabbed a box of tissues and figured the best she could do was to let her mother cry this out. When she finally calmed down and had a face full of running makeup, she realized this was the most real and honest emotion she'd ever witnessed.

"Better?" she asked as her mother wiped her face.

With a small nod, Georgia agreed. "I want to thank you."

"For what?"

"For caring enough to want to come here and have this conversation," she said quietly. "I promise to do better."

"Thanks, Mom." This time the hug was less awkward and possibly the best hug she'd ever shared with her mother because there was real emotion there.

Things were changing.

Getting better.

When they pulled apart, Georgia cupped her daughter's cheek. "I'm very proud of you, Peyton. And, believe it or not, it makes me feel good just knowing you're in such a healthy relationship."

"What do you...?" It was an odd statement because her mother didn't really know much about her relationship with Ryder to be saying something like that.

"The fact that the two of you talk about your struggles and you share interests...those are very important things." She paused and took Peyton's hand in hers. "Just...promise me one thing."

She nodded.

"You may think that I ran the show around here, but... that didn't happen until much later in our marriage. There were many years where your father made all the decisions and would tell me what was for the best and what wasn't." She sighed. "It was the way he was raised, too. He didn't think it was important to include me in important decisions. Don't let Ryder do that to you."

Her soft laughter was out even as she shook her head.

"Trust me, that is not an issue. I've made it abundantly clear from the very beginning that I not only have an opinion on just about everything but that I won't tolerate him thinking for me."

"You're very fortunate, Peyton. You found one of the good ones."

And she had to agree.

"What do you mean the plans weren't approved?" Ryder yelled into the phone. The town had been jerking him around for weeks now on his resort plans and he'd hit his limit. "Dammit, Austin! What the hell else could we possibly have to do?"

"I'm working on it, Ryder. I've got a meeting with the town planners tomorrow and hopefully we'll get things cleared up once and for all. You have your set of plans at home with you, right?"

"Of course. But what difference does that make?"

"Just...look them over again and see if I missed anything. I don't know why they're being so difficult on this but...I swear this has never happened before."

"And what about the restaurant? Where are permits at with that?"

"We'll be discussing that at the meeting tomorrow as well."

"Can I come to this meeting?" he asked, knowing full well that he shouldn't.

"No. That is definitely not going to help," Austin confirmed. "Look, what are you doing right now?"

"Fantasizing about strangling someone in the town planning office."

"Ha, ha. Very funny. Listen, Jake is here with me and maybe the three of us can look things over and talk it through so I can go in there with more of a plan tomorrow. Can we stop by?"

"Yeah, sure," he said wearily. "Or maybe I should come to the office?"

"Nah, we're in the car after going and looking at a site we're bidding on and we're not far from you. We'll see you soon."

"Thanks." After he hung up, Ryder had to fight the urge to throw the phone across the room. This project was taking way too long to get off the ground. Both projects were and he was beginning to feel like it was a sign or that he was jinxed. All his plans to contribute to Magnolia Sound–put his stamp on it–were definitely not going the way he envisioned, and it made him think back to the day in Austin's office when Peyton first confronted him. Maybe he was wrong for trying to force his way and his ideas on a town steeped in tradition.

With a snort, he pushed the thought aside because it was ridiculous. It was all just a coincidence and once everything got cleared up, he had no doubt that the planners would admit they were in the wrong.

And I can't wait for it.

In the distance, he heard the soft knock on the front door as Peyton let herself in. "Hey," she called out softly. "It's just me."

And just like that, all the tension left his body as she walked up the stairs toward him. The best part of his day was when he got to hold her and kiss her, so he did just that. Then, he led her into the kitchen and grabbed her a bottle of water.

"How about some wine?" she asked with a nervous

laugh. When he turned to question her, she added, "It's been a rough day."

"Uh-oh. That doesn't sound good."

"Ugh...I decided to finally go and confront my mother today," she told him as she sat down.

He poured her wine and handed her the glass, opting to grab a bottle of water for himself. "What made you decide to do that today?"

"I've been thinking about it more and more ever since your parents came to visit." She took a sip of her wine before shaking her head. "I can't even explain it, I just knew I had to go and do it today."

"And...?"

"And...it was very eye-opening and very emotional and...I guess I'm afraid to get my hopes up."

"I'm not really sure what to say. I mean...I guess I understand why you felt like you needed to do it, but I have to agree about not getting your hopes up. Your mother's been the way she is for far too long for her to suddenly morph into the kind of person you want her to be."

"Maybe, but...she seemed to really listen this time." She gave him a sad smile. "Only time will tell, right?"

He nodded.

"So, what about you? How's your day been?"

Groaning, he leaned against the island beside her and told her about his call with Austin. "He and Jake are on their way over and hopefully we'll come up with something to appease the town so we can finally get things back on track."

"What about the restaurant? Are the permits still stalled there too?"

"Unfortunately." Just thinking about it was making him

angry all over again. Before he could say anything else, however, the doorbell rang. "That'll be them."

"I'll get it," she said as she went to stand, but Ryder stopped her.

"No, you relax and enjoy your wine. I'll get it." Then he gave her a quick kiss before going down to the door.

He welcomed Jake and Austin and motioned for them to go up the stairs and smiled when he heard them talking with Peyton.

"Promise me you'll call Mallory and go out for a girls' day," Jake was saying. "Between the shop and the kids, she doesn't take nearly as much time for herself as she should. And she's mentioned more than once how long it's been since the two of you went to lunch and got pedicures."

"Ooh...that is true," she agreed. "I'll call her tomorrow and set something up."

"Oh, and that also reminds me," Jake went on. "I've got some clients coming in next week and I want to have lunch brought in. Any chance you can cater on such short notice?"

She smiled. "For you? Of course! Have your assistant call me tomorrow and we'll set it all up."

"Thanks, Peyton. You're the best."

Ryder was about to chime in when his phone rang. His brother's name came up on the screen and he knew he should take it, so he excused himself and walked over to the living room. He was only half paying attention, but saw Austin put his iPad on the kitchen table while talking to Peyton.

"Hey," he said distractedly, as he answered the phone. "What's up?"

"Hey, Ryder. You busy?"

"A little."

"Um...so I had dinner with Mom and Dad last night and thanks for the heads-up on what's going on with Mom!"

Ugh...he really didn't want to get into this right now. "It wasn't my place to tell you and besides, it's been less than a week, Patrick. It's not like we talk that often." Looking across the room, it looked like Austin was showing something to Peyton on his tablet. Maybe he was showing her the resort plans? But...that wouldn't be right. Why would he pull them out?

"Yeah, well...I had dinner with them last night and Mom wasn't looking so good. She said she was tired and I didn't think much of it. Then she raved about your new girlfriend. Again, thanks for the heads-up. Now she's after me to meet a nice girl like yours."

"Wait...that's not right," he heard Peyton say. She looked up at him and frowned before returning her attention to the tablet.

What's not right?

"You know this is going to be a wild time with them," his brother was saying. "I mean...we should make a joint effort to spend more time with Mom. I know she's definitely looking to spend more time with you and Peyton. Me? Not so much. She didn't ask about when I'd be around, only you."

"Don't be ridiculous, Patrick. Of course she wants to spend time with both of us," he reasoned. "I'm sure it's nothing personal."

"It feels personal," he murmured.

"This looks nothing like it's supposed to!" Peyton's voice got a little louder and he couldn't figure out why she was getting so worked up about the resort property. They had nothing to do with the kitchens for the restaurant or the café.

"Don't obsess about this. It's all going to be okay."

"Aren't you the least bit concerned? Our mother has cancer, Ryder. Cancer!"

"Of course I'm concerned," he said with a huff of annoyance. "I just think..."

"What the hell, Ryder?" Peyton cried, and he suddenly put everything that was going on around him together.

Her restaurant plans.

Not the resort.

And the changes he never told her about.

"I have to go," he said quickly into the phone before hanging up. Ryder knew he could deal with his brother later, but this...this needed his full attention right now. Stalking across the room, he kept his eyes on her. "Peyton, I..."

"You changed everything, Ryder!" she said frantically. "Everything!"

"In his defense," Austin started, but she cut him right off.

"He has no defense! Those were my plans. *My* plans!" She stepped around both men and stormed toward him. "You said you were building *my* restaurant, Ryder! Those plans barely resemble anything of mine!"

Holding up a hand to stop her, he knew one of them had to stay calm and be the voice of reason. "There were issues with the plans," he explained. "In order to maximize the potential of the property, some changes needed to be made. It's not a big deal. If you take a breath and just look at what we did, you'll see that the changes are no big deal. If anything, it made everything better. More efficient."

Her eyes narrowed to near slits and he nervously glanced at Austin and Jake—who both turned away.

"Peyton, come on. Be reasonable. You can't possibly

think that your plans were so perfect that nothing needed to change," he went on casually, even though he had a feeling he was digging an even deeper hole for himself. "You drew that design yourself. You can't possibly know everything there is to know about architecture and all it entails to make sure a building is safely placed on a piece of property."

Glancing over her shoulder toward her cousin, she asked, "Was the design safe, Austin?"

"Um...yes?" he said weakly. "But there were..."

She wasn't listening. Turning back to Ryder, she said, "And you know what? I could have handled the changes if you had bothered to talk to me about them. I'm not a child and I'm not an idiot and this feels all too familiar, Ryder."

"What does that mean?"

"It's like we're right back to when we first met. You're not taking me seriously and it feels like you...you lied to me to get your way!"

"How did I...?"

"You thought you could throw cash at me and when that didn't work, you promised to build my restaurant! We agreed it would be seventy-five, twenty-five and yet you had no intention of sticking to that, did you?"

"Of course I did! If you'd just calm down..."

"And I'm sure once we started sleeping together you really didn't think you had to honor our agreement!" She groaned as she shook her head with disgust. "I can't believe I trusted you!"

"Um...maybe we should go," Jake said as he and Austin began gathering their things.

"No," Peyton said loudly, firmly. "You guys stay. Apparently you have all kinds of plans to discuss that don't involve me. I'll go." She stormed around gathering her things and rather than feeling bad, it angered Ryder.

"You know what, Peyton? Yes, you should go. Go and calm down and think about all the crazy shit you just said." When she turned and glared at him, he didn't back down. "I made a mistake and didn't talk to you about the plans, but it wasn't intentional and I certainly didn't do it because I don't value your opinion!"

"Right," she snorted as she picked up her purse.

"I don't see what the big deal here is," he went on. "It's a few tweaks and a tree, for crying out loud!"

"Not to me!" she countered. "Don't you get it? You gave me your word on this! How many times did I ask about the plans, huh? How many?" Before he could reply, she was already speaking again. "And not once did you mention anything changing! You just let me believe that everything was fine." Her shoulders sagged as she looked at him sadly. "You lied to my face, Ryder. Repeatedly."

Ryder hated when people doubted him, but he hated it even more that she did. After everything they'd shared and everything they'd been building together, for her to think so little of him was beyond hurtful and insulting.

It gutted him.

As she started walking down the stairs to the front door, he followed. "When you're done having a hissy fit and prepared to have an adult conversation about this, let me know," he said.

Her only response was to slam the door behind her.

Fine, he thought. Let her go and calm down. He was trying to put out too many fires to be able to deal with her being hysterical and unreasonable. Raking his hand through his hair, he heaved out a sigh and walked back up to the kitchen.

"Okay, where were we?" he asked as if nothing happened. "What time is your meeting tomorrow?"

Jake looked at him as if he were crazy and Austin looked ready to punch him. "What?"

"Are you seriously just going to let her leave like that?" Austin demanded.

"She's upset. Nothing I'm going to say is going to calm her down right now so...it's better this way. Let's figure this stuff out and by then she'll hopefully be willing to have a rational conversation." He motioned to the tablet. "Can we use your plans or should I go and grab mine?"

"Ryder," Jake began cautiously. "Can I offer you a little advice?"

He wanted to say no, but nodded instead.

"It sounded like Peyton had a point. You kept pertinent information from her after promising she'd have more than just a small say in this project. I'm sure you think I don't know what I'm talking about, but believe me, I do. I made a similar mistake with Mallory when we first got back together. Misunderstandings can kill a relationship."

"Yeah," Austin agreed. "And if that didn't do it, talking to her like she was a child you were reprimanding certainly will. Jeez, man, what were you thinking?"

It would have been easy to argue but...they were right. He knew he was wrong about not sharing the changes with her, but he wasn't wrong about her reaction to it and nothing either of them said was going to change his mind on it–which is exactly what he told them.

"It's your funeral," Austin murmured.

"So...wait. The restaurant–the single standing structure–that's Peyton's?" Jake asked.

"No, it's mine, but I told her I'd build the restaurant she was planning on for the property."

"When was Peyton going to buy that property?"

Beside them, Austin groaned. "She'd been planning on

it for over a year and then Ryder swooped in and stole it out from under her."

"Hey! I didn't steal it from anyone!" he argued.

"Like that matters right now," Austin said, his tone dripping sarcasm. "The fact is you got the property and she didn't and then you made some sort of cockamamie deal where you promised to use her plans and then didn't."

"Yeah, but..."

"And," Austin went on, "you neglected to tell me any of that. Peyton and I had talked about her plans for the restaurant and if you would have mentioned even once that these were her plans, I would have gone to her directly and saved your sorry ass."

"My ass isn't..."

"It's sorry," Jake chimed in. "Trust me."

"Well...shit." Sighing, he sat in one of the kitchen chairs. "I'm not used to having to take anyone else into consideration—not in business and not in my personal life. I honestly didn't think any of this was a big deal. It was a couple of walls...a tree..."

"And turning the building, and changing the size of a deck, and..."

"Okay, I get it!" he snapped. "So now what do I do?"

Both Jake and Austin looked at each other before Jake spoke. "She is going to need some time to cool off because she is definitely mad at you. But don't give her too long."

"And please leave me out of it," Austin added. "The two of you are exhausting."

Jake ignored that statement and tried to focus on the business at hand. "As for what we're here for, I honestly don't think there's anything else you can offer that Austin and I haven't thought of. Do you trust us to talk to the town planners and try to come up with a solution?"

He hated not being involved, but Jake was right. This was totally out of his hands. Nodding, he said, "Yeah. I trust you both. Just let me know how it goes."

They said their goodbyes and once he was alone, Ryder walked out onto the back deck and stared out at the ocean and wondered how his day had gone so horribly out of control.

Didn't Peyton trust him to make the right decisions for her and the restaurant? Didn't she realize his success rate with all the businesses he'd invested in? Why would she take this so personally? Maybe she was just naturally untrusting, or maybe it was because...

Then it hit him—he'd never had the contracts drawn up. They kept negotiating in the weeks following the initial discussion and then...then their relationship changed.

Shit.

"Well, I know what I have to do right now," he muttered as he pulled out his phone to call his attorney. It was important for Peyton to know she could trust him and if that meant a signed contract and a promise to include her in any and all discussions moving forward for the restaurant, then so be it.

So much for love, he thought, and it left him struggling with relief for not saying he loved her and disappointment because he was obviously the only one who felt that way. All this time he kept telling himself she was different—that she wasn't with him because of his last name or for his money—but clearly he was wrong.

And he wouldn't make the same mistake again.

12

"I can't believe you're here."

"Well...believe it."

"I mean...what were you thinking? This is totally unlike you!"

It was after midnight and Peyton was putting her feet up on her sister's couch after over seven hours of driving. "We talked about this when I called to tell you I was on my way. I just needed to get away for a few days. You've been begging me to come and visit and here I am. Can't you just let it go at that?"

"Absolutely not! I mean...look at you! You're nearly delirious from driving for so long and I can't believe you just left the café on such short notice!"

"Parker..." she whined.

"Nuh-uh. Out with it." She plopped down on the opposite end of the couch and crossed her arms, and Peyton knew her sister would sit there like that all night until she got some answers. "And you know what? I'm here in my comfy jammies without a care in the world. I just had a bowl of cookies and cream ice cream with chocolate syrup so I'm all sugared up and wide awake."

Crap.

"Ooh...can I have a bowl?"

"No."

"But..."

"Tell me why you're really here and then you can have ice cream," Parker said firmly.

"Ugh...fine!" Then she proceeded to tell her about the argument with Ryder. She unloaded everything from their initial agreement months ago to him not honoring it, as she found out today. "So obviously I don't really even *know* him! I mean...I trusted him! Loved him! And thank God I never said the words to him because I'd feel like even more of an idiot than I do right now!"

Without a word, Parker stood and went to the kitchen and prepared a massive bowl of ice cream. When she handed it to Peyton and sat back down, she smiled. "There. Doesn't that feel better to get all that off your chest?"

Peyton couldn't help but nod. "It really does." She took a spoonful of ice cream and hummed with appreciation.

"It's good, right?"

"Definitely. Thank you."

"You're very welcome," she said sweetly. "So...did the drive all the way down here help at all? Did you come to any conclusions about your relationship with Ryder?"

"Honestly? The drive did help, and it made me realize that I'm too gullible. He never gave me the contracts he said he would, and I was foolish enough to take his word for everything." She sighed and took another spoonful of ice cream before shaking her spoon at Parker. "I'm second-guessing everything. Was he just using me all along? Was he sleeping with me so he could get help with his precious resort–which, FYI, is totally never going to fit in with Magnolia no matter what he thinks and I think that's why the permits keep getting denied–and did sleeping with me help him get in even closer with our family?"

Frowning, Parker took the spoon from her and helped herself to some of the ice cream. "Why would he sleep with you to get to our family? He was already friends with just about everyone; he didn't need you for that."

"Yeah, but...he feels like this...connection to everyone. Like we're the family he's always wanted. And by we I don't just mean us, the Bishops, I'm talking about the extended family. He loves how everyone is so close and happy and supportive of one another."

"We are awesome..."

"Okay, so maybe that part had nothing to do with me and was just a perk, but I'm still convinced he was just using me for the help I was giving him."

Her sister handed the spoon back with a dramatic sigh. "Oh, Peyton...I hate to be the one to burst your bubble, but...you're not that awesome."

"Um...excuse me?"

With a nod, Parker explained. "You're good at what you do, but Ryder's a millionaire who could hire some of the best restauranteurs in the business to help him. There wasn't anything you were going to help him with that he couldn't get from a more qualified source. It's obvious he wanted you for a reason."

"I told him to hire someone more qualified, but he insisted he wanted me! That I was perfect for the job!"

"Or maybe you were perfect for *him*!" She groaned. "You can't be this clueless!"

Rather than respond, Peyton ate a few more spoonfuls

of ice cream way too fast and got brain freeze. When she winced, Parker laughed. "It's not funny."

"Oh, please, it totally is, and you deserve it. I can't believe you blew this so badly, Peyton!"

"I didn't blow anything. He did by lying to me." And because she was childish, she shoveled even more ice cream in her mouth even though it felt like her head was literally going to explode.

"Okay, yes. I will agree that he was wrong to make changes to the plans without talking to you about them, but...so what? Nothing was done yet. It's not like the place got built and you were completely blindsided. Everything is still in the planning stage. Maybe if you would have told Austin and Jake to scram so you and Ryder could talk, you would have realized that he'd listen to you."

"He should have been listening already. He promised..."

"Oh my God! Enough with the promise!" Parker shouted. "Are you seriously going to sit there and tell me that you've never made a mistake in a relationship? That you never said or did anything that you wish with all your heart you could change or take back?" Jumping to her feet, she paced in front of the sofa. "And I'm not talking about this situation with Ryder because I know that's what you were thinking, but I'm talking ever, Peyton. Ever!"

"Um..."

"Like...if someone shared how they felt to you and you blew them off and ruined everything. Or...or made light of something you should have taken seriously and lost something special. Can you really sit there and tell me that's never happened to you?" she demanded.

"I kind of have a feeling we're not talking about me anymore..."

Parker stopped and hovered over her. "You have to be

honest with yourself, Peyton, and deal with the conse-
quences. None of us is blameless in any situation and if you
have the chance to make things right with Ryder–if you
really do love him–then you have to deal with the fact that
you behaved kind of bratty."

"I did not..."

"You did! Maybe after a good night's sleep you'll realize
it too. You were both wrong in this scenario and if you are
able to walk away so easily, then maybe you were the one
using him."

Slamming the bowl on the end table, Peyton stood and
got in her sister's face. "It wasn't like that! I would never do
something like that! I love Ryder!" Tears stung her eyes.
"That's why this hurts so much. Don't you get it?" She
immediately sat back down. "God, it feels like my heart is
literally ripping in two!" Looking up at Parker, her vision
blurred as the tears fell in earnest. "I wanted him to fight
with me–to tell me he was sorry–but instead he insulted me
in front of Austin and Jake and talked to me like I was a
child. It was humiliating."

Fortunately, her sister sat down beside her, hugging her.
"I'm so sorry, Peyton. I really am." She sighed. "Okay, let's
drop this subject for tonight. You're exhausted and I think
you need some sleep. You've had a rough day."

They sat in companionable silence for several minutes
while Peyton cried it out. When she finally felt a bit better,
she straightened and accepted the tissues Parker got for her.
"Thanks."

"Come on. I know there's a guest room, but you're
crashing with me."

That just made her chuckle. "It's not like we haven't
done that a hundred times before." And by the time they
were both in the bed, all the exhaustion of the day caught

up with her. "Oh, and I forgot to tell you the other big news of the day."

Yawning, Parker asked, "There's more?"

"Yup. I went and confronted Mom today."

"What?! And you're just telling me this now?" she cried before flopping over onto her back. "I know I said you needed sleep, but I have to hear how that all played out first."

"Parks, come on. It's so late and this bed is really comfy..."

"Ugh...fine. Just give me the highlights. Did you yell?"

"Not really."

Frowning, Parker shook her head. "That's not particularly helpful. Did she show any emotion?"

"She cried."

"What?! You made Mom cry and now you think I'm going to let you sleep?" She gave Peyton a small shove. "This is huge! I've never seen or heard Mom cry! It's like seeing Bigfoot and a unicorn having tea together!"

Okay, that did make her laugh a little. "Yeah, well...she just sort of burst into tears at one point and I didn't know what to do. And it wasn't the genteel sobs of a Southern belle. It was an ugly cry."

"You are so lucky..."

Peyton gave her sister a hard look. "That's really not very nice."

"To be fair, neither is she, so..."

"You have a point." Rolling onto her back, she stared up at the ceiling and sighed. So basically her day consisted of bullying her mother, arguing with Ryder, and running away and keeping her sister up all night with her nonsense. Unable to help herself, she groaned.

"What? What's the matter?"

"This day has just been awful and the common denominator in all of it is me." Turning her head, she looked at Parker. "I don't think I like the person I've become."

"To be fair, you've been a bit of a marshmallow for most of your life and I think you're trying to make up for lost time." Reaching over, she squeezed Peyton's hand. "Maybe don't try to be such a badass to everyone who loves you and...you know...baby steps."

"A little too late for that now, don't you think?"

"Actually, no. I think everyone's entitled to a little bad behavior and if the people around you love you like they claim to, then you should be forgiven. I can't imagine Mom disowning you or Ryder just being willing to walk away from you because you dared to respond in a way that he didn't like. I mean...no two people can think the same thing and feel the same way all the time, right? And...and...sometimes you need to just think for a bit before making life-altering decisions! People need to realize that and stop punishing...you know...people who just need time!"

Peyton's frown returned. "Okay, again...I have a feeling we're not talking about me anymore. What's going on with you? Is everything okay?"

Parker's blue eyes went wide before she rolled over and turned out the light. "You know what? It's late, and the day has caught up to me, too. Get some sleep and we'll talk more about getting you back to Magnolia and Ryder in the morning. Night!"

There was a part of her that really wanted to argue and push to find out just what in the world was going on with her sister, but it was hard to keep her eyes open or to even think straight right now.

She missed Ryder. Even as mad as she was at him, she missed him. As much as she adored her sister and appreciated her opening up her home and bed to her, this wasn't where Peyton wanted to be.

Why did I have to run away? Why couldn't I have just gone home and stayed there while I calmed down? Did I really have to go to such an extreme?

Her phone was out in the living room, and even though she hadn't checked it since she crossed the South Carolina/Georgia state line, she couldn't help but wonder if Ryder had tried to reach out to her. And knowing him, her silence just made her seem more childish to him.

Great.

She considered getting up and getting her phone and calling him to apologize, but...her body just wouldn't cooperate. She was tired but she was also an early riser. So, she'd sleep now and get up tomorrow and call him first thing.

It was a good plan.

The right plan.

And hopefully by this time tomorrow night, she'd be sleeping beside Ryder instead of her snoring sister.

"Thanks, Cal. I appreciate you putting a rush on this," Ryder said to his attorney the next morning when the contracts were sent over. When the bank opened, he'd go and get the cashier's check and have everything ready to give to her by lunchtime so he could put this all behind him.

And damn, did it hurt to think like that.

She'd obviously turned her phone off last night because he hadn't been able to reach her so today after he went to the bank, he planned on going to the café and speaking to her privately and giving her the check for the hundred thousand and the contract regarding the restaurant. Moving forward, she could be the one to talk to Austin about the plans because he was going to stay out of it.

Even though it was his money bankrolling the whole damn thing, but...whatever.

Last night, he hadn't slept at all. He'd tossed and turned and found himself reaching for her more times than he could count. He missed her, ached for her, but...the reality was that he was going to have to get used to being alone again.

And possibly consider leaving Magnolia Sound.

There was no way he could stay here and have it be the utopia he had planned on making it while knowing Peyton was there, moving on with her life without him. There'd come a time when she'd start dating another man–possibly marrying him–and adding to the amazing Coleman extended family. He'd lose not only her, but them. He knew he'd get over losing the Colemans, but Ryder didn't think he'd ever get over losing Peyton.

"Great way to start the day, sinking further and further into misery and self-loathing," he murmured before making himself a second cup of coffee.

It was going to be a long day.

"It's going to be an even longer life," he mused darkly, taking his mug. He needed to shower and get dressed and get going. The only way he was going to survive was to keep moving. If the plans for the resort got denied again, he'd pull the plug on the whole thing, sell the property and move on.

Feeling better about having a plan, he went to shower.

Leaving the house an hour later, Ryder wasn't looking forward to anything he was about to do. He knew he was doing what was best for Peyton, but it still felt wrong on so many levels. In the car, he glanced at his phone and decided to try calling her again, but it went directly to voicemail.

God, why was she so stubborn?

It was after ten in the morning and he knew her schedule as well as he knew his own. The fact that her phone was still off was very telling.

She didn't want to hear from him.

Letting out a long breath, he frowned as he pulled out of the driveway. Whether she liked it or not, she was going to have to hear from him one more time because once he went to the bank, he was showing up at the café and wasn't leaving until everything was signed, sealed, and delivered. He was sure she'd be glad to see him go. After all, she never was thrilled with the plans he was making to her precious town so...again, maybe it was all for the best.

But why did it have to hurt so badly?

"Shake it off, Ryder," he muttered as he made his way across town.

Dealing with the bank took a little longer than he wanted, but he simply reasoned it was because they were dealing with such a large amount of money. Once he was done there and back in his car, he nearly jumped when his phone rang. His heart hammered in his chest as he prayed it was Peyton, but...it wasn't. With a muttered curse, he answered. "Hey, Austin. What's up?"

"Hey," he began slowly, and Ryder knew he wasn't calling with good news.

"The plans didn't get approved again, did they?"

"I'm afraid not."

Part of him wanted to rail and carry on and demand to know what their problem was, but...he didn't.

"We can go back to the drawing board and modify your plans again, Ry," Austin explained. "It seems part of the issue is..."

But he didn't want to hear it. It didn't matter. "Don't

worry about it, Austin. I appreciate the call. Let's just call this done."

"Done? Ryder, come on. You can't be serious!"

"I am," he replied solemnly. "Listen, I appreciate everything you've done, but I know it's time to pull the plug. It just wasn't meant to be."

"O-kay...so what are you going to do with the property? I'm sure you already have alternate plans."

"Yeah. I'm going to sell it."

"What?!" Austin cried with disbelief. "Why? Why would you do that? You were so psyched to utilize the property! Just because this one design didn't work doesn't mean something else won't! Why don't we meet for lunch and talk about it?"

"I can't, Austin. My day is booked. I'll be in touch, though. Thanks." And he hung up before his friend could say anything else. It was just one more thing he couldn't deal with right now.

Within minutes, he was in front of the café but didn't see Peyton's car. Maybe she was out running an errand, but he could easily wait for her inside. Maybe he could have something to eat to pass the time.

When he walked in, Dana greeted him. "Hey, Ryder! What can I do for you?"

"Hey, Dana. I'm here to see Peyton. Is she around?"

She looked at him funny, like she was mildly confused. "Um...I'm sorry, but...she's not here. She decided to take a few days off."

"Oh, okay. Thanks. Have a good day," he said as he forced a smile. Walking out of the café, he felt incredibly foolish and wondered if the entire staff would now be talking about how there was obviously trouble between him and Peyton that he didn't even know where she was.

But he immediately pushed that train of thought aside and drove over to Peyton's.

She wasn't there.

Now he wasn't sure what else he could do but wait.

Which wasn't his strong point.

He considered going to her parents' place or simply driving around town in hopes of spotting her out and about, but that seemed a little stalkerish. With nothing else to do, he began to drive home.

But at the last minute, he turned around and drove to the Coleman Construction offices. He knew Austin was working there today and walked in as if he owned the place. When he spotted his friend, he said, "I need Parker's number."

"Why? We were just on the phone like ten minutes ago. What's going on?"

"I can't reach Peyton and..."

"Dammit, I told you I didn't want to be in the middle of this!"

"Then just give me her number and I'll be on my way."

"No. Absolutely not. I'm done with this whole situation so...no." His phone rang and the man practically dove for it. "I have to take this. You know the way out."

It was pointless to argue, and Ryder knew he could simply search for himself for Parker's number. He just thought this would be quicker.

Back to square one, he was walking back to his car when he spotted Mallory Summerford–Jake's wife and Peyton's cousin.

And said a silent prayer that she had no idea about what went down yesterday.

"Hey, Ryder!" Mallory approached him with a smile. "How are you?"

"Good," he replied easily. "Good. Where are the kids?"

"Oh, they're with my mom so Jake and I can have lunch together," she told him. "It's easier to sneak out during the day than to go out for dinner. Bedtime is rough when Jake and I aren't there."

He nodded because he had no clue about kids, so he had to take her word for it. "I was just in with Austin but he had to hop on a call but I was looking for Parker's number. Do you happen to have it handy?"

She eyed him curiously. "Why not just ask Peyton?"

Waving her off with an easy laugh, he said, "Well, I'm hoping to surprise Peyton with something and if I ask her for Parker's number, she'll get suspicious."

That seemed to relax her. "Aren't you sweet?" She pulled out her phone and gave him the number. "When you talk to her, please tell her I said hi." Then, taking a step around him, she said, "I really need to get inside. Jake's only got an hour before he needs to be back on the jobsite and I don't want to be late. It was good to see you, Ryder!"

"You too, Mallory!" With a smile and wave, he made a hasty retreat just in case Jake or Austin decided to fill her in on his relationship drama.

He dialed and Parker's phone was ringing as he pulled away from the Coleman Construction offices. Honestly, he had no idea what Parker did for a living other than housesit for friends down in Florida, and he hoped she was available to talk.

"Hey, it's Parker! Leave a message and I'll call you back! Thanks!" the recording said and with a muttered curse, Ryder hung up.

Now what? He wondered. He didn't want to leave a message; he wanted to talk to her. No, he wanted to talk to

Peyton, but clearly that wasn't happening any time soon either, so...where did that leave him?

Going home held little appeal, but...all the people he knew here in town were related to Peyton, and it didn't seem like a good idea to go and reach out to any of them. He thought about all the plans he had for this town and for his future, and it didn't seem possible that it was all just going to go away.

Turning the car around one more time, he drove to the northernmost part of town, to the property that would never house The Ashford. All of his dreams were supposed to go into this project and it died before it ever got off the ground. It was depressing as hell, but there wasn't anything he could do about it. The town wasn't on board with it and he should have listened to Peyton on that from the beginning. She had been the only one brave enough to tell him that his plan was flawed, and looking back, he should have listened.

Hindsight and all that crap...

The drive didn't take long, and after parking on the edge of the property, he climbed out and stared at the expanse of cleared land. It was nothing but plowed dirt with some random markers for where the buildings were supposed to go, but in his mind, Ryder saw so much more. He saw the white buildings, the lush greenery, and the fountain out front. Maybe at some other point in life he'd get another opportunity to make this happen.

Just not in Magnolia.

And not with the people he had come to love.

Peyton's face instantly came to mind, but he pushed it away.

Ryder had no idea how long he stood there and just stared out at the empty space, but eventually he turned away, got back in his car, and started to drive home.

But he stopped back at the café first.

Inside, he handed Dana the envelope that held the contracts and the check. "If you could please leave that for Peyton in her office, I'd appreciate it," he told her before finally going home.

Normally he'd throw himself into work–there was always something that needed his attention, but his head just wasn't in it. That should have alarmed him because it had never happened to him before, but as he sat down on his sofa, he just sort of accepted it.

Tomorrow was another day, and he'd have to start thinking about transitioning out of Magnolia and deciding where he was going to go. Scrubbing a hand over his face, he yawned and considered taking a nap right here on the couch. There was no way he'd get any sleep in the bed. So he kicked off his shoes and decided to get comfortable.

His eyes closed and he felt himself relax. His mind wandered back to the property, but this time he envisioned something different there. Something *very* different from The Ashford. It was funny how inspiration hit at the oddest times, but Ryder knew better than to ignore it. The next thing he knew, he was in his office pulling up different websites and feeling more inspired than he had in a long time.

There was no way he was giving up–not on Magnolia and definitely not on Peyton.

13

There had been an accident on I-95 and a drive that should have taken seven and a half hours took closer to ten. By the time Peyton crossed into Magnolia Sound, she was near delirious with exhaustion.

And starving.

She had stayed an extra day with her sister just because she wanted to. They went for mani-pedis and out for lunch in the afternoon before joining several of Parker's friends for dinner. It was the perfect break from life that Peyton needed before going home. Now it was time to deal with the fallout with Ryder.

It was a little after nine and the café would be closing soon, but she figured she could stop in and grab something to eat and make sure everything was okay there before going home. She considered going to Ryder's but figured it would be smarter to wait until tomorrow considering she'd been on the road all day.

There were still a few customers enjoying their meals when she walked in, and she smiled and waved on her way to the kitchen. She chatted with everyone and got caught up on the local gossip and felt some of the tension from the long drive starting to leave her. There had been no issues while she was gone—not that she expected any. Her staff was amazing. So she made herself a plate of grilled scallops with a side salad and took it to her office.

The first thing she noticed when she sat down was the large envelope with her name on it standing against her computer monitor.

"Hmm...what's this?" she murmured as she reached in and pulled out the stack of papers. A check fell free and floated to the floor and when she picked it up, Peyton swore she was having a stroke. "What the hell?"

With trembling fingers, she sorted through the papers and realized they were the contracts they had originally discussed when they first started working together. She scanned the document and saw it was everything she and Ryder talked about, but...did he honestly think this was what she wanted? The moment they started dating, she never once thought of their business arrangement. In her mind and in her heart, this was about the two of them just being together.

Maybe he was just using you...

No. She refused to believe that. Standing, she grabbed everything—the contract, the check, her purse and keys—and stormed from her office. "Can someone please throw away my dinner?" she called out on her way out the door. "I need to go!"

It was a good thing Ryder didn't live far from the café because even as mad as she was, getting back in the car was the equivalent of climbing Mount Everest right now.

She slammed her car door when she parked in his driveway and stomped up the front steps. It was tempting to use her key and totally surprise him like that, but if a business relationship was what he wanted, then dammit, that was what he was going to get. So she rang the bell and knocked on the door consistently until he opened it.

He was disheveled. That was her immediate thought. His hair was a mess, there were dark circles under his eyes, and the most shocking...

He was in shorts and a t-shirt.

"What the hell is all this?" she yelled, waving the envelope in his face, refusing to be distracted by his appearance.

His eyes went a little wide before he cleared his throat. "The contracts. We uh...we never signed them."

Next, she pulled the check out of the envelope and made a big show of ripping it up and letting the pieces fall at his feet. "It's insulting. That's what it is," she told him. "How dare you do that to me after everything we've shared! I thought I meant more to you than that, but obviously my first impression was correct. You just throw money around to get what you want. And since what you want is to pay me off and send me on my way since we're done, then fine. But I don't want or need your money, Ryder Ashford. I never did."

She was feeling pretty damn proud of herself for getting through that little speech without crying. And with what she hoped was a scathing look, she turned to walk away.

Only...Ryder's hand grasped her arm to stop her. He spun her around and she realized he no longer looked quite so disheveled. Now he looked big and menacing.

Uh-oh...

"You think I did this to get rid of you?" he asked incredulously.

Yanking her arm free, she nodded. "Yes. Yes, I do."

Muttering a curse, he took a step back into the house. "Can you please come inside so we can talk about this?"

"There's nothing to say. This little packet said more than enough."

"For the love of it, Peyton. Please? Just...five minutes?"

With a snort, she stepped inside. "Right. Like I haven't heard that line from you before."

And yet...here I am giving him the damn minutes...

She stomped up to the kitchen and saw it was a mess. This was all so unlike him, and as much as she hoped it was because of her, she couldn't seem to let herself believe it. The man was too self-sufficient, and he was obviously done with her, so...this all had to be for some other reason.

Crossing her arms and doing her best to look defiant, she waited him out.

"Look, like it or not, we made a deal months ago, a deal that I neglected to follow through on. That's not who I am, Peyton. You did everything you promised to do and I didn't, so...that's what the contract and check are about. I want you to know that I appreciate all that you did and all that I learned from you." He paused and looked like he wanted to touch her, but...he didn't. "About restaurants," he quickly corrected. "I learned a lot about the restaurant business and hopefully–maybe sometime in the future–I'll be able to put all of it to good use."

"In the future? What are you talking about? What about The Ashford and my restaurant? Or rather, your restaurant with some of my ideas?"

Because yeah...it still stung.

His broad shoulders sagged and at that moment, Peyton felt like the worst kind of person. She was being mean and a brat and a bully in a way that only he brought out in her.

With a weary sigh, she quietly said, "Ryder, I appreciate that you're a man of your word. But the day we got...romantically involved, that whole deal went away." Then she realized she was lying. "Well...most of it. I didn't want the money. I never did. That was your negotiating tactic. And I thought you wanted to build my restaurant because... because you thought my plan was good. That you trusted me enough and believed in me enough to want to build it. So...that's on me. I'm sorry for the things I said and for my bad behavior. I won't stand in your way so you can build whatever it is that you want. After all, it's your money, not mine."

Then, even though it nearly killed her, she forced herself to smile as she held out a hand to him.

"It's been a pleasure doing business with you, Ryder Ashford, but I'm not going to sign any contract. I enjoyed helping you and thank you for being willing to take a chance on me."

This was the very last thing she wanted to be saying to him. The entire drive back from Parker's, she rehearsed how she was going to apologize and how he'd hopefully do the same and they'd make up in spectacular fashion. Once she saw that contract and check, however, everything changed.

So she was back to being the broken-hearted woman she was when she arrived on her sister's doorstep and she had a feeling that was who she was going to be for a long time.

Glancing down at her hand, she realized he still hadn't taken it.

O-kay...

Dropping it, she kept her smile in place. "I should go." She'd taken no more than three steps when his words stopped her.

"What is it you want from me, Peyton?" His voice was so low and so gruff, she almost threw herself at him. But when she turned around, she saw the same sadness there that she'd seen in her own reflection for the last two days.

Was it possible she was reading this all wrong? Could Ryder have missed her as much as she missed him, and this was his completely misguided way of showing it? Or was she just seeing what she wanted to see?

Then, because she had nothing left to lose, she figured she'd tell him exactly what was on her mind.

"You want to know what I want, Ryder?" she asked firmly, confidently.

He nodded.

"You, you idiot! Just you! Though God only knows why! You're impossible to deal with! You're bossy and condescending and completely clueless about how to be in a relationship! We had a fight, Ryder! A fight!" she went on, her voice getting louder with each word. "And instead of insulting me about being childish, maybe you should look at your actions, buddy! I at least was honest about how I felt whereas you hurled insults and then tried to pay me off to get you out of your life! If I had known this was what I was going to come home to, I would have just..."

She never got to finish.

In typical Ryder fashion, he hauled her into his arms and kissed her senseless.

There was nothing sweet or romantic about it. It was wet and urgent and needy. Peyton had already been breathless, but as she reached out and grabbed his shirt in her fists, it felt like she was holding on for dear life.

Ryder abruptly broke the kiss—as breathless as she was—and stared down at her. "Do you have any idea how much you have turned my world upside down?" he growled. "Every single day since the moment I met you I've felt completely off-kilter." His arms were banded tightly around her, and he didn't seem in a hurry to let her go.

Luckily, Peyton was more than happy to stay exactly where she was.

"You're right," he went on. "I am bossy and condescending and completely clueless. I know exactly how to handle myself in business, but with you...you're not like any woman I've ever known. I keep thinking that I'm giving you what you want and yet somehow you keep proving me wrong." Dark eyes scanned her face, and she saw a vulnerability there that she'd never seen before. "Don't leave me, Peyton. I need you." Pausing, he reached up and caressed her face. "I love you."

Right then, at that moment, she was fairly certain her heart stopped.

He loved her.

A slow smile crossed her face as she reached up and cupped his strong jaw. "I love you too," she told him. "Even though..."

He cut her off again with a kiss, and Peyton simply melted against him. It was much better than talking anyway.

There was nothing sweeter than victory, Ryder thought as Peyton's curvy body pressed closer to him. But this one was definitely the sweetest.

She loved him.

He held her tighter and poured everything he had into the kiss, but there were so many things he wanted to say to her that couldn't wait. So...reluctantly–again–he ended the kiss. With his forehead resting against hers, he breathlessly confessed how this was his favorite way to stop an argument.

Fortunately, she laughed with him and he took her hand in his and led her over to the sofa so he could sit with her in his arms. As soon as they were comfortable—her back to his chest and his arms around her—Ryder felt himself relax.

"I missed you," he murmured, placing a soft kiss on her temple.

"Mmm...I missed you too."

They sat in companionable silence for barely a minute because he knew they needed to talk. "Where did you go?" he quietly asked.

"What do you mean?"

"You said if you had known this was what you were going to come home to. I took that to mean you went somewhere."

"Oh. I went to see Parker."

"You drove all the way to Florida?" he asked, unable to hide his shock.

"I was really mad and sometimes driving helps. Before I knew it, I was on I-95 heading south." She shrugged. "I got there around midnight and was too exhausted the next day to get back in the car, so I left there this morning. My plan was to come right here, but there was an accident and I sat in traffic for an additional three hours. By the time I got into town, it was late and I was in a pissy mood and starving. I decided to swing by the café and when I did, I saw your envelope."

"You have to know I honestly thought I was doing the right thing. I thought part of the reason you were so upset was because I wasn't honoring our agreement. That's when I realized we never did sign a contract so..."

Peyton turned in his arms and met his gaze. "Ryder, I was upset because you—the man I love—weren't treating me like an equal. It felt like you were deliberately leaving me out of things. I know you're used to being in charge of projects, but I trusted you to work with me on the restaurant and you weren't."

"I see that now," he agreed solemnly. "But in my defense, I truly believed I was doing the right thing, that I was saving you some of the grief and aggravation of the planning stages. Once things got the green light, it was going to be all you."

Now she fully maneuvered until she was straddling his lap. "I need you to listen very carefully to what I'm about to say," she warned.

"O-kay..."

"While I appreciate what you were trying to do, I don't need you to save me! I am more than capable of saving myself. Believe it or not, I was looking forward to all aspects of the planning phase! I wanted to learn!"

"Peyton..."

"And you know what else? You're the one who needs saving, Ryder, and I'm going to be the one to do it!"

Ryder was pretty sure his eyes were comically wide, but...

"I need to be saved?"

"Uh-huh. Definitely."

"Definitely? How do you figure that?" Honestly, he knew she was right. There had been several eye-opening things about himself that had come to light in the last year and most of them happened since meeting Peyton. But he was curious just what it was she saw.

"I think you've spent far too much time on your own and doing things for yourself because no one else did. I mean, no offense, I've met your parents, and it's obvious they weren't overly nurturing."

He nodded. "Go on."

"And because your parents are so much like mine—well, at least my mother—I imagine you don't know what it's like to be loved and accepted just for you. That's why you throw money at things and take control of projects. This way people have to look up to you or be thankful for you." She cupped his jaw a little harder as she leaned in closer. "But I'm here to tell you that I don't give a damn about your bank account. If you ever try to get your way with me by writing a check, I will strangle you."

Swallowing hard, he nodded again. "Understood."

Peyton relaxed and moved back a little, her hands sliding down to rest on his chest. "Good." She smiled. "Ryder Ashford, I love our conversations and all the things we do together. I love laughing with you and all of our sexy time together." She paused for a moment before adding, "And I do love the way you take care of me and look out for me. But I need you to respect me enough to let me make decisions for myself even if you might not agree with them."

"I do respect you, Peyton. I swear. But...just like you pointed out, my whole life has been spent seeing how most people don't really care about me as an individual. It's always been about the money. I promise I'm going to work on it, but I can't undo a lifetime of habits overnight." His arms tightened around her. "So I think you'll just have to be with me all the time to keep me in line."

She smiled. "I like the sound of that."

Ryder did too, but...he didn't love it.

The master negotiator in him told him he needed to sweeten this deal to give them both—hopefully—what they wanted.

Taking one of her hands in his, he gave it a gentle squeeze. "All the time seems a little vague, don't you think?"

"Well...obviously we both have to work so we know we

can't be together every minute of the day, but...it's still good," she reasoned.

His free hand reached up and cupped her cheek, his thumb gently stroking her soft skin. "I'm thinking forever, Peyton." His statement was low and a little hoarse and he'd never been more serious about anything in his entire life. "I don't want vague and I don't want possibilities. I want you– forever." Her soft gasp as those beautiful eyes went wide gave him pause. But then those perfect lips started to smile. "I know I should have planned this better, but I'm sitting here looking at everything I could possibly want in this world."

"Ryder," she whispered.

"You've opened my eyes to things I never knew I could have." Then he laughed softly. "And that's saying something since I grew up in a family where we could afford every-thing we could ever want. But you, my beautiful girl, are more than a want. You're a need. The fact that you're sitting here in my arms and you love me and accept all my flaws is...well...it's humbling. And wonderful." Shaking his head, he laughed again. "I feel like there are a million words trying to get out at the same time and I'm fumbling with them all."

Leaning in, Peyton gave him a quick kiss on the lips. "You're doing better than you think." Then she kissed him again and lingered a bit longer. When she pulled back, she smiled warmly at him. "You once shared with me why you liked being around my family so much, and it was weird to me that you considered us such an oddity because we're just us. This is the way we are and always have been. We all have flaws, but when you love somebody, you love their flaws too."

This all felt too good to be true. Ryder knew he'd closed

dozens of deals that had made him tons of money, and he'd traveled the world and saw every wonder there was to see. But this moment in the living room of an investment property was the most perfect moment he'd ever experienced. "I love you," he said, just because he could.

Her smile grew. "I love you too."

"I'm never going to get tired of saying that or hearing it so...you've been warned," he teased.

"Well, just so you know...I feel the same way." She squirmed against him in the sexiest of ways. "How about we take this inside and finish making up properly?"

This girl...

"Great minds, Peyton. This is why we're perfect for each other." And in one swift move, Ryder was on his feet with her in his arms. Her legs wrapped around his waist as he walked to the bedroom.

Their bedroom.

Gently, he laid her down and couldn't help but marvel at the sight of her there. "I haven't slept in days. It's not the same when you're not here. I don't sleep, I can't concentrate...you're my home, Peyton. My rock. My everything."

Tears welled in her eyes as she reached up to him. "You're going to make me cry," she whispered. "You have to stop saying such sweet and romantic things."

"Never," he vowed. "Every day for the rest of our lives you're going to know that you are loved for who you are. I'm going to be your biggest supporter and cheerleader and I can't wait to see the great things you're going to do."

As soon as the words were out, he realized now was not the time to bring up business. Instead, she pulled him down on top of her and wrapped herself around him, and it was like everything felt right again.

Her hands raked through his hair–her nails gently

scratching his scalp–causing him to moan with pleasure. She knew exactly how to touch him to get a response, and right now, Peyton was doing her best to make him crazy with need.

The kiss was hot and possessive one minute, languid and sweet the next. Every touch, every moan, every sigh turned him on. In his mind, he envisioned them making love slowly, tenderly, but it was obvious that wasn't what either of them truly wanted right now. It was hard to say who stripped faster; the only thing Ryder knew was that he was glad he was dressed casually. The skin-to-skin contact was beyond satisfying, and when she let out a throaty purr as she wrapped herself around him again, it spurred him on.

Everything was a blur after that. It was sensory overload and as they moved together, sharing messy kisses while laughing and sighing pleasure, he finally knew what true happiness was.

And it was all thanks to the magnificent woman in his arms.

"Oh my goodness, this is heavenly."

"Mmm..." he hummed beside her. "I have to agree."

"No, seriously...I can't believe how amazing this is!"

Shaking his head, Ryder chuckled. "Peyton, it's a BLT, and you made it yourself. I don't see what the big deal is."

She waved the sandwich in his face. "Are you kidding me? Are your taste buds not working? This sandwich is spectacular! The avocado really gave it a pop of flavor and the candied bacon is just decadent. Yum!"

"Watching you fry up bacon in nothing but my t-shirt was way more decadent," he corrected. "The sandwich is good. Catching a glimpse of your incredibly sexy bottom peeking out from under my shirt was simply spectacular."

"Such a guy," she murmured around a giggle.

It was after midnight, but when Peyton told him she hadn't eaten dinner–after her stomach growled loudly and repeatedly–he dragged her from the bed and into the kitchen. It was too late to order anything to be delivered, but they had been stocking his kitchen over the last several months, so he knew they'd be able to put some kind of meal together.

He just didn't expect it to be this good.

Off in the distance, he heard his phone chime with an incoming text. Frowning, he got up and walked across the room to see who it could be.

"And for the record, you walking around in nothing but those snug boxer briefs is pretty spectacular too," she called out, winking at him when he turned around.

It was hard not to preen under her praise, but the message he was reading stopped him in his tracks.

"Ryder? Is everything okay?"

He reread the message again just to make sure he understood it. "Um...yeah," he murmured, frowning, before turning the phone off and putting it down. When he sat back beside her and picked up his sandwich, he could feel the weight of her stare. "What?"

"Seriously? You're not going to tell me why your face got all scrunchy?"

Laughing, he turned to look at her. "Scrunchy? My face got scrunchy? Is that even a thing?"

"Trust me," she said solemnly. "It is." But then she started laughing too, so...

"It's nothing," he said before taking a bite of his sandwich. Unfortunately, even the crunch of the extra crispy bacon wasn't enough to drown out Peyton's sigh. "I'd tell you, but...I feel like it's something I should tell Austin first. And Garrett."

With wide eyes, she dropped her sandwich. "Oh my God! It's about Uncle Cash, isn't it? Was that who texted you? Did he tell you where he was? Is he here in Magnolia? Is he going to try to see Aunt Grace again?" She shook his arm. "Or...or...did he tell you why he disappeared? Is it too late to call Austin?" Looking around wildly, Peyton tried to see the clock on the microwave.

"First of all, calm down," he told her. "Yes, it's too late to call Austin or Garrett. No, it wasn't Cash who messaged me. He's not here in Magnolia though so there's no worry about him going to see Grace or anyone."

That took some of the wind out of her sails. "So...who was it?"

"Peyton..."

"Ryder," she mimicked. "Oh, come on. It clearly has something to do with Uncle Cash and you know once you call Austin and Garrett, everyone's going to know. Come on. Please!"

Rolling his eyes, he knew she wouldn't let up, and he also knew she wasn't going to be the one to gossip to anyone about it until her cousins brought it up first, so...

"Okay, so my guy had last tracked Cash to Seattle and..."

"Wait. I'm sorry. Your guy? For real?"

He nodded. "Yeah. My guy."

It was her turn to roll her eyes. "You know, I heard everyone mentioning him like that, and I thought they just couldn't remember his name. But you really just call him your guy? Why?"

"His name isn't important and he doesn't like to draw attention to himself."

"Yeah, but..."

"Do you want to know what he texted me or not?" he asked with a combination of humor and frustration.

"I do. I do. Sorry."

With a nod, he gave her the basics. "It seems as if Cash is living with a woman in a little town just outside of Seattle."

"Oh." Her shoulders sagged. "That's a little anticlimactic. I mean...obviously he's involved with someone. What's the big deal?"

"This woman is a bit...younger than Cash," he said carefully. "Like...younger than Jackson."

It took a minute for the implication to hit her, and then her eyes went wide. "Oh my goodness! No! You think this woman is his daughter?"

"We don't know yet, but she's obviously someone important to him if he just packed up and left Magnolia without saying goodbye to the family he was supposedly reconnecting with." He shrugged. "If you think about it, it just makes sense. He's got a second family."

"Wow," she sighed. "That is going to hit everyone hard. Ugh...so much drama. I mean...why come back at all?"

"I think he was truly interested in the inheritance, but maybe got a little caught up in nostalgia when he saw Garrett that day. Who knows?"

"It's just wrong that he dangled that money at the guys and then left town with it. So he gets to be a millionaire and share the wealth with his other family." She shuddered. "He's the worst."

"Actually..." he began slowly, unsure he should be sharing this, but... "He never cashed the check."

"What?! How do you even know that? And why wouldn't he? I mean...two million dollars! Who wouldn't take that money and run?"

"I'm not even going to begin to try to understand Cash's thought process. All I know is my guy was able to check it all out and the check was never cashed. Maybe he does still plan on giving your cousins the money. Who knows?"

Picking up her sandwich again, Peyton frowned. "Well, I don't even want to think about any of it. It's giving me a headache and I wish I didn't know any of it."

"You begged me to tell you!"

"I didn't realize it was going to be such awful news!"

It would be wrong to argue that she should have known by his...scrunchy face–which he still didn't think was a thing–but honestly, the last thing he wanted to be talking about right now was Cash Coleman and all the ways he'd done his family wrong. Instead, he finished his sandwich and washed it down with a bottle of water. Once he saw that Peyton was done, he took both their plates and cleaned up.

"I can help," she said as she got up, tugging the t-shirt down to cover her bottom.

Which was completely adorable.

Once everything was put away, Ryder took her by the hand and led her back to bed. "Come on, Duchess. I think we're both ready for a good night's sleep, right?"

As if on cue, she yawned. "Definitely."

Five minutes later and with his girl in his arms, Ryder turned off the light.

And was asleep before the room went fully dark.

14

"Do you have to go into the café this morning?"

They were sitting at the kitchen island sipping their coffees, and Peyton found herself torn. She'd already been irresponsible by taking off the way she did, so what kind of example would she be setting if she took yet another day off?

"I really should," she said with a sigh. "I stopped in last night, but...I didn't get anything accomplished. How come?"

"Well...I did some thinking after you left the other night—about The Ashford, your restaurant, and a few other things—and I'd like to run some ideas by you."

"Really? Did Austin finally get the permits approved?" Last night they hadn't talked about business and she was more than okay with it. But she also loved that Ryder was sharing the things he was working and asking her opinion on them.

As long as they were discussing and he wasn't keeping secrets about the things that directly involved her.

"No, the permits got denied again," he told her, shaking his head.

"I'm so sorry, Ryder." Reaching over, she placed her hand over his. Truthfully, she did feel bad about his plans not working out. She might not have agreed with what he wanted to do with the property, but she hated that the project he was so passionate about wasn't going to happen. "So what happens now?"

"Are you sure you have time? I don't want to keep you if you need to go. We can talk about all of this tonight over dinner if that's better for you."

Smiling, she leaned over and kissed him. "I'm never on the schedule unless someone's out or on vacation. And considering the mood I was in last night when I left the café, I'm guessing no one's expecting me in this morning."

That made him laugh softly. "I don't even want to think about that."

"Anyway..."

"Give me a minute to get my laptop so I can show you what I'm working on." He got up and left the room and Peyton couldn't help but smile. She hated how they'd fought, but she seriously loved the way they made up.

Last night and again this morning.

Still, she realized something about herself through all of this. For years she'd lacked confidence in herself, thanks to her upbringing. Then when she finally started believing in herself, the only one still doubting her was her mother. And when Ryder came on the scene, there was just something about him that made her feel comfortable standing up for herself and her ideas.

At least...she thought she was comfortable.

The truth was, she'd reacted like such a brat because he managed to hit her trigger. Peyton knew Ryder was nothing like her parents–especially her mother–but something in the way he had spoken to her just had her reacting as if he was. From now on, she knew she would have to be aware of that and not fly off the handle. It was impossible to say it would never happen again because...well...it was Ryder. It would be foolish for her to think she could keep up with him and everything he knew about business, and she knew she was going to be reminding him again and again that she could handle more than he thought. If they were going to work together, they were going to have to learn to communicate better.

And considering his mention of forever last night...

Yeah, that one was still sinking in. He hadn't formally proposed, but she knew that was exactly what he was talking about. It felt like maybe she was dreaming–too many things were falling into place for her that it didn't feel real–and yet...here she was.

"Okay," Ryder said excitedly as he came back into the kitchen, laptop in hand. When he sat back down beside her, he seemed to take a moment to collect his thoughts before looking at her. "When the permits didn't get approved, I gave up. I threw in the towel and was convinced the universe was trying to tell me something."

"Oh, Ryder..."

"You were gone, and I thought we were through and I told myself it was a good thing I wasn't going to build the resort because there was no way I wanted to stay here in Magnolia without you."

His admission made her heart both ache and soar. She wanted to wrap her arms around him and tell him she wasn't going anywhere, but she knew he was leading up to something.

"My plan was to sell the property, leave the plans for your restaurant with Austin for you to tweak and I'd pay to build it when you were ready."

She moaned his name again because...she couldn't believe he would do such a thing.

"But then a little inspiration hit. I had no idea what was going to happen between you and me, but...you were the inspiration behind the inspiration," he said with a wink.

"I'm not even sure what that means."

Opening the laptop, he pulled something up and then turned the screen toward her.

It was a picture of a hotel–bright colors and very retro. "What am I looking at? It reminds me of the hotel we stayed at back in Missouri."

Beside her, he nodded. "That's what I was going for. Instead of The Ashford, I'd like to reach out to Austin to design this–a family-friendly hotel with a retro vibe. Bright bold colors, mid-century modern décor...there would be a pool, playground, an ice cream shop...I'm not sure what else, but I plan on researching a bit more and seeing what else would be desirable."

She was reading the small proposal he had written under the picture and it sounded absolutely perfect for Magnolia. "Ryder...I can't believe you thought of this! It's amazing!"

"I haven't even gotten to the best part," he said smoothly, scrolling down the screen until he got to a picture of a diner. "This would be your retro diner you talked about. We can either incorporate it into the main building or separate it. I think we'd have to talk to Austin about it and see which version the town would be more likely to sign off on, but..."

She couldn't let him finish. Awkwardly, Peyton launched herself into his lap, wrapping herself around him before kissing him soundly. When she raised her head, she knew she was on the verge of tears. "You remembered," she said with awe.

"Of course I remembered," he softly replied. "Duchess, I remember everything you say, and I want to give you everything you want. You have to know that."

Reaching up, she cupped his jaw. "I don't care if you never gave me another thing, Ryder Ashford. I don't need a restaurant or a diner–although I love them and appreciate them–but I'd love you even if you couldn't give them to me. Do you understand that? My feelings for you don't hinge on these grand gestures. It's you that I love, not the things you can give me."

His smile was sweet and a little boyish and endearing. "I know that and you have no idea how much that means to me, but...you're going to have to get used to me spoiling you." And with a quick, chaste kiss, he put her back in her seat. "So...we'll talk to Austin and see which version is more likely to get approved."

"Ryder, I don't even know what to say. I can't believe you came up with this so quickly!"

"Like I said, I was inspired."

"Okay, but...what about The Ashford? I hate that you just have to scrub all those plans."

His smile grew. "Funny you should mention that..." He opened up another tab on the screen and motioned for her to look at it.

"Wait...is that...is that Shawn's listing?"

He nodded.

"I'm lost. What does this house have to do with your resort?"

This time he was the one to reach for her hand, and with it clasped in his, he explained. "When we first met and I told you about the resort, you had a...strong reaction to it."

"I pitched a fit," she reminded him.

"Still, behind all your anger toward me was a very real statement. The Ashford–in theory–was a good idea. Just not for Magnolia Sound."

Peyton did her best not to gloat because she knew this was hard for him. "Will you build it someplace else?"

With a small shrug, he said, "Eventually. I'm considering checking out property in the next town over."

"Laurel Bay? Really?"

"I didn't think there was a place smaller than Magnolia Sound, but...there is quite literally nothing there. It's a clean slate and possibly the better choice for the resort somewhere down the line."

"Oh. Then...what's with the listing?"

"That, Duchess, is going to be The Ashford." He grinned. "Or should I say, the home of *the* Ashfords–me and you."

Now she knew her eyes were ridiculously huge as she stared at him in shock. "But... I mean...that place...and your house that Austin...how...?"

Fortunately, he took pity on her and explained. "It was a little wishful thinking, but...that property–once it's renovated–is everything I wanted for the resort. The grounds are incredible, the rooms are going to be gorgeous, and it's the kind of luxury I enjoy living in. Don't get me wrong, I love the house on the beach where Austin and Mia are staying, but...I still haven't been able to live in it and I don't know if it would ever feel like home. I think with you and I overseeing everything we want done on the house, it could be the perfect home for us. And our family."

"Our...family?" she croaked.

He nodded. "Yeah. Our family. Me, you, our kids, and... a place where our extended family can come and stay.

Including our parents. I know it won't be ready by the time my mother has her surgery, but...I thought about what you said that night and realized how selfless that was. She was awful to you and yet you were still trying to comfort her." Pausing, he let out a long breath. "You inspire me to be a better person. So I want a home that makes everyone feel welcome. The beach house it great, but it's not big enough for me to feel comfortable inviting anyone to stay for an extended period of time."

"I can understand that, but I'm just completely over-whelmed. This is...it's a lot to take in."

"I know, but I'm excited by all the possibilities."

"It's a lot, Ryder. I mean...this is all just so much! A resort, the diner, the restaurant, the house, the other resort... I mean...how can you do all of it?"

Standing, he gently pulled her to her feet as his arms banded around her. "Because I won't be alone. You're going to be right there by my side—as my partner, my equal, and hopefully...my wife."

Her knees went weak, but before she could say anything, he went on.

"I said it last night and I'm saying it again this morning and yet I still don't have a ring to make it official, but you have to know that it's what I want, Peyton. Maybe I should have waited until I did have the ring, but...it wasn't going to change anything for me. We could get in the car right now and get one, but..."

He dropped to one knee with her hands in his.

"Peyton Bishop, I love you. You may not want the world, but I want to give it to you. There has never been anyone that I've wanted to share my life with, but from almost the moment we met, I've wanted to share everything with you. You don't have to say yes today. We can wait because...well...you know me. I go after what I want. But I'm also willing to wait for your response. I'll wait as long as it takes. I just wanted you to know my intentions." He kissed her fingers and was about to rise when she sank down in front of him.

"Ryder Ashford, the day you walked into my café in a tuxedo, I lost a little piece of my heart. Now you have all of it. I don't need a ring and I don't need the world because...I already have it. You. You are my world and everything you just proposed is scary and exciting and there isn't anyone else I could do it with except for you. I love you."

Tears were clouding her vision, but Peyton didn't mind. This time when he kissed her, it was slow and sweet and reverent.

Perfect.

She had no idea how much time had passed before they stopped and got to their feet, but she was more than a little thankful to be off of the kitchen floor.

"So what do you say? We can leave right now and go get a ring or we can be responsible adults and go to work? Which do you want?"

It was a funny question. "There isn't a jewelry store here in Magnolia, but the drive to Wilmington won't take too long. We can still be responsible and go to work after lunch, right?"

"Um...no," he said with a hint of amusement. "I was thinking we'd fly up to New York and shop at Tiffany's and find you the perfect ring. Then we'd have a fantastic dinner someplace, stay at the Plaza before coming home tomorrow and *then* being responsible adults."

"Oh...wow! That sounds very tempting."

"Come on, Duchess," he urged, resting his forehead against hers. "Indulge me. Let's do this."

It truly was tempting. Peyton spent most of her life being responsible and unwilling to take risks, but...she was beginning to see the upside to being a bit more carefree. Ryder studied her face as she pretended to think about it for a moment. "Hmm...I just have one request."

"Anything, and it's yours."

"You're not allowed to fly us there."

Ryder's bark of laughter echoed around them as he hugged her tightly. "My little negotiator, you got it!"

They packed quickly as Ryder made arrangements with his pilot. Peyton took a few minutes to call the café and made arrangements with her staff and talked to Dana to make sure there wasn't anything urgent that needed her attention. Once that was done, she wasn't sure what to do with herself.

Ryder's laptop was still open on the kitchen island, and she walked over and tapped the screen, wanting to look at his plans for the new resort and the diner. But the tab labeled "Peyton's" caught her eye.

"Um, Ryder?" she called out.

"Hmm?"

"Would you mind showing me the plans for the restaurant? You know...the ones Austin showed me the other night?"

He casually strode back into the room and smiled warily at her. "Are you sure you want to look at them right now? They really set you off the last time you looked at them."

"I'm fine, I promise. I was just a little shocked, that's all."

While he didn't look completely convinced, he still honored her request and pulled up the plans.

And then took a giant step back.

Now that she knew what to expect, she was able to view everything with a clear and calm head. There were a few questions she had to ask and he answered them all without elaborating on them and as she sat back and closed her eyes, she realized she could still envision it all just as she had before. Even with the modifications. With a sad sigh, she looked at him. "I'm so sorry."

"For what?"

"If I had just talked to you that night instead of hurling accusations, I would have saved us both a lot of grief."

"I disagree."

Okay, that was not the response she was expecting. "Excuse me?"

Nodding, he moved in close. "Peyton, it's okay for us to argue and disagree. You had every right to be angry with me. We had an agreement and I broke it by not coming to you immediately with the changes that needed to be made."

"Maybe..."

"Plus, I think that bit of a reality check really helped me put things in perspective. You see, I was so laser-focused on The Ashford and why I wanted it here that I didn't pay attention to all the reasons why it shouldn't be here."

"Shouldn't?"

With another nod, he explained. "Peyton, you were right when you accused me of coming in here and wanting to change the town. In my mind I thought it needed to be changed–improved–but I realize now that was just arrogance on my part. This town is perfect."

"Well, I don't know if I'd call it perfect..."

"It's perfect because it brought me to you. These projects we're hopefully going to do will only enhance the town and if this new resort doesn't work out, then...I don't know...we'll sit down with the entire population of Magnolia and ask everyone what it is that they want."

Unable to help it, she laughed. "That's a little extreme, don't you think?"

"Not at all. Your great-grandfather created something wonderful here, Peyton. I'm just sorry that I never got to meet him and that I tried to discredit all that he accomplished. It's time for me to stop thinking only about what I want and start listening to where there's a need."

"You've already done that. What you did for Garrett with the veterinary clinic was exactly that."

"Yeah, well...Emma had more to do with that than I did, so..."

"So you're a slow learner," she teased. "But the important thing is that you're learning." Leaning in, she kissed him. "What time do we have to head to the airport?"

"We need to leave here in about forty minutes." A slow smile spread across his face. "Why? What did you have in mind?"

With a sexy smile of her own, Peyton took him by the hand and led him back to the bedroom. "I'm embracing being a little irresponsible," she told him. "Let's see if we can push the limits on getting to the plane on time."

His grin was downright lethal. "I really do love the way you think, Duchess. Our lives are never going to be boring, that's for sure."

And she couldn't agree more.

EPILOGUE

ONE MONTH LATER...

"Is this really necessary?"

"Oh, absolutely."

Peyton frowned, not quite sure she believed him. "It seems a bit excessive."

"We are all about safety, Duchess. Can't have you getting hurt on the jobsite."

Well, she supposed that was true. "Did it have to be a hot pink hardhat, though? I stick out like a sore thumb."

With a swift kiss, Ryder took his place beside her. "That's the point. I want everyone to know who you are when you stop by to check on the progress of all of this."

The "this" he was referring to was her restaurant.

Hers.

It was an extremely exciting day, and she knew they were just breaking ground, but it still felt huge to her. The entire Bishop family was there to celebrate with her–including Parker–as well as the whole extended Coleman family.

And Ryder's parents.

They had to close off the street to accommodate all of them, and it was wonderful.

Ryder insisted on making a big deal out of it with a ribbon cutting and everything before the bulldozers went to work. Afterwards, they were all going back to Peyton's brother's place to celebrate.

And she wasn't catering it either.

"Can I please have everyone's attention?" Ryder called out, interrupting her thoughts. He handed Peyton a megaphone and led her over to a makeshift stage he had put out for her. She held his hand as she stepped up on it and looked out at so many familiar faces. When he smiled up at her, she felt like her heart was beyond full. "You got this, Peyton."

She was trembling and her voice was a little shaky when she began to speak, but when she glanced at Ryder and she saw the confidence and pride in his smile, she knew she could do this.

"I want to thank everyone for coming out today," she began timidly, but Parker gave her a thumbs up and she knew she could be louder.

She could finally be who she was truly meant to be.

"As many of you know, I've wanted to own my own restaurant since I was a little girl. Pops understood that and gave me my first opportunity when he left the café to me. I've loved that place and it will always be special to me because of the connection to him, but...I don't feel like it's truly mine." Pausing, she shifted the hardhat on her head. "If anyone had told me a year ago that I'd be breaking ground on a place all my own, I wouldn't have believed it. I had no idea the way those plans would change and how that change would be for the better. Thanks to my wonderful fiancé, I can not only build the restaurant of my dreams, but I can do it with the very best man by my side."

There was a round of applause as she smiled down at Ryder.

"So I am very pleased to announce the official ground-breaking of Peyton's," she said with a smile. "For years I played around with what I was going to name this place. Back when Ryder and I first met, he had plans for a resort here in town that he was going to name after himself, well... his family name. At the time, I called it egotistical, but the truth is, I understood it because...this place, this restaurant, was always going to be called Peyton's because it's finally the place that I always dreamed of–always planned for–and I can't wait to share it with all of you. Thank you so much for coming out to support me today. I love you all!"

Then, right on cue, the machines started and dug the first patch of ground up.

Ryder stepped up onto the stage and spun her around before kissing her. It was far too loud with the bulldozers doing their thing behind them to really say anything to each other, but the kiss he gave her said everything.

With another round of applause, they stepped off the stage and walked over to their little crowd of supporters. Peyton was immediately embraced by her sister, then her parents, and then her brother. After that, it was a bit of a blur. When the heavy machinery shut down a few minutes later–thanks to Ryder–she was finally able to hear what everyone was saying to her.

"We'll see everyone at our place!" Mason called out as he and Scarlett separated from the group. Little by little, people began to leave and Peyton was anxious to follow too.

"Peyton?"

Turning, she saw Ryder's mother walking toward her.

She looked great and apparently was feeling a little better as she got closer to her surgery.

"Hey, Helen!" she said, giving her a hug. "Thank you so much for coming out for this."

"After listening to you and Ryder talking about it last week when I called, I knew I had to be here."

"Thank you. I know it's not much–just some dirt getting moved around–but...it's a lot to me."

"As it should be." Helen gave her a serene smile. "I want you to know that I am beyond grateful to you."

"To me? Why?"

"For starters, I've never seen my son so happy. Honestly, I don't think I've ever seen anyone quite as happy as Ryder."

Blushing, Peyton nodded.

"And I'm grateful for all you're doing for me. You've... you've welcomed me into your life, your home, your family and...it means the world to me, Peyton, so...thank you."

"You'll always have a place here with us," Peyton assured her. "I wish the new house was going to be done sooner so you could come and recuperate here, but..."

"It will be nice to know I can come and see all the wonderful work you've done when I'm feeling stronger." She kissed Peyton on the cheek. "We'll see you at your brother's house."

Looking around, it was down to just a handful of people, including herself and Ryder. Parker came strolling over and hugged her again. "I am so proud of you!"

"Thank you! I'm so glad you're here. It would have felt wrong without you."

Pulling back, her sister grinned at her. "And I appreciate you keeping the bungalow for me to use. It was nice having the bed to myself this time and not having to go and sleep in my childhood room while getting pressured by Mom to move back."

"Well, damn. I was about to pressure you to move back." Peyton teased.

"Ugh...not you too. Not today..."

"Okay, fine. But I can't guarantee the bungalow will be here the next time. I'm almost completely moved in with Ryder and there's no reason to keep it."

"Can we put that on hold for today?" Parker asked. "I don't want to talk about my messed up life when today is your big day." She squeezed Peyton's hand and smiled again.

"What? What are you smiling at?"

"Your ring! My God, how is it possible for one man to have such good taste in everything? Jewelry? Women? Clothes? I mean...just look at him, Peyton! Ryder is just..."

"He's like James Bond," she said with a small laugh. "The first time he walked into the café, that's what I thought. And I can say with great confidence that he is the best in every single way."

"TMI, Peyton," her sister murmured, kissing her on the cheek. "I'm going to go. I'll see you over at Mason's."

They hugged again and Peyton stood and watched as Parker ran over and hugged Ryder.

And possibly whispered something in his ear.

Ryder nodded and Parker turned and walked to her car while Ryder walked directly to her.

"What was that all about?"

"What was what all about?"

"My sister. What did she say to you?"

He waved her off and began to lead her over to his car. "Just telling me how awesome I am and how nobody's better than me," he said with a laugh.

"Somebody's rather full of themselves. Again."

"Part of my charm," he replied, helping her into the car.

"It certainly is," she agreed. And as Ryder walked around the front of the car, she couldn't help but smile. When he climbed in beside her, she was nodding.

"What? Now what did I do?" he asked.

"Everything. You truly are the best, Ryder Ashford, and I love you."

"I love you too. Now let's go celebrate!"

A LOOK BACK AT THE BISHOP
FAMILY WITH
IN CASE YOU DIDN'T KNOW

"Success." Mason Bishop looked around the room with a satisfied grin. Sure he was alone and talking to himself, but he was alone in a place of his own and it was beyond exciting. It was something he should have done long ago, but he'd let himself be guilted long enough.

Collapsing down on his new sectional, he studied his surroundings with a sense of accomplishment. It was something he was always going to do, but a week ago he had hit his limit at home and decided the time had finally come.

Of course the fact that his cousin Sam kept poking at him because he still lived with his parents had helped, but...

As if on cue, his phone rang and there was Sam's name on the screen.

"Hey!"

"So?" Sam asked giddily. "Is it glorious? Please tell me it's glorious!"

Mason couldn't help but laugh. "I just put the last of the boxes in the trash so I haven't had the time for it to feel particularly glorious yet, but..."

"Okay, fine. Pretend, for crying out loud. You're in your

own place and it's filled with your own stuff. Doesn't it feel great?"

It would be fun to keep needling one another, but to what end? "You know what? It does," he said with a big grin. "I slept here last night but there were boxes and crap everywhere. Now everything is put away and...yeah, I guess it is kind of glorious."

"There you go! Now don't you feel like a complete idiot for waiting for so long?"

"Weren't you living with your mom up until a couple of months ago?"

"Dude, that was totally different. I'd been living on my own up in Virginia for years. It was only when I was forced to move here that I *chose* to live with my mother. Apples and oranges."

"Maybe."

"No maybes about it," Sam countered. "And now Shelby and I are living together and it's awesome."

"You sure that's a good idea? Moving in together so soon? Her father's a pastor. The gossip mill must be going crazy with the news!"

"Thanks. Like I needed the reminder," Sam deadpanned.

"And?"

"And what?"

"C'mon, are you telling me there's been no backlash? No one spouting how you're living in sin and whatnot?"

Sam let out a low laugh. "Oh, they spout it all the time, but we're good with it. We both know this is it for us and if anyone really starting hassling us, we're more than okay with going to the courthouse, making it legal, and shutting everyone up."

Mason was pretty sure his jaw hit the floor. "Wait...

what? Are you serious? Making it...? Who are you and what have you done with my cousin!"

That just made Sam laugh harder. "When you know, you know. And with Shelby...I know."

And damn if he couldn't hear his cousin's smile.

It was enough to make a guy sick.

"Wow...just..." He let out a long breath. "I never thought I'd live to see the day."

"Yeah, well...me either. But like I said, she's it for me. But I appreciate the uh...concern." He laughed again. "That's what that was, right? You being concerned?"

"Um...yeah. Sure. We can call it that," Mason said with a snicker. "We're family and we just look out for one another, right?"

"Yes, we do. But enough about me. Weren't we talking about you and the decisions you're making for your own life?" He paused. "You know I was seriously just thinking of your own sanity, Mason. Every day I watched you die a little more while under your parents' thumbs."

"I know and now that it's done, I can't believe I didn't do it sooner–like as soon as I graduated college."

"Hell, I'm still surprised you opted to move back here at all."

Raking a hand through his hair, he looked up at the ceiling. "I tossed around the idea of moving somewhere else, but...believe it or not, I like it here. I see all the things I want to do and help change. And if it means I have to live under the watchful eye of my folks, I'll live."

"They'll get hobbies eventually, right?" Sam teased.

"God I hope so."

"They will. And either way, this move is going to be great for you. Trust me."

He didn't need his cousin to tell him that, he already knew it.

Could feel it too.

Last night when he'd carried in the last box and closed the door behind him, Mason felt like he had taken his first free breath.

Sad, right?

"I do trust you and I know the time was right because everything fell into place. The house - even though it's only a rental - is the perfect size for me. A couple of years from now I might be ready to buy a place, but for now this works."

"If you'd make a damn decision on the bar Pops left you, you know you could have afforded something of your own. I mean, why are you holding on to this place? Let it go already!"

Yeah, everyone had been in his face about the Mystic Magnolia and Mason had to admit, the whole thing still stumped him. Everyone else got an inheritance that made sense except him. Granted, he never felt the closeness to Pops his sisters or his cousins did, but to be left a decrepit old dive bar just seemed like a slap in the face.

Although–if he was being honest–he'd admit there was one *tiny* reason he was still holding on to it...

"I'll deal with it when I'm ready," he stated, unwilling to let his mind wander any more than it already had. "The lawyer said there wasn't a rush and everything is being handled - bills are being paid and all so...I'm still trying to wrap my brain around it all."

"You mean why Pops gave you the place only old locals go to?" Sam teased. "And I mean *old*! No one under the age of sixty-five goes there!"

"Okay, that's not *that* old..."

"C'mon, fess up. Pops took you there when you were younger, didn't he," Sam prodded. "The place must hold some significance to you and that's why he felt like you should be the one to have it."

"Why would I go to a bar with my great-grandfather? That's just...it's weird, Sam."

"Some could say it was like bonding, but whatever."

"Look, Pops never took me to the Mystic Magnolia or any other bar so...I'm stumped."

"Did he give you a letter? I thought we all got letters."

Rubbing a hand over his face, Mason let out a long breath. "He said a lot of things in my letter but none explained why he thought I should get that place."

"Really? Huh...that's strange. What did he say?"

"It was like he was channeling his inner Yoda or something. He spoke in all kinds of riddles. It was weird."

"Like what?"

Ugh...this really wasn't something he wanted to talk about right now. He was feeling all good and proud of himself and had been ready to order a pizza and kick back and enjoy it here in his new place and now his cousin was crapping all over his good mood.

"Look, you um...you wanna come over for some pizza?" he said, hoping to change the subject. "I was just getting ready to order one when you called."

Luckily Sam could be easily distracted.

"Wish I could, but rain check, okay? Shelby and I have dinner plans with Jake and Mallory. You wanna join us?"

The laugh escaped before he could stop it. "Right. Why wouldn't I want to be the fifth wheel at dinner? I think I'll pass."

Catching his meaning, Sam laughed. "Yeah. Okay, I get it. Are you going to the benefit concert tomorrow night?"

"Shit," he murmured. "Is that tomorrow?"

Sam chuckled. "Yup. I think your mom bought out the entire VIP section."

He groaned. "Of course she did." He paused. "Wait, the Magnolia Amphitheater has a VIP section? Seriously?"

"Sure. Most places do."

"Still, that place isn't all that big–like 2,500 seats max."

"And that has to do with VIP seats...why?"

He groaned again. "Never mind. It doesn't really matter. We'll all be there so...wait, who's playing?"

"A couple of bands, I think. I didn't pay much attention either, but they're all somewhat local."

For the life of him, the name of the band escaped him, but it didn't really matter. "Go have dinner and tell everyone I said hey and I'll see you all at the show tomorrow."

"Yeah, sure. Sounds like a plan. Have a good night."

"You too."

After he hung up, Mason stretched his arms out along the top of the sofa cushions and smiled. He could order some pizza and maybe invite some friends over and not have to hear about what other people his age were doing or who had just gotten married or engaged or who would be a suitable spouse for him. Seriously, he loved his parents but their obsession with his life had gotten out of control.

Ten days ago had been the breaking point.

He had come home from work to find his mother having wine with a woman he'd never met before. Leslie....something. Mason had figured she was involved in one of his mother's many charity projects and said a brief hello and went to go change so he could go for a run.

That's when it all went wrong.

"Mason, sweetie," his mother said in her best southern

drawl. "You can't go for a run. You have dinner reservations in thirty minutes with Leslie."

The rage he had felt in that moment had been like nothing he'd ever felt before. In the past he'd dealt with being introduced to women his parents thought would be a good match for him or being asked to take out one of their friends' daughters, but this was the first time he had been so blatantly ambushed in his own home.

Forcing a smile onto his face, he looked at Leslie and said, "I'm so sorry you were misled, but...I already have plans this evening." When he turned to leave the room, his mother had jumped to her feet and come after him, berating him for being rude.

"Rude?" he snapped. "You made dinner reservations for me with a stranger without talking to me about it and *I'm* being rude? This is it! I'm not doing this anymore! You have interfered with my life for the last time!"

The argument had gone on for hours and even though his father had come home and tried to calm things down, it was too late. The damage was done. Mason had walked to his room, packed a bag and walked out.

And hadn't talked to either parent since.

He spent a week staying at Magnolia on the Beach - a small local hotel - and frantically combed the real estate ads looking for a place to live. The house was a complete godsend and when it was available immediately, he knew it was meant to be his. Furnishing it had been a breeze since his cousin Mallory owned the local decor place in town and helped him and then his sisters had both taken turns bringing some of his things from home over to him. They could be total pains in the ass at times, but he was thankful for them right now.

It was quiet and for a long minute he sat there and

enjoyed it and then...not so much. He wasn't used to it and he had a feeling it would be a while before he was. Suddenly the thought of sitting home eating pizza wasn't quite so appealing, but then again, neither was going out to a bar or going out to eat alone.

Maybe he should've been the fifth wheel.

"This is ridiculous," he murmured coming to his feet. He'd lived in this town his entire life. Surely he could go out and grab something to eat and maybe run into a friend or two and kill some time before coming back here alone.

Or maybe...not alone.

Hell, he could finally bring a woman home instead of either going to her place or going to a motel!

The idea had merit.

But then...it didn't.

Honestly, he was tired, sweaty, and hungry. There was no shame in admitting that a quiet night in his own home was really what he wanted. Still, now he didn't want pizza, he wanted something with a little more substance. Feeling like he had a bit of a plan, he walked with purpose into his new en suite bathroom to shower so he could go out and grab something to eat before settling in for the night with some Netflix.

"I think my virginity is growing back."

"Engine grease under your fingernails isn't very attractive, Scar. Maybe that's why guys aren't banging down your door to ask you out. But that's just my opinion."

Scarlett Jones looked down at her hands and frowned.

Damn.

With a shrug, she walked back into her bathroom to

rewash her hands. Yeah, she wasn't a girly girl. She grew up working in her father's garage alongside him and her three brothers and it turned out she really had a gift for working on motorcycles. If the engine grease and the smell of gasoline on her didn't turn guys off, the fact that she was fiercely independent did.

Did it bother her? Yes.

Enough to make her quit? No.

Glancing up at her reflection, Scarlett couldn't help but wonder what was wrong with her. In just about every other aspect of her life, she was confident–sometimes overly so. She was smart and caring and always willing to help out anyone in need. Everyone was always saying how great she was.

And yet, she hadn't been in a relationship in a long time.

Like...a really long time.

Hence the fear of her virginity growing back.

Turning off the water, she shook out her hands as she continued to stare at herself. While there wasn't anything particularly remarkable about her, she was bold enough to know she was attractive–long, wavy brown hair, dark brown eyes, and -if she did say so herself, a pretty kickass body. So why couldn't she seem to attract a decent guy?

"You're not pissed at me, are you?"

Reaching for a hand towel, Scarlett pulled herself from her thoughts and looked over at her best friend Courtney. With a smile, she replied, "Nah. That would be a pretty stupid reason to be mad. I had grease under my nails and you were just pointing it out. No biggie."

Only...it did bother her.

Not that Courtney had pointed it out, but that it was there in the first place and she hadn't noticed it.

And it probably wasn't the first time.

"Are you sure? Because you just sort of up and walked away."

Scarlett tossed the towel aside before holding up her hands and wiggling her fingers. "To get rid of the grease!" With a small laugh, she walked past Courtney and back out into her bedroom. "Okay, where are we going tonight? Do I need to change?"

Looking down at herself, she seriously hoped not. She was comfortable. For the most part, they stuck to the local pubs and going out in jeans and a nice top were fine. But lately, Courtney had been wanting to broaden their horizons and that meant dressing up more.

She bit her tongue to prevent her from complaining out loud.

Courtney walked across the room and flopped down on the bed with a dramatic sigh.

That can't be good, Scarlett thought, but waited her friend out.

Busying herself with straightening up her room and not looking for something else to wear, she mentally prayed Courtney would just say what was on her mind.

"I think I want to move," she finally said and Scarlett immediately gasped in shock.

"What? Why? Where?"

Sitting up, Courtney flipped her hair over her shoulder and sighed again. "Anywhere. I'm just never going to do anything or meet anyone if I stay here. I'm over small-town life."

They'd had this conversation multiple times and for the most part, Scarlett was used to it. Walking over, she sat down on the bed beside her. "Okay, what brought this on? Last weekend we went out and had a great time and I seem to remember seeing you make out with Mike Ryan." Then she winked. "And I distinctly remember watching you wave goodbye to me as you left with him."

Courtney fell back on the bed. "Yeah, and it was good and the sex was good, but...it's like it's always the same guys! We've been hanging out with the same people we've known since elementary school!"

"That's not true. We're heading into the peak tourist season! You know it's going to be crazy around here for the next six weeks or so. Maybe you'll meet someone..."

"You don't get it, Scar. I don't want to be the girl the tourists hook up with for a quick weekend fling or the girl the locals pass the time with until they can hit on the tourists! I'm just...I'm ready for a change!"

"Okay, okay," she soothed, falling back next to Courtney. "How about this...let's just go out tonight and grab something to eat and then we'll pick up some ice cream on the way home and just have a mellow night? How does that sound?"

"Boring," Courtney said with a pout. "And the exact reason why I'm done with small town life."

"Hey! I'm kind of taking offense to that! I know I'm not the most exciting person in the world, but..." Sitting up, Scarlett immediately bounced off the bed.

"You're right, you're right, you're right," Courtney said, standing up. "That was uncalled for." She gave Scarlett a long hug before pulling back. "I'm just in a funk and I'm bored and...don't listen to me. I'll get over it."

And the thing was, Scarlett knew she would, but it didn't mean she could just ignore the situation either.

"Look," she began cautiously, "I'm bored too. It's not like a whole lot of exciting stuff happens around here or that I've got all kinds of interesting things going on..."

"Now that's not true. You could be doing so much more if you would just share your hobby with…"

"Lalalalala!" Scarlett cried out before stopping to glare at her friend. "I swore you to secrecy and you promised to never bring it up!"

Courtney looked around the room in confusion. "Who's going to hear me? It's just the two of us!"

There was a slight chance she was being paranoid, but there was no way she was going to tell anyone other than Courtney what she'd been doing in her spare time.

"Fine. Whatever," she murmured. "Can we go grab something to eat now? I'm starving."

And yeah, there was a little snap in her voice that she was regretting.

They walked out of the bedroom and Scarlett picked up her purse and keys and followed Courtney out the door.

"So not the fun night I was hoping for," she said under her breath. At her car, she paused and apologized. "I'm sorry I snapped at you. That was wrong of me."

Courtney–ever the drama queen–merely shrugged.

Awesome.

"You want to go to Café Magnolia or The Sand Bar for burgers?"

"Ugh…I know their burgers are legendary, but why won't they change the name of the damn place! It's not very appetizing to go and eat someplace that has the word sand in their title."

"So you want to go to the café?"

"I didn't say that," Courtney was quick to amend. "I mean, we both know a girls night requires burgers."

"And fries," Scarlett said with a grin as they climbed into her car.

The Sand Bar was like most of the businesses in

Magnolia Sound–an institution. It had been around for at least twenty years and was in need of a renovation, but business was too good to close down and get it done. When the hurricane hit a little more than six months ago, it seemed like the logical time to finally freshen the place up. Unfortunately, old Mr. Hawkins simply fixed the roof and replaced a couple of windows and declared The Sand Bar open once again for business a week after Hurricane Amelia blew through.

"I'm getting the bacon cheeseburger, fries, and possibly onion rings," Courtney declared as they drove along Main Street. Turning her head, she grinned at Scarlett. "And I think you should share an order of fried pickles with me."

Her stomach hurt just thinking about all the food, but she kept that to herself. Fried pickles definitely weren't her thing, but she'd eat a couple and move on. "Sure. Why not?"

The parking lot was crowded, but that wasn't anything new. The location was prime–on the beach side of the street–and there was indoor and outdoor seating, live entertainment, and a full bar. Honestly, Scarlett never cared much for coming here to drink, she was all about the food. Once she was parked and they were making their way toward the front entrance, the smell of food had her stomach growling.

Loudly.

"Totally not lady-like, Scar," Courtney teased even as she worked her way through the crowd and managed to find them a small booth in the corner.

"How do you do that?"

"Do what?"

"Always find us a place to sit?"

"It's my lone super-power," she said dryly as she flagged a waiter over. Once their orders were placed, Courtney began scanning the room. "I swear, even the tourists are the same ones."

Scarlett looked around and frowned. "Seriously? How can you tell?"

"Because we've been doing this for what feels like forever. Maybe they'll be some different faces at the concert tomorrow. You're still coming with me, right?"

Their server came back and placed their drinks down and Scarlett eagerly reached for hers. There was no way she could admit she wasn't looking forward to the concert, but she still needed a little sweet tea to bide her time.

"Nice delay tactic." Courtney knew her too well. With a weary sigh, she asked, "Tell me why you don't want to go."

"I don't know, Court. The amphitheater is small and the crowds are going to be crazy! We're going to be up in the nosebleed section and packed in like sardines! And on top of that, it's going to be ninety degrees out! Call me crazy, but that is not my idea of a good time."

"Why are you like this?" Courtney whined. "It's like you just refuse to have fun!"

"That's ridiculous! I have fun all the time! I just don't find it enjoyable to stand around and sweat when I don't have to!"

"You spend so much time working in your dad's garage and it's always hot in there! Every time I've ever seen you there, you're sweating!"

"And that's because I have to be there!" she cried with more than a little frustration. "When I'm there, I'm working. I work, because I need money! And sometimes that means working in a building with little to no air conditioning!"

"Scarlett..."

"I'm forced to do it for work so why would I opt to do it on a night out when I'm supposed to be having fun?"

"Look, we both know you don't have to work at the garage, you choose to."

"I need the income…"

"Yeah, yeah, yeah…I get it. You use the second job to feed your hobby supplies," she said with a hint of sarcasm. "You work too much and you're always saving and you live frugally. It's admirable."

"But…?"

"But…you are way too uptight! No one is thinking about it being hot out, Scarlett! We're all like 'Yay! Concert!' Why can't you do the same?"

Seriously? "When have I ever simply followed the herd, Court? That's not me."

"Okay, fine. It's not, but…can't you just do it this once? C'mon! It's going to be so much fun! For one night can't you forget about your jobs and be a little carefree? You might actually enjoy it."

So many comments were on the tip of her tongue–most of them snarky–but Scarlett opted to keep them to herself. It was easy for people like Courtney to be carefree and not obsess about their finances. And while she didn't begrudge her friend having a family who always was and probably always would be financially stable, there was also no way for her to fully understand the anxiety that plagued her daily.

Growing up poor–and knowing that everyone you knew wasn't–wasn't something you got over. From the time Scarlett first started school, she knew she was different. Besides never having anything new for herself, she was dressed more like a boy than a girl. Looking back now she could almost laugh about it, but back then, it had been beyond painful. Her father had done the best he could and she loved him for it. She just wished someone had stepped in and tried to explain to Dominic Jones that raising a daughter was very different from raising sons. Her brothers were all fine–in their own annoying way. All three of them. But they were boys who had been raised by a strong male role model.

They'd also had more time with their mother before she died from colon cancer when Scarlett was only four. Kandace Jones had fought hard to win her battle with the deadly disease, but it was too much for her. There were days when her memories of her mother were so strong it was as if she were sitting right there with her, and other days it was like she couldn't remember a thing and would be devastated.

Either way, her father had struggled to raise four kids on his own and apparently it was easier to treat them all equally–like boys–rather than figuring out that Scarlett wanted nothing more than to be treated like a girl.

Something she still struggled with.

Maybe that was another reason why she couldn't seem to find anyone she was interested in dating. It was hard to find the balance between being the girly-girl she longed to be and the tough-as-nails mechanic she presented to the world.

A damn dilemma indeed.

Although if anyone dared to look in her closet who didn't know anything about her, they'd only see the girly stuff.

Way too much of it.

"Hey," Courtney said with a growing smile. "Just when you thought there were no new faces in the crowd..."

Scarlett turned her head and tried to see who her friend was talking about. "Who are you looking at?"

"I don't think I've seen him here before. I mean...I suppose it's possible, but I always heard he tended to hit bars and restaurants out of town–especially since we graduated."

Frowning, Scarlett continued to scan the crowd. "So it's someone we know?"

"Oh, good lord. I think he got even better looking..."

Now her curiosity was seriously piqued. Still, not one face in the crowd looked familiar and with a huff of frustration, she faced Courtney again. "Who the hell are you talking about?"

"Mason Bishop," she replied before taking a sip of her beer. "He's a little too pretty for my taste, but still, you have to appreciate a fine looking man." Putting her drink down, she looked at Scarlett. "What's with the face?"

Doing her best to put a relaxed smile on her face, she replied, "What do you mean?"

"You were practically scowling. Why?"

With a shrug, Scarlett reached for her own drink and wished it was alcohol. "I really wasn't."

"Yes, you were. Now spill it. What's up?"

If there was one thing Scarlett was certain of, it was that Courtney would continue to badger her until she told her what was up.

So she did.

"Guys like him? Like Mason? They're what's wrong with the world!"

Courtney's eyes went wide. "Um...what?"

Nodding, she looked over her shoulder and spotted him and glared briefly. When she turned back to Courtney, she explained. "Everything comes easy to guys like him. Like it's not enough that he comes from one of the founding families here in town, but his folks are wealthy and successful, his sisters are both super nice and pretty, and he looks like a damn model!"

"Scarlett..."

"No, I'm serious! Do you remember what he was like in school?"

"Uh...yeah..."

"Mister Popularity! Captain of the baseball team, student body president, homecoming king, prom king...ugh! It was enough to make me sick!"

"Okay, if I didn't know him, I'd agree with you. All those things combined are a bit much. But Mason was always a nice guy, so..." She shrugged. "It's just who he is, Scar. What's the big deal?"

Rolling her eyes, she was about to go off on a rant when their server returned with their food. With a muttered thanks, she opted to reach for her burger and take a huge bite instead.

And damn...as far as distractions went, this was the best one yet. It was almost enough for her to forget what they were talking about.

"You should probably get to know him before you get so judgy," Courtney said as she picked up her own burger. "I bet if you spent some time talking to him..."

"Oh, I know him, Court. Back in middle school we were lab partners for a short time. He was semi-decent and kind of nice, but once high school hit, it was like he didn't even know me. So...I stand by my earlier opinion, thank you very much."

"Look, I get you have issues with people you think lead a privileged life...

"You have no idea."

Courtney gave her a hard stare before she continued. "However, sometimes you have to remember that looks can be deceiving and you have no idea what goes on behind closed doors."

Doing her best to appear bored, she reached for an onion ring. "And sometimes it's all exactly as it seemed. Sometimes shiny happy people are exactly that–shiny happy people with no substance."

"Well damn."

With a shrug, Scarlett took another bite of her burger and pushed all thoughts of Mason Bishop completely out of her mind.

IN CASE YOU DIDN'T KNOW is available now!
https://www.chasing-romance.com/in-case-you-didnt-know

ALSO BY SAMANTHA CHASE

The Magnolia Sound Series:

Sunkissed Days

Remind Me

A Girl Like You

In Case You Didn't Know

All the Befores

And Then One Day

Can't Help Falling in Love

Last Beautiful Girl

The Way the Story Goes

Since You've Been Gone

Nobody Does It Better

Meet Me at the Altar:

The Engagement Embargo

With this Cake

You May Kiss the Groomsman

The Enchanted Bridal Series:

The Wedding Season

Friday Night Brides

The Bridal Squad

Glam Squad & Groomsmen

Bride & Seek

The RoadTripping Series:

Drive Me Crazy

Wrong Turn

Test Drive

Head Over Wheels

The Montgomery Brothers Series:

Wait for Me

Trust in Me

Stay with Me

More of Me

Return to You

Meant for You

I'll Be There

Until There Was Us

Suddenly Mine

A Dash of Christmas

The Shaughnessy Brothers Series:

Made for Us

Love Walks In

Always My Girl

This is Our Song

Sky Full of Stars

Holiday Spice

Tangled Up in You

Band on the Run Series:

One More Kiss

One More Promise

One More Moment

The Christmas Cottage Series:

The Christmas Cottage

Ever After

Silver Bell Falls Series:

Christmas in Silver Bell Falls

Christmas On Pointe

A Very Married Christmas

A Christmas Rescue

Christmas Inn Love

The Christmas Plan

Life, Love & Babies Series:

The Baby Arrangement

Baby, Be Mine

Baby, I'm Yours

Preston's Mill Series:

Roommating

Speed Dating

Complicating

The Protectors Series:

Protecting His Best Friend's Sister

Protecting the Enemy

Protecting the Girl Next Door

Protecting the Movie Star

7 Brides for 7 Soldiers

Ford

7 Brides for 7 Blackthornes

Logan

Standalone Novels:

Jordan's Return

Catering to the CEO

In the Eye of the Storm

A Touch of Heaven

Moonlight in Winter Park

Waiting for Midnight

Mistletoe Between Friends

Snowflake Inn

Wildest Dreams (currently unavailable)

Going My Way (currently unavailable)

Going to Be Yours (currently unavailable)

ABOUT SAMANTHA CHASE

Samantha Chase is a *New York Times* and *USA Today* bestseller of contemporary romance that's hotter than sweet, sweeter than hot. She released her debut novel in 2011 and currently has more than seventy titles under her belt – including *THE CHRISTMAS COTTAGE* which was a Hallmark Christmas movie in 2017! She's a Disney enthusiast who still happily listens to 80's rock. When she's not working on a new story, she spends her time reading romances, playing way too many games of Solitaire on Facebook, wearing a tiara while playing with her sassy pug Maylene...oh, and spending time with her husband of 30 years and their two sons in Wake Forest, North Carolina.

Sign up for my mailing list and get exclusive content and chances to win members-only prizes!
https://www.chasing-romance.com/newsletter

Where to Find Me:
Website: www.chasing-romance.com
Facebook: www.facebook.com/SamanthaChaseFanClub
Instagram: https://www.
instagram.com/samanthachaseromance/
Twitter: https://twitter.com/SamanthaChase3
Reader Group: https://www.facebook.com/
groups/1034673493228089/